# Holly, Joanne and Steph

*By*

*Peter Karl*

**Peter Karl**

Copyright © 2025

All rights reserved.



# Dedication

I dedicate this to no one in particular as this is all my work. I will say my inspiration derived from stories I've read in newspapers, TV shows I've seen and thought-provoking processes in my head to build a story. This story is completely fictional and never meant to resemble anyone, any business, or entity. It would be purely unintentional.

# Acknowledgment

To the readers who buy and read this book. I hope you enjoy reading it as much as I did writing it. I have written others, so please look for them if you've become a fan.

Thank you, Peter Karl.

# About the Author

**Peter Karl**

Peter Karl (author's real name is Peter Ortmueller) was born in Germany on 9 October 1952. His family immigrated to Australia, arriving in Fremantle on 23 February 1954.

Fast forward to July 1969, I began a three-and-a-half-year apprenticeship as a motor mechanic in Kalgoorlie and won the Apprentice of the Year Award in 1973. I started 'dabbling' in writing my biography in the early '90s, but never continued until 2015.

I retired in 2021 and made serious inroads into writing, completing three novels, one a narrative non-fiction. My goal is to publish in 2025, or even earlier.

I hope you find this read enjoyable and engaging.

**Also by Peter Karl**

*Working for Davies*

# Table of Content

# Prologue

Three ladies influence each other's lives. Along the way, as the dynamics in their lives changed, Steph was there for Holly during high school in Geraldton, and for Joanne during the time Holly spent on a brief stay working in Sydney.

Joanne did eventually meet up with Steph, under unusual circumstances. Their experiences, with the twists and turns they encountered, and other influences, certainly took their toll.

This is a story of murder, assassination, and revenge. The girls won out in the end, not surprisingly.

# Chapter 1: Joanne Holland

A young twenty-six-year-old was up for most of the night. She was standing with her back against the railings on the balcony of the Ocean Centre Hotel on the third floor. She was in a state of delirium and was about to succumb to the drugs coursing through her veins. Her mind was whirling, her consciousness waning, and her vision was blurring. She was looking back into the room and thought she saw something, or someone, moving toward her. She felt the railing press hard into the small of her back, and then suddenly she seemed to be falling. The sensation was surreal, and the world seemed to spin and spin again.

She was in a blue silk nightdress, having made herself ready to retire to bed long before now. However, something was playing on her mind, and a couple of stiff drinks should have helped. But there was something not quite right. It was playing on her mind, and things now seemed to move too fast. She didn't think the drugs would treat her so harshly. They never did before, or when she was with Roberto. She appeared to have overcome her anguish of the past, but deep-rooted emotions were coming to the surface. Nobody noticed, and nobody cared. If only Steph were here, her closest friend.

She was soaring through the air with grace and elegance.

'Steph, help me,' she whispered, as the falling sensation seemed to overwhelm her.

The street was bare when she fell. The early morning traffic was almost non-existent at this hour, especially along the foreshore, which only served as a minor road for car parking areas. There were no cars, no pedestrians, and no witnesses. The last thing she saw was the fading stars in the dawning sky before everything went black.

Her body now lay in a gathering pool of blood, mostly around her head and upper body. She lay face upwards, gazing into the sky with lifeless eyes still open.

A scream from the restaurant of the hotel broke the silence on the second floor. Hotel guests waiting for breakfast had wandered out to take in the vista of the beautiful scenery of the harbour this early in the morning and looked down from the restaurant's balcony, only to see Holly's lifeless body on the ground below. Blood now thickened around the body and soaked into her nightdress.

The woman who screamed gasped for breath, put a hand over her mouth in horror, and backed away from the railing into the restaurant. A man staring down at the awful sight immediately replaced her. He mouthed some inaudible words and went inside to use a phone.

It only seemed like a matter of minutes before a police car arrived, followed by another, then a third.

The police gathered around Holly's lifeless body and surveyed the area for clues. One officer returned to his car and retrieved some tape to cordon off the area, now a potential crime scene. A few minutes later, a plain car arrived with well-dressed, suited men inside. Two detectives stepped out of the car and began talking to the police officers on the scene.

Senior Detective Jonathan Ralph had been a homicide detective for nearly twenty years and had developed a keen eye with that length of experience. You always questioned everything and took nothing at face value. The obvious wasn't necessarily the truth.

Detective Matthew Robert Wilson was new to homicide and was developing into a very astute investigator. The senior detective was training him well and letting him in on the trade secrets. Matthew was learning quickly and, at twenty-eight, still had a long career ahead.

They got on very well and, early in their association, both insisted on a first-name basis.

Senior Detective Ralph crouched over Holly's body to have a closer look, then stood and surveyed the immediate area around the body, shaking his head. People mingled and stood behind the taped-off area, craning their necks to see what was happening. Early morning runners and joggers alike took in the scene.

'Suicide?' one asked.

'Does her throat look cut?' said another.

'I don't know, young people these days,' said an older onlooker, shaking her head.

'Okay, everyone, there's not much to see, so move away,' said a police officer, trying to get the gathering crowd to disperse. Another officer placed a sheet over the body.

Senior Detective Ralph stepped back onto the street and looked up at the floors above as he moved backwards. He found what he was looking for.

'Matt, looks like she jumped from up there,' he said, pointing up to the third-floor middle balcony. 'There's a curtain flapping in the breeze, and I can see the glass door is open. Let's have a look.'

As they made their way into the hotel, an ambulance came around the corner. Two paramedics alighted, ran to the rear, and retrieved a stretcher. They stood there for a moment and asked the police officer, 'Can we shift her?'

The police officer gestured to hold for a moment and walked over to the Sergeant. He said something, and a shake of the head was the reply.

'No,' the police officer said. 'Forensics hasn't been here yet. You can move her after they've finished.'

An additional police car showed up at the scene. A detective with a large black suitcase got out and walked over to the body. Cautiously, he positioned the case nearby and opened it. He pulled out plastic bags and rubber gloves and began looking around for items of interest. He pulled on the gloves and began examining the area around the body. His companion joined him, removed the cover from the body, and began taking pictures from different angles. After completing the photography, he covered the body again and signalled the paramedics to take it away.

By now, Detectives John Ralph and Matt Wilson were on the balcony looking down as the forensic team performed their tasks. Matt looked down and observed how Holly's body had landed on the ground.

'I have a problem with the way the body landed on the ground, particularly if she had jumped from here,' Matt announced as he kept looking down at Holly's body.

'What makes you say that?' John replied.

'If she jumped, her body would be face down. If she rolled forward off the balcony and somersaulted in the air, her head would face upwards and toward the hotel,' Matt opined. 'Here she is facing upwards and with her head away from the hotel.'

'I see where you are going with this. The way she landed shows she had fallen backwards.'

'Maybe someone pushed her,' Matt suggested.

John looked down again at the body and was deep in thought over Matt's observation. There was some serious substance coming to the surface.

'I think you are absolutely on the money.'

Both now looked down at the body, covered up again. Forensics had finished and showed the paramedics all was clear.

'All we need is just that. You can take her away,' they said to the paramedics.

'Stop! Just before you do,' John yelled down. 'I'm coming down.'

John hurried off, and Matt stayed behind. The forensic team was on its way up to sweep the room. He wanted to see if they would find anything important.

John reached the paramedics, who were waiting patiently near Holly's body.

'Where are you taking her from here?' John asked.

'We'll be taking her to the morgue. Why?' one paramedic asked.

'The coroner will have to conduct an autopsy, so be careful how you handle her.'

The two paramedics placed the stretcher near the woman's body.

'Watch out for the blood,' said the first one.

'Yeah, no worries,' came the reply.

The two lifted the stretcher and wheeled it to the ambulance. Once the stretcher was inside and secured, they got into the ambulance and drove off at a steady pace, with only the lights flashing.

The police photographer snapped a few more shots, then he and John headed back inside the hotel. They entered and walked toward the elevator. An attractive-looking blonde woman entered the lift behind them. As John observed her from behind, he thought she possessed lovely features and was dressed to kill.

The lift stopped at the third floor, and the doors opened. As the blonde woman walked into the passage, she sensed something was not quite right. Suddenly, she came to a halt and stood still. Approaching Holly's door, she saw someone in the room with his back to her. She turned and almost bumped into John and the photographer.

'Ma'am?' John queried as he stopped her retreat. The photographer maintained his pace and continued on.

'I... I'm here to meet a friend,' she stammered.

'And which room is she in?' the detective asked.

'Room 302, this one here.'

'What is your friend's name?' John asked.

She replied, saying, 'Holly Jamieson.'

'What is your name?'

'Joanne Holland,' was the blonde's reply.

'Miss Holland, is it?' John continued with the questions.

'Yes, that is correct. What is the reason for your query, may I ask?'

'We've had a person fall from up here. I believe she could be the person who occupies this room. We are trying to ID her,' he told her. 'We think it could be this friend of yours.'

'Oh!' she retorted, her hand moving to cover her mouth as she took a couple of steps backward. 'It couldn't be Holly!'

'Miss Holland, can you answer a few more questions?' John asked. 'I hope that's alright?'

Joanne nodded in approval, wanting to find out more about what had happened to Holly. John extended his arm and beckoned her to come in his direction, saying, 'Come this way.'

Both of them made their way into the room. She stopped a few steps inside and looked around. The window to the balcony was open, the white lace curtains still flying in the light breeze. John, right behind her, pushed past and walked over to the table. He pulled up a chair and beckoned her to sit down, which she did.

Matt came in from the balcony after talking to the photographer.

'Miss Holland, this is Detective Matt Wilson,' John introduced.

'Miss Holland,' Matt acknowledged with a polite tone in his voice.

Joanne looked around the room, her mind racing. What happened to Holly last night? The room looked immaculate, and so did she, as she always did, with nothing out of place and no evidence of anything untoward.

The realisation of Holly being gone suddenly hit Joanne. Tears brimmed in her eyes and flowed down her cheeks. She wept openly as John turned away, not wishing to make it any harder for her. Matt stood beside her and waited a moment before asking about Holly.

Unfortunately, some questions had to be asked. Matt tried to use some compassion when he started.

'How long have you known Holly?' he began.

'We only met about six months ago in Sydney. She said there was a friend in Perth she wanted to catch up with,' she replied. 'So she came back here and brought me with her.'

'What was your relationship with her?' Matt gingerly asked.

At that point, Joanne sat up a little straighter, clasped her hands in her lap, and looked at Matt with piercing blue eyes.

'We were in an extremely close relationship. Lovers, if you like!' came her quick, snappy reply.

'I'm sorry to ask you a personal question. It must be difficult to come to terms with what has happened,' Matt said, trying to console her.

'Yes, thank you,' she replied in a lower voice.

'Were you with her last night, Miss Holland?' Matt asked.

'Only for a short time, as she was hoping her school friend would drop by,' she replied.

'And who might that be?'

'The person's name is Stephanie Winters. They have been close friends since high school, I think.'

'Is she living here in Geraldton?'

'Yes, she has family here in Forrester Park.'

'Well, Miss Holland, that is all for now. Thank you for your cooperation,' Matt said, appreciating the valuable information she had given. 'Oh, by the way, where were you last night?'

'Currently, I am living at the residence of a close friend. Holly and I had a slight disagreement, and I suggested I'd stay out of her way for the night.'

'Who was that with?' Matt asked.

'Someone I met earlier,' Joanne replied.

'I inquired about the person whom you met. The person's name?' Matt insisted.

'I just know him as Lewis.'

'You met a man?' Matt asked, a little confused by her answer.

'Yes, I enjoy the company of a man occasionally,' Joanne replied, putting on her airs and graces.

'I see,' Matt replied, a little bemused by her frankness.

'Will that be all?' she asked. 'I'd like to collect some of my things.'

'Not just yet. Leave me your phone number and where you are staying. I'll contact you when we've finished, or if we need to see you again,' he replied.

She scribbled down her number and the address on a hotel pad on the table and handed it to Matt. She glared at him for a moment and then left.

'Don't leave town either,' Matt called after her as she headed towards the stairs.

# Chapter 2: Holly's Degree

Stephanie was a little puzzled as to why Holly had not called her on the phone. They were supposed to organise a get-together with Joanne for a few drinks and maybe go out for tea. Perhaps she had made other plans at the last minute.

Holly was a little impetuous and somewhat unpredictable, especially since her return from Sydney. She'd had a hard time with the boyfriend she was seeing, and Steph suspected he had bashed her occasionally. Steph also learned that the boyfriend belonged to an undesirable element involved in drug trafficking, though no one had convicted them so far. She was concerned for Holly's safety and well-being and had said as much to her on the phone.

'It's all good, Steph,' Holly used to say. 'Roberto and I are good together.'

Steph had doubts, but she had no choice but to accept Holly's statement.

* * *

They met in high school on an occasion when Holly was being taunted by some bullies because of the tartan-coloured jacket she was wearing one morning.

Stephanie knew how to handle herself. She had recently earned her brown belt in Jujitsu, and could pin, joint lock, throw, or manipulate a movement to defend herself with ease. She had also competed in a national tournament and had managed third spot overall. The bullies were in for a shock.

Steph saw one bully lash out at Holly, but miss. That was the signal she was waiting for.

'Hey! Leave her alone!' she yelled as she hurried in to defend Holly.

'It's alright,' Holly said to Steph. 'I can handle it.'

'Not from where I was watching. Three ganging up on you is unfair in my book.'

'What are you going to do about it, you blonde bimbo?' one of them sneered, trying to get a reaction from Steph.

Steph stood her ground and said nothing, just stared with cold, steely eyes as her anger rose. Holly was no match for them at all.

'Go on, slap the bitch,' one said to the apparent pack leader.

All she needed was their encouragement. She stepped forward and swung a fist at Steph. Steph saw it coming, moved just enough for the punch to sail past, and the offender was thrown off balance. Steph grabbed her arm, locked it under hers, and applied a little pressure.

'Ahh, you bloody bitch!' she squealed as the pain of her elbow bending backwards registered.

Steph drew her close and, in a low voice, said, 'I suggest you crawl back into the hole you came from and leave her alone, or next time I'll break it, maybe both of them.'

She applied a bit more pressure, and the offender's eyes widened at the stabbing pain.

'Okay, okay,' she squealed again, louder this time. 'You made your point.'

'Then don't forget it.'

'Okay, okay.'

Steph released her arm, and the offender rubbed her elbow and flexed it gingerly. Steph's quick reaction and ability to make her submit still bewildered the other two. They exchanged only long looks as they turned and left.

Once they had gone out of sight, Holly turned to Steph and said, 'Thanks.'

'Are you okay?' Steph asked, concern in her voice.

'Yeah, I'm fine now,' Holly replied with a sigh of relief.

'I'm Stephanie Winters,' Steph said formally, introducing herself.

'I'm Holly Jamieson,' Holly replied.

'Hi.'

'Yeah, hi,' Holly said, shaking Steph's hand.

'Where did you learn to do that?' Holly asked.

'One of my hobbies is practising martial arts. Not that I advertise it,' Steph replied. 'So, what's your next class?'

'Maths is my next subject,' Holly replied enthusiastically. 'What about you?'

'Science,' Steph answered.

'I'm supposed to hand in an assignment today, but I'm stuck on one equation,' Holly complained.

'Can you get an extension?' 'Why?'

Holly enquired.

'I can give you a hand after school if you like,' Steph offered. 'I can come around to your place too, if you'd like.'

'Cool!' Holly replied, wide-eyed. 'Thank you.'

'It's not a problem at all. We'll catch up after school.'

Holly and Steph went their separate ways to their next lesson. Holly was beaming inwardly as she sat down in class. She hoped she had found someone she could call a friend, and she sounded like maths was her forte.

This was the start of a firm friendship. Steph helped her with maths, breaking it down into terms Holly could understand.

'There's always more than one way to skin a cat,' she told Holly.

**Holly, Joanne and Steph**

There was only one other occasion the bullies tried to torment Holly, but Steph was close by, and they gave up as soon as she appeared. She just pointed a finger at them, and they retreated.

* * *

Holly and Steph became firm friends throughout the rest of high school and into college. Steph studied nursing, and Holly trained to become an accountant. They drifted apart for a while but kept in contact via phone and email.

Steph stayed in Perth and finished her nursing training, always intending to return to Geraldton, where her family lived. Holly had an ambition to make it big in Sydney and couldn't move there quickly enough. It seemed to Steph that this was about the time Holly began to change. She wasn't the innocent, bullied girl from high school anymore. She had matured and had the guts to look you in the eye and tell you to piss off, without actually saying the words, if she didn't like you.

It puzzled Steph that their contact had become less frequent. Holly was clearly moving in a different circle, and Steph hoped she was looking after herself and taking care not to fall into poor company.

One morning, Holly rang Steph, full of excitement. She had just found out she'd passed her accountancy with flying colours and had applied to become a CPA.

'I did it!' she babbled over the phone to Steph. 'I got my degree!'

'Well, good for you, girl,' Steph replied. 'It's about time your hard work paid off.'

'Thank you,' she said.

'You're welcome, Holly.'

'I know I haven't contacted you lately, but I was studying for my finals,' Holly explained.

'That's okay, as long as everything is well with you.'

'It's great. I met a guy as well, and it looks like it will be a regular thing,' Holly informed her.

'That is good news. What's he like?'

'We've only met twice, and I told him I had exams to think about before I got into any relationship. He was fine with that, so fingers crossed,' Holly said excitedly at the prospect.

'That's good news, Holly. I'm really pleased for you. What's his name?'

'Roberto,' Holly replied.

'Have you got a job yet?'

'Yes, I'm working for Roberto's dad. He imports heavy machinery and spare parts. I'm to start in the accounts receivable department next week.'

Finally, Holly appeared to have some luck going her way. She now had an accounting degree, a job, and a boyfriend.

'Steph, I have to get ready. I'm going out for lunch with Roberto to celebrate,' Holly informed her. 'Ok. You look after yourself.'

'Thanks, Steph, I will. Bye.'

Holly hung up, and the phone went silent. Steph stood there for a moment, pondering the fortune that had suddenly come Holly's way. She shouldn't doubt it for one minute. She'd worked hard for it and deserved to reap the rewards.

Steph finally smiled to herself, thinking about how eager Holly seemed to be and the future she had in front of her.

No one could have guessed the misfortune that lay ahead.

* * *

Steph, bumped into by a blonde-haired woman in jeans and a blue top, saw her rushing out of the hotel. The woman quickly got into a red BMW parked a short distance up the street and drove off at speed.

'Nice! An "excuse me" would have been the order of the day,' Steph muttered under her breath.

She watched the woman drive away in a hurry, then entered the hotel and headed upstairs. As she approached Holly's room, she noticed the door was slightly ajar and heard voices coming from inside.

'We're finished here,' one voice said.

'Okay. Give us a report as soon as you can,' said another.

Steph was startled as the door swung open and a well-dressed man carrying a suitcase came out. He glanced at Steph as he hurried off down the stairs. Then another man appeared at the door. Their eyes met and held.

'Can I help you, ma'am?' he asked.

'Umm, this is my friend's room. What's going on?' Steph asked, somewhat bewildered.

'You are?' the man asked.

Steph quickly regained her composure and quipped, 'More to the point, who are you?' she fired back.

'I'm sorry, ma'am. I'm Detective Matt Wilson,' he replied as he pulled out his ID.

'Stephanie Winters,' Steph replied, a little surprised.

'Miss Winters, please come inside.'

Steph entered the room and looked around. She was still wondering why the police were there. Where was Holly?

'Where is Holly?' she finally asked.

'Miss Winters, please take a seat,' Matt instructed.

'Please tell me what is going on,' Steph insisted politely as she sat down.

'Your friend, Miss Jamieson, has fallen from the balcony. I'm sorry to inform you that her injuries were fatal.'

Steph stared at Matt for a moment. Her heart felt like it skipped a beat, and a shock wave through her body gave her an ache deep inside. Tears welled up in her eyes. She blinked and looked away as the tears trickled down her cheeks.

'When did this happen?' Steph asked, looking back at Matt through watery eyes.

'We believe in the early hours of this morning,' was Matt's reply.

'How did she fall? She didn't jump. She wouldn't!'

'We are still looking at all avenues, and there is nothing conclusive yet. You seem certain about her decision not to jump.'

'Holly was never suicidal. I can vouch for that,' Steph asserted.

'We also need to identify the body to confirm that it is Holly Jamieson,' Matt informed her.

Steph looked straight ahead, remembering the plans they had made and the experiences they had shared. Even though Holly had been distant until recently, the bond between them had always been strong since high school.

'Where is she?' Steph asked.

'They have taken her away for an autopsy. The coroner is to make a report on his findings.'

'I'd like to see her one last time,' Steph said, fighting back more tears.

Matt looked at her and felt sorry for her. They had obviously been very close friends. Even with grief clouding her face and her eyes puffy from crying, he thought Steph was quite an attractive woman. But that was as far as he would venture for now.

'Did you drive here?' Matt asked.

'Yes, I did.'

'I'll take you to identify her if you like. I don't think you're in a fit state to drive at the moment.'

'Yes, thank you,' Steph replied in agreement. 'I'm ready when you are.'

All this time, Senior Detective Ralph was out on the balcony, watching Matt interview Steph. He was quite content to let Matt handle the questioning, especially given the state Steph was in. He would have been a little more brazen in his approach, and that wouldn't have done anyone any good. From what he'd heard, it seemed Holly had been the victim of someone pushing her off the balcony, and he was determined to find out who had committed the act. Murder was definitely on the cards. So far, two people were suspects, Joanne and Steph. Neither fitted the profile of a murderer. It seemed someone else had been in the room with Holly in the early hours of the morning.

Matt made a quick phone call and was informed that Holly's body would be available for identification by the time he arrived at the morgue with Steph.

'We're heading off to identify the body,' he informed Senior Detective Ralph.

'Good. We're nearly finished here anyway, so I'll meet you back at the station,' Ralph replied.

'Okay, I'll bring Steph to make a statement if she's still up to it by then.'

'Anytime she's ready. Even tomorrow morning will do.'

Matt nodded and followed Steph out of the room and down the stairs. He showed her to his car and opened the door for her. She nodded him a quiet 'thanks' and got in. There was no conversation on the way to the morgue.

They arrived, and both got out. Matt hurried to open the morgue door for Steph. Inside, they met a nurse who had been expecting them. She led them to the viewing room and said to Matt, 'I'll tell them you're here for a viewing.'

Matt nodded and turned to Steph, who was fidgeting with her hands in anticipation. She faced the large window, behind which a black curtain was drawn. Matt came up and stood beside her.

Behind the curtain and on the other side, there was a gurney with a body covered with a white sheet. The nurse who met them stood beside the gurney waiting for a signal to uncover the face of the body underneath.

Steph clasped her hands together tightly, her knuckles turning white. She took a deep breath and then nodded to the nurse. The sheet was pulled back, revealing the face of a woman. It was Holly.

Steph felt her legs go weak, and Matt instantly reacted, catching hold of her. She pressed her hands against her face as the tears flowed. Turning to Matt, she sobbed, eyes closed, and leant on his shoulder. Matt wrapped his arms around her and felt her grief. She continued to sob, seemingly uncontrollably.

After a minute, she pulled away and turned back to the window. The nurse had left, and Holly remained uncovered. Steph tried to calm herself and regain some composure.

'Oh, Holly, you poor dear. Who did this to you?' Steph sobbed.

'Miss Winters, I'm sorry, but I still have to ask you. Is that Holly Jamieson?'

Steph pressed her hands against the window, slightly leaning against it, looking down at the still form of Holly. She turned away from the window at Matt's question and, with teary eyes, replied.

'Yes, it is Holly Jamieson.'

She made her way to the door, Matt following. The nurse reappeared and gently covered Holly's face again. Steph turned back for one last look and whispered, 'Goodbye, Holly.'

With her arms folded and her posture leaning forward, Steph slowly made her way out. Matt caught up and put an arm around her. She took the opportunity and rested her head against his shoulder.

'I don't understand why she would take her own life. Believe me, she wouldn't do that.'

'Why do you say that?' Matt asked.

'It's not the Holly I knew. She loved life. That's not in her character.'
'People change, and they do the unthinkable.'

'No, not Holly. She would never do that.'

'So, what are you trying to say?' Matt asked.

'I don't know. It just doesn't make any rhyme or reason for her to do that,' Steph replied in frustration.

They stepped outside, and Matt opened the car door for Steph. She got in, and Steph got it. They drove back to the hotel where Steph had parked her car, and Matt parked his car close to Steph's car.

'Are you alright to drive?' he asked, concerned. She seemed to have calmed down somewhat. Steph sat there without moving for a moment, then said,

'I know Holly went through some drama in Sydney, and I know she came back here to get away from it all.'

'Away from what exactly?' Matt queried.

'She hooked up with this bloke over there, and I'm sure things went a bit pear-shaped,' Steph replied. 'She told me some scary things.'

'Do you want to come down to the station and give us the details of your concerns?' Matt pressed.

'Yes, I can do that if you want me to,' Steph replied with a queer look on her face.

'Miss Winters, we have some issues with Miss Jamieson's death. It's not as straightforward as it appears.'

'What do you mean?'

'I can tell you more at the station,' Matt replied.

'Okay, when do you want me there?'

'Whenever you're ready to make a statement.'

'You don't suspect me?' Steph asked, a little alarmed.

'Not at all, Miss Winters. We just want to know more about Miss Jamieson's background and, hopefully, solve the puzzle of her death.' 'I thought it was straightforward?' Steph questioned. 'You were contemplating suicide?'

'No, there's more to it than that,' Matt replied.

'What are you saying?' Steph asked. 'You believed me when I said Holly wouldn't have killed herself?'

'I'll tell you more at the station.'

'Okay, I'll be there shortly.'

Steph got out of the car and went over to her own. Matt pulled away, and she hesitated for a moment, watching him drive off. He was talking in riddles, and she wanted to find out why. What wasn't he telling her?

# Chapter 3: Find Him

On the way to the police station, Steph went through the McCafé drive-thru for a coffee and a bun. She had skipped breakfast to meet Holly and maybe go to the Dome for something to eat, but that didn't happen.

With Holly's demise, her appetite diminished, though she still needed a caffeine fix. She was still pondering the detective's insinuation about Holly's death as she pulled up outside the police station. She locked the car and went inside with the coffee in hand.

'I'm here to see Detective Matthew Wilson,' she announced to the desk clerk.

'Is he expecting you?' the clerk asked.

'Yes, he is,' Steph replied.

The clerk was about to pick up the phone to call Matt when the door in the hallway opened and he said, 'Miss Winters, this way, please.'

Steph smiled at Matt, gave the clerk a quick sideways glance, and followed him down the hallway to an interview room.

'Take a seat, please,' Matt offered. 'I won't be a moment.'

He left the room and came back shortly with Senior Detective Ralph.

'Miss Winters, this is Senior Detective Ralph. He is in charge of this investigation.'

'Investigation?' Steph echoed, taken aback by Matt's introduction and the announcement that this was an investigation.

'Yes, Miss Winters,' Ralph confirmed. 'We suspect foul play surrounding Miss Jamieson's death.'

'How so?' Steph asked, somewhat bewildered that the police were thinking along those lines already.

'We believe someone pushed her over the balcony railings,' Matt replied. 'The coroner supports that theory as well, from his initial examination.'

Steph tried to fathom what was being said. She was surprised and perplexed when the police stated Holly had been murdered. That's what the detectives were suggesting, but by whom?

'I'm a bit surprised at what you are saying. But are you sure someone murdered her?'

'Look, Miss Winters,' Matt began. 'May I call you Stephanie?'

'Steph is fine.'

'Steph,' he continued, 'we are certain someone else was involved in her death. If you can tell us all you know about Miss Jamieson, where she worked, who her friends were, people she associated with, that sort of thing, we have a chance of piecing this together and finding the culprit.'

'Am I a suspect?' Steph asked seriously this time.

'Everyone is at the moment,' Ralph replied. 'Hence this interview, and hopefully eliminating you from suspicion.'

Steph felt a little uneasy in the chair but realised that, under the circumstances of Holly's "murder", they were only doing their job. She had believed Holly never jumped from the beginning. Taking a deep breath, she asked,

'What do you want to know?'

'First,' Ralph began, 'where were you last night?'

'I was at home. I live with my parents.'

'And where is that?'

'Pinyali Way, Forrester Park.'

'You were home all night?' Ralph continued.

'Yes.'

'Tell us about your relationship with Miss Jamieson.'

'Well, where do you want me to start?' 'At

the beginning, when you first met.'

Steph looked at Ralph and then at Matt, who was leaning on the table. He sat back in his chair, seeming to get comfortable, with a frown on his face. She then looked back at Ralph's expressionless face. He was a seasoned investigator with many years behind him.

Ralph had probably endured many sleepless nights in the past, unravelling the truth from the lies spun by the scumbags he arrested would tell him. Steph got more comfortable in the chair as well.

'We met in high school,' she began. She mentioned the incident of Holly being taunted by some of the "low-life" girls at school and even helped fend off one in particular. They struck up a firm friendship almost right from the start.

'I helped her with some of the schoolwork, especially maths, and we got on fine,' she continued. 'We even went to college together for a while until I pursued my nursing career and she went to Sydney to complete her accountancy studies.'

'Did you lose contact with her?' Ralph asked.

'No, we kept in contact regularly via phone, text messages, Facebook, and the occasional email. The distance didn't create any barriers to communicating,' Steph replied.

'What made her come back here?' Matt asked this time.

'Oh, my God!' Steph said, recalling a conversation from the past. 'She had a torrid time over there.'

Both detectives' jaws seemed to drop, and they sat up straighter in their chairs.

'When was this?' Ralph quickly asked.

Steph frowned as she remembered the details of what Holly had told her. She wanted to get the information out quickly and babbled a little.

'Slow down, Steph,' Matt intervened. 'Take it slow.' Steph looked at Matt, then sighed.

'She rang one day in a terrible state, about a month ago. Having finished her accountancy course, she applied for the CPA. She met this Roberto character, who got her a job in his father's business. After hiring her, they assigned her to manage the creditors' accounts for their machinery-importing business.'

'Roberto who?' Ralph interjected.

'Roberto Rosetti, or Rosetta, something like that,' Steph replied.

'Did Miss Jamieson mention the business name at all?' Ralph asked.

'I think it was Emporium Machinery Imports,' Steph said. 'It just stuck in my head, probably because it sounded odd to me.'

Matt scribbled something on his notepad and got up, leaving the room.

'I'll be back in a minute,' he said as he went.

'Tell me about the murder she reckoned she saw?' Ralph asked, pressing Steph for the information.

Steph took another deep breath and then continued.

According to her, she and Roberto were getting along fairly well, and they were doing drugs in his flat on the third floor. In a neighbouring building across the alley from his flat, she saw what she believed was a shooting.

'They were both high on drugs and lying on the floor. Holly got up to get a drink or go to the toilet or something when she saw a man pointing a gun at a woman. She couldn't hear what was going on, but the woman seemed frantic. At that point, the man shot her.' 'Where did he shoot her?' Ralph pressed.

Just then, Matt came back into the room and sat down.

'Holly didn't say. She was high and thought she was hallucinating. Then she saw Roberto's father come into the room. She motioned for

Roberto to come and see what she was seeing. Roberto's father noticed they were both looking at him in the room and a woman, presumably on the floor, with the gunman standing over her.'

'What happened?' Matt asked as he came back into the room.

'Miss Jamieson appears to have witnessed a murder with her boyfriend across from his flat,' Ralph informed him.

'Yes, you said that before I left,' he replied, slightly surprised. 'Did she identify the killer?'

'No, she only saw him once before that night,' Steph replied.

'So you don't know who it was?' 'No,

I don't,' Steph said.

Just then there was a knock on the door, and a well-dressed uniformed officer opened it. He stepped inside and handed Matt some papers.

'Here is the information you were looking for, Detective,' he said.

'Thank you,' Matt replied.

The officer left the room and closed the door behind him. Matt flicked through the pages and had a surprised look on his face when he finished.

'Well,' he began. 'Roberto Vincenso Rosetti is the son of Dominic Roberto Rosetti and Teresa Marie Rosetti. They own Emporium Machinery Imports P/L and import machinery and spare parts. Roberto has been in trouble with the police on drug charges, assault with a deadly weapon, theft, and so on. Quite a list, I may add.'

'Did Miss Jamieson know anything about this?' Ralph asked Steph.

'I'm not sure. She mentioned nothing like that to me.'

'It's something you wouldn't brag about,' Matt observed.

Steph went on, saying Holly told her that the day after the shooting she was upset about what had happened. Roberto's father spoke to both of them in his office and told Holly that if she said anything, he would have to take matters into his own hands and seek an alternative solution.

'Why didn't you go to the police and tell them what Miss Jamieson told you?' Ralph asked.

'Would they have believed me?' Steph fired back.

There was another knock on the door, and the officer who had given Matt the information earlier poked his head in and said to Ralph, 'Senior, do you have a minute?'

'Yes, sir, we will finish in a couple of minutes.' 'Good,'

the officer replied and closed the door.

'Miss Winters, that's all for now,' Ralph said. 'You've had a hell of a day, and we appreciate the help you've given us so far. Leave your details at the front desk as we'll probably need to talk with you again.'

Steph got up and left the room, followed by Ralph and Matt. Ralph headed to the Super's office, while Matt walked Steph to the door.

'Steph, we really appreciate your help,' he said to her. 'If you need anything, call me.'

She smiled as he handed her his card, then she returned to her car and drove away.

Matt went back inside and joined Ralph, who was now with the boss, the Superintendent.

***

'Have a seat, Matt,' the Superintendent said as he entered his office. 'I've just received some alarming information faxed through from Sydney.'

Matt took a seat next to Ralph and waited for the news.

'The Rossetti family has been a thorn in the side of the New South Wales police for a decade,' the Super read. 'They are under suspicion for importing stolen goods, dubious machinery parts, and drugs.

Despite multiple arrests, the police were unsuccessful in making any charges stick.'

'What's the problem? Not enough evidence?' Ralph asked.

'You could say that. Most of the evidence is circumstantial, and witnesses miraculously disappear,' the Superintendent said. 'Rumour has it they have a hitman in their employ.'

'Do we know who it might be?' Matt asked.

'The Federal Police are involved as well, and it's believed that a Russian, Sergio Stromnikov, is the man.'

'If the Feds are involved, this could be a serious case,' Matt observed.

'What about Immigration? Do they have his details?' Ralph asked.

'They did, but the information is no longer useful. He's in hiding somewhere, having fallen off the radar, it would seem.'

Matt and Ralph looked at each other and then back at the Superintendent.

'I bet they have lawyers who can manipulate the law when they can. How does this affect the case?' Ralph asked.

'I think we need to tread carefully. We don't know who handled Miss Jamieson's murder, and the coroner's report I just received shows she may have had an unwanted intruder,' the Superintendent warned. 'A cocktail of drugs was in her system. It was a lethal dose.' 'What do we know about this hitman?' Matt asked.

'Not much. He came into the country three months ago via Singapore from Kyiv in Ukraine and then fell off the radar. Immigration cannot find him, and the Feds are looking out for him as well,' the Superintendent informed them.

'Why do they believe the Rossettis employed him?' Ralph asked.

'Here is a photo they managed to get. He saw Dominic twice.'

'If what Miss Jamieson told Miss Winters is correct, then the Rossettis are involved in her murder as well,' Matt said.

The Superintendent agreed. They had to be careful that this Russian wasn't still in Geraldton getting rid of the evidence.

Steph flashed through Matt's mind as well. Was she in danger, too? Matt got up and wandered around the room, deep in thought.

'What is it, Detective Wilson?' the Superintendent asked.

'I was wondering, could Miss Winters be in danger, and Miss Holland?'

'Do you think he knows about them?' the Superintendent asked.

'I don't see how at this stage,' Matt replied. 'He's a mean-looking bloke too. We don't know what instructions he received before leaving Sydney.'

Matt handed the photo to Ralph, who took a long look at it, then handed it back.

'Do you recognise the man, Senior?' the Superintendent asked.

'No, I don't, but he strikes me as someone who is heartless and calculating. I've seen his kind before,' he replied.

'Where, Sydney?'

'Yes,' he replied. 'It's the "Sydney way" of how people go missing,' Ralph continued. 'Shooting people is too messy, so they throw the bodies overboard with both hands tied and feet in cement. You can't swim, so you sink to the bottom and drown. It may be impossible to recover the body.'

'Charming bunch of mongrels,' Matt said.

'Yep, and then some.'

Matt handed the photo back to the Superintendent, who placed it in the file. He picked up some documents and handed them to Ralph.

'The coroner's report supports your theory, Matt. Miss Jamieson had some bruising in the kidney area not consistent with falling. Someone had forcefully pushed her against the balcony railing and then pushed her over.'

Ralph flicked through the pages and read something that caught his eye. He frowned at the section relating to drugs.

'Rohypnol,' he exclaimed. 'That's the "date rape" drug.'

Matt peered over at the report to check if Ralph was mistaken, but he wasn't.

'Yes, that caught my eye as well, and look at the level,' the Superintendent pointed out. 'That with alcohol, it's a wonder she was still standing.'

'Maybe she wasn't,' Matt suggested. 'If those are the levels, then she would almost be unconscious and unable to struggle.'

Someone pushed her hard against the railing before she toppled over. The injuries she received when she hit the ground would have killed her instantly. The Superintendent pointed out that someone had pushed her hard against the railing before she toppled over, resulting in a fractured skull, broken neck, six fractured vertebrae, fractured pelvis, and ribs. 'It appeared as if a train had hit the poor girl.' 'Falling the way she did, it's little wonder,' Ralph replied.

'That means someone murdered her,' Matt responded.

'Yes,' the Superintendent agreed. 'The evidence definitely points that way, and I'm prepared to call it "wilful murder". Let's use every method to find the person who did it. My money is on the Russian, and he's still in town. Find him.'

Both Ralph and Matt stood up in unison and nodded to the Superintendent, before leaving his office. Matt had several things going through his mind. He was concerned about Steph's safety and then asked Ralph, 'What's the plan of attack?'

'I think we need to get Miss Joanne Holland in here and see what else she can tell us about Miss Jamieson,' Ralph replied. 'Today would be nice, because we need to move on this fast!'

'I'll get her brought back in,' Matt said. 'I have her address.'

# **Chapter 4: Hit and Run**

Steph suspected that someone had murdered Holly, and she couldn't shake off the idea. It didn't gel with her one bit. She knew Holly was having issues with Roberto and his father, and that was why she wanted to move back to WA. Was it possible that someone had followed her here intending to kill her? Her mind was racing.

She pulled up at the mall to stop for another cup of coffee and to dwell on Holly and the times they had shared together. It was strange how someone tormented at high school could sort out her life, only to succumb to this tragedy in such a traumatic way.

Steph got out of the car with a tear in her eye. Without hesitation, she made her way to the cafe on the other side of the road. She didn't stop to look for traffic; she didn't hear the car speeding towards her, but at the last moment, she became aware of the vehicle bearing down on her.

Amid the screams and passers-by shouting, 'Look out!' it was all too late. The car clipped her and flung her through the air. Steph landed heavily, looking like a rag doll on the ground, unconscious.

The onlookers felt horror at what they had just witnessed.

'Get the rego number of that car!' someone shouted.

'Call an ambulance!' There was another shout, 'and the police.'

A shop assistant from the nearby pharmacy came out to see what the commotion was about, then quickly dashed back inside, shouting. 'There's been an accident!'

'Two more staff came out, and one knelt down beside Steph's seemingly lifeless form.

'I'm a nurse,' she announced. 'Has anyone rung for an ambulance?'

'I did,' a voice came from the crowd. 'They should be here shortly.' 'Get me a neck brace, a blow-up splint, and a pillow,' the nurse requested from the shop assistant.

'You can use my cardigan for a pillow,' an onlooker offered.

The nurse checked Steph's neck and ran her hand along her spine. A trickle of blood came from Steph's ear and nose. The nurse put the neck brace on Steph when the shop assistant returned and then darted off again. The nurse fitted the neck brace, then rolled up the cardigan and gently placed it under Steph's head. She secured the inflatable splint around Steph's broken lower leg.

The shop assistant returned with more items the nurse had requested. One onlooker picked up a handbag and car keys lying a short distance away and handed them over.

'These might be hers,' he said.

Steph moaned.

'It's okay. You're in expert hands,' the nurse assured her.

Steph lapsed back into unconsciousness as the sound of the approaching ambulance grew louder. First onto the scene was a police car, sirens blaring and lights flashing. It stopped a short distance up the street to allow enough room for the ambulance. It was close behind the police car and pulled in alongside Steph.

The paramedics were quickly at her side. The nurse introduced herself and explained what treatment she had given. They acknowledged her help, then placed Steph on the gurney and into the ambulance.

Meanwhile, two police officers approached. One asked, 'Can anyone tell us what happened? Any witnesses?'

'It was a hit and run,' someone piped up.

'It was a red car!' said another. Comment erupted from the rest of the onlookers.

'Okay!' the officer exclaimed. 'Those of you who didn't witness the incident, please move on. I'd like to hear from those who actually saw what took place.'

The ambulance headed off to the hospital with lights and sirens blaring up the mall.

One onlooker stepped forward.

'I saw what happened,' he said. 'A red Mazda 6 came roaring up the mall, clipped the lady, and took off without stopping.'

'Did you get a rego number?' the officer asked.

'No, but someone else apparently did.'

'That's me,' came another voice. 'I saw it too, just like this man said. Here's the rego number I wrote down.'

'That's handy,' the officer replied, noticing the man's work attire. 'You always carry a notepad?'

'Yes, for work,' the man explained.

He tore out the page and handed it over. A third man came forward, saying he had only caught part of the rego number, 347. The officer looked at the notepad given to him by the second man, and he nodded in approval.

'That's what's written here as well. Thank you,' he said. 'Was it a male or female driver you saw?'

'Male driver,' two onlookers replied.

'It was awful seeing her run down like that,' said a woman in the crowd.

'I've seen nothing like it,' added another.

'Whose cardigan is this?' the officer asked, pointing to it.

'That's mine,' another onlooker said. 'The nurse used it as a pillow for the poor girl's head.'

The nurse stepped forward and gave the officer the handbag and keys someone had found near the accident.

'I think these are hers,' she told the officer as she handed him the items. The officer addressed the witnesses. 'Thank you all for being so observant. I think the lady who suffered the injury would thank you as well. Well done, everyone!'

The two officers walked back to their vehicle, and the crowd dispersed. One officer opened the handbag and found Steph's driving licence in her wallet. A moment later, they drove off back to the station to file their reports.

***

Senior Detective John Ralph was reading through the reports on Holly's death when an officer handed him the full coroner's report. He immediately began studying it. Detective Matt Wilson hadn't yet returned with Joanne Holland.

As Ralph leaned back in his chair, reading, the Superintendent poked his head around the corner of his office.

'Senior, what was the name of the deceased woman's friend? Stephanie Winters?'

'Yes, they'd been friends since high school. Why?' Ralph asked.

'I just received this report from traffic. Stephanie Winters was run down in a hit-and-run accident at the mall about twenty minutes ago.' Ralph immediately sat up straight and then sprang to his feet.

'What?' he reacted, his face astonished and his mouth agape.

'I just rang the hospital, and she's at St John's. Her condition isn't clear yet.'

'Fuck!' Ralph yelled as he dropped back into his seat.

'Senior,' the Superintendent warned. 'Language.'

'Sorry, Sir, but really! What's this place coming to?'

'Hurry and find out before more people get hurt,' the Superintendent urged.

Just then, Matt walked in, and he didn't look too pleased with himself either. He was alone. A quick glance at both Ralph and the Superintendent told him something was wrong.

'You didn't find her,' Ralph said, stating the obvious.

'I'd delay sending a uniform to find her and bring her in,' the Superintendent said, then left. 'Ralph will explain.'

'We have a problem,' Ralph began. 'In a terrible turn of events at the mall, a car driven by a hit-and-run driver struck Stephanie Winters, leaving her with serious injuries.'

Matt froze on the spot, his face turning pale as the blood drained away. It took a moment to sink in. Matt was keen on Steph, and this wasn't the outcome he had expected. Someone must think Steph is a threat as well. Were they planning to do away with Joanne Holland next, or had they already done so?

'How is she?' Matt finally asked.

'She is in St John's Hospital,' Ralph replied. 'We're not sure of her condition.'

Matt sat down in a chair and stared at nothing in particular. He then looked over at the Senior, who was reading the accident report. After flicking through the pages and then back again, Ralph sat back in his chair, fixed his eyes on Matt, and said,

'The Super's right. That fucking bastard's still in town.'

'What was he driving?'

'It's a red Mazda. Here's the rego number.'

'We'll alert the traffic authorities to look out for the Mazda with this rego number.'

'It would be a hire car,' Matt suggested. 'I'll ring around the rentals and see if we can find it.'

Matt left the room and headed to his own office. He rang the rental car companies in town and finally found one that owned the car. It was a rental from Avis at the airport. According to the paperwork, the person who rented it had it for three days and was supposed to return it in the afternoon.

Matt took Stromnikov's photo to see if the receptionist at Avis would recognise him. He went to see Ralph.

'It's an Avis rental from the airport, picked up two days ago. It's due to be returned this afternoon,' Matt informed him.

'He's leaving on the evening flight to Perth.'

'I'll show the photo to the girl out there and see if she recognises him,' Matt said.

'We'll both go,' Ralph insisted. 'I want this asshole found too!'

It was a ten-minute drive to the airport. Matt and Ralph went to the Avis counter, where a smartly dressed young lady in a polka dot blouse and red scarf, the Avis car rental uniform, greeted them.

'Morning, gentlemen, how can I help?' was her pleasant greeting.

'I'm Senior Detective Ralph, and this is Detective Wilson,' Ralph introduced. The receptionist's smile disappeared quickly, becoming nervous about what was going to happen next. After all, it's not every day two detectives come in and flash their ID cards at you.

'Have you seen this man before?' Matt asked, showing her the photo.

The young lady quickly composed herself, possibly relieved that she could help the detectives. She took a deep breath and replied.

'Yes, I have. He came and picked up a car a couple of days ago. I have his name here in the register.'

She flicked through the pages, and it was only a couple of seconds before she stopped and pointed to the entry in the register as she gave it to Ralph.

'Serge Strom,' Ralph read. 'Is that the name he used? Did he show you any ID?'

'Clever,' Matt muttered. 'He's using an alias similar to his real name.'

'He showed me his driver's licence. There's the number, and it was a New South Wales licence,' she informed Ralph.

Matt noted down the driver's licence number and date of issue.

'Can you remember what he was wearing at the time?' Ralph asked.

I recall seeing faded jeans and a navy-blue jacket, notwithstanding the refined appearance of the other customers.'

'Was the car pre-booked, or was it a spot booking?' Matt asked.

'No, it was a pre-booking,' she replied.

'How did he pay for the car hire?' Ralph asked.

The receptionist turned the register around, searched for the receipt number, then opened the 'booking' file and found the copy hire form. A quick glance gave her the answer.

'It was cash.'

'Is that unusual for clients to pay cash for a hire car?' Ralph asked.

'Yes, it doesn't happen that often.'

'Who did the booking?' Matt asked.

'Emporium Machinery.' She replied. 'I've never heard of them.'

'Right,' Ralph said. 'Thanks for your help. It's been most valuable.'

'You're welcome,' she replied, finding her pleasant smile again.

Matt and Ralph went back to the car and drove to the station.

# Chapter 5: Turning Point

Two uniformed police officers escorted Joanne Holland into the police station. She looked a little flushed, as if she had been through an ordeal of some sort. A couple of minutes passed before the Superintendent came into the room.

'Miss Holland,' he began. 'Apologies for this intrusion, but we need you to help us some more with our enquiries, if you will.'

'Sure, but I don't see what else I can say that I didn't this morning,' she replied, somewhat perplexed.

'Senior Detective Ralph and Detective Wilson will be returning shortly and will interview you once they're back, he informed her. 'Would you like a drink in the meantime? Coffee or tea perhaps?'

'Coffee would be nice, thank you,' she said, accepting the offer. White, no sugar.'

The Superintendent left and returned a couple of minutes later with the coffee. He placed the cup in front of Joanne and said, 'I'll leave you to it. The detectives shouldn't be much longer.'

Joanne was curious about what more information they needed. She wasn't really in the mood for more interviews, but if it helped solve Holly's demise, she wanted that at any cost. Holly having her life taken in such a fashion was traumatic in the extreme. She wondered if they had already spoken with Steph as well.

It wasn't long before Ralph and Matt came into the room and sat down.

'We're grateful for your coming in again to help us with our investigation, Miss Holland,' Ralph began. 'It must be stressful under the circumstances.'

'Yes, you could put it like that.'

'Where were you this morning? You weren't at the address you gave us,' Ralph asked.

'Lewis and I went for coffee at the Dome. We also wanted to see if we were still being followed.'

'Followed?' Matt asked. 'By whom?'

'There was a guy in a red car parked a short distance up the road from Lewis's house. Our suspicions were right because he followed us into town. 'I think it was a Mazda.'

'What time was this?' Matt pressed.

'Mid-morning, just before 10 am,' Joanne replied.

Matt looked over at Ralph, who returned the glance.

'Miss Holland,' Ralph continued. 'Was this the man who was driving the car?'

Joanne looked at the photo he handed her and, after a moment, shook her head before giving it back.

'It could be, but I'm uncertain,' she replied. 'I know this man.'

'Miss Holland,' Ralph said. 'A male driving a red Mazda 6 ran Miss Stephanie Winters down in the mall just after 10 am this morning. This person is also a person of interest concerning the death of Holly Jamieson.'

Joanne, blonde with very fair skin, turned whiter than white at Ralph's words and sat transfixed. She put her hands to her face and caught her breath.

'Oh, my God! Is Stephanie okay?' she finally blurted.

'Where do you know him from?' Ralph quickly asked, ignoring Joanne's question.

'I saw him at a nightclub in Sydney some time ago. Do you think he's responsible for Holly's death?' Joanne asked frantically.

'Yes, we believe so,' Ralph said, careful not to divulge too much in an ongoing investigation.

'Oh, shit!' she exclaimed. 'I could be next. What about Steph? How is she?'

'Miss Winters is in an induced coma and is in a bad way, according to the latest hospital report, Matt informed her. 'The good news is she's in a stable condition.'

'So tell us more about this man and his connection with Miss Jamieson,' Ralph asked sternly.

'There's not much to tell. I saw him only once or twice, and both times he was talking to Holly's boyfriend.'

'That's Miss Jamieson's boyfriend, Roberto Rosetti, also known as Robbie,' Ralph clarified.

'Yes.'

'How did the two of you meet?' Matt asked.

'I was at a nightclub, Club77 in the Cross, and I saw Holly come in one evening, distraught. She ordered a drink and then sat down in a corner on her own. I went over to her and noticed bruising on her cheek. She was sobbing.'

'You engaged in conversation with her?' Ralph prompted.

'Yes, exactly,' Joanne replied. 'I thought she could do with some female company.'

'That was the night you became friends?' Ralph inquired.

'No, not really. Holly came in a few more times after that with a man, Roberto, and on one occasion asked me to join them. She introduced me to Robbie, as she called him. That night we had a few drinks and something to eat.'

'The first time you spoke to Miss Jamieson, did she tell you where she got the bruising from?' Matt asked.

'Robbie had been hitting her, she said, and it wasn't the first incident either. She was in the hospital for a week. I found out later he had something to do with it,' Joanne said, pointing to Sergio's photo.

'What was it she saw that warranted a beating like that?' Matt asked, his voice concerned.

'She wouldn't say, and I never found out. I mentioned it once or twice, and it was a touchy subject with her. So I let it go.'

'How did the three of you get on?' Matt continued.

'Holly and I were fine. I just couldn't stand the animal she was with,' Joanne declared. He wanted a threesome one night, and I told him to "fuck off". I'm not into that stuff. It's one-on-one or nothing, male or female.'

'Were you friends with Holly at first, or did you start by having a relationship?' Matt asked.

'We became firm friends first, and I was there to help Holly stand up when she got knocked down. That pissed me off,' Joanne continued. 'She got bashed or slapped around by Robbie, and I was her crutch. The relationship started around that time.'

'That must have upset you, knowing what was happening to her,' Matt said.

'Yes,' Joanne agreed. 'Especially the last time she came with a swollen lip and a black eye! She also had bruising down her left side, where he used her as a punching bag.'

'What did you do then?' Matt asked.

'We moved to my friend's place and laid low for about a week. Once Holly was feeling better, we had plans to buy a car and head to WA. She wanted to catch up with her friend Stephanie in Perth.' 'But

she wasn't in Perth,' Matt pointed out.

'No, she moved back to Geraldton and was staying with her family,' Joanne said.

Just then, there was a knock on the door, and the Superintendent opened it. He beckoned to Ralph to go with him.

'Senior,' he said.

Ralph got up, excused himself, and followed the Superintendent out into the corridor.

'The red Mazda identified as being involved in the hit-and-run this morning has been located on Eighth Street, in front of the basketball stadium, abandoned,' the Superintendent informed Ralph.

'Is it the vehicle?' Ralph asked.

'Yes,' the Superintendent replied. 'The rego number matches the witness statements, and it has damage to the left-hand-side front panel consistent with a collision with a person. Forensics is still examining the vehicle and will confirm its findings.'

'Stromnikov must still be in town,' Ralph suggested.

'Or he's grabbed another vehicle and has already left, the Superintendent said. 'An eyewitness living across the road from the stadium said she saw the vehicle parked less than an hour ago by a man answering his description.'

'Did she report it abandoned?' Ralph asked.

'No, two officers on routine patrol radioed it in as suspicious and stopped to inspect it. That's when the witness caught their attention and gave them the information about when it was left there. She also provided an excellent description of the suspect.'

'How long ago was the report radioed in?' Ralph asked, trying to gauge how much time Stromnikov had to cover his tracks.

'The report came in about half an hour ago, and the witness said it was there for only about three-quarters of an hour,' the Superintendent said.

'I wonder where that fucking arsehole has gone!'

'Senior, if you please,' the Superintendent said, clearly displeased with Ralph's language.

'Sorry, Sir, but we have a small window of opportunity to catch the mongrel,' Ralph said in defence of his outburst. 'He's already got an hour on us.'

'Agreed. You'd better get with it, then,' the Superintendent advised.

The Superintendent went back to his office, and Ralph returned to the interview room, finding Matt still questioning Joanne.

'How are we going here?' Ralph asked no one in particular.

'I think we're almost finished,' Matt replied. 'I was just offering Miss Holland a lift back to where the uniforms picked her up.'

'Good,' Ralph said. 'You organise that for Miss Holland. I have a couple of urgent phone calls to make.'

Ralph left the room and went to his own office to make the calls. Two other car rental businesses operated in town, one being quite close to where the Mazda was dumped. He dialled the number.

It rang only once before someone quickly answered. Ralph introduced himself and asked about a car being hired in the last hour.

'Yeah,' came the reply. 'A bloke came in about an hour ago and hired a Commodore to travel to Perth. He was tall, had a shaved head, and spoke with an accent.'

'What's the registration number of the vehicle?' Ralph asked.

The man gave Ralph the rego number, and Ralph thanked him for the info before hanging up. Matt wandered into Ralph's office and asked, 'What's going on?'

'How did you get on with Miss Holland?' Ralph asked instead of answering'.

'Okay, I drove her back to where she's staying.'

'Right,' Ralph acknowledged. 'We have to move quickly. We found the red Mazda parked in front of the basketball stadium. Stromnikov hired another car from the Auto Barn just up the road about an hour ago.'

'Really? That's not good news,' Matt replied, surprised by the turn of events but eager now the suspect was close. 'Where's he heading?'

'Perth.'

'We have to cut him off, and quickly,' Matt suggested.

'Agreed. So we'll let the highway patrol know to keep a lookout but not to stop him. You ring Dongara and find out where highway patrol currently is,' Ralph instructed. 'I'll ring through to Eneabba and alert them.'

Matt went to his desk and rang the Dongara police. Ralph rang through to Eneabba and two of the surrounding townships. The idea was to trap Stromnikov on the long stretch of highway north of Eneabba, where there were no minor roads to turn off from.

The only option Stromnikov had on that section was to flee on foot. This area was low scrubland for kilometres in any direction, and concealment from being sighted wasn't possible.

Ralph also reached out to the Police Air Wing, which had a chopper conducting night exercises in the area, to determine if it could transport them to the proposed roadblock location if required.

Both Ralph and Matt had to move fast, and with the help of the highway patrol, catch Stromnikov before he got too close to Perth. The opportunity to deviate onto a couple of alternative side routes would make his capture difficult. Eneabba could be the turning point.

# Chapter 6: Roberto Rossetti

Roberto Vincenso Rossetti was the younger son of Dominic Roberto Rossetti and Teresa Maria. He had an older sister, Maria, and a brother, Dominic Jr, the eldest of the three children. Dominic died three years ago from injuries he sustained in a car accident while allegedly being pursued by the police.

His death weighed heavily on the family, and there was no love lost between them and the authorities. Even the Federal Police and Customs actively monitored their imports of parts from China, but they found nothing that could be classified as illegal.

By mastering the art of drug smuggling, the Rossettis could outwit the police at every turn. Before the ship berthed, the 'crooked' sailors onboard opened the sea containers just offshore and stashed the drugs elsewhere. The criminals then resealed the containers with the proper equipment, ensuring Customs remained clueless. Customs documented the container seals, and everything looked legitimate.

At departure, someone sealed the containers and recorded the seal codes. However, some codes were left unrecorded, and the Chinese didn't initially notice the omissions in the register. After removing the drugs and attaching new seals, they filled in the blank spaces.

Once the ship docked in Sydney, the register appeared complete, and Customs Officers were none the wiser about the later entries. Even the electronic files were tidy, with alterations undetectable unless you knew exactly where to look.

Roberto was being groomed to take over from his father. Dominic, now in his late seventies, was planning to step back and let Roberto run the organisation. Roberto had travelled to China to introduce himself to the suppliers and discuss future shipments to Australia. Everything seemed to run smoothly. Cocaine and opium were big money earners.

On his return, Dominic called a 'family' meeting. Roberto's sister, Sylvia, wanted no part in the business and only visited her mum and dad at Easter and Christmas, mainly for the sake of the grandkids. Teresa didn't play any major role in the business either, but lingered in the background with a small yet significant task, monitoring inventory transactions and the bookkeeping.

The meetings usually comprised Dominic and two of his lieutenants, with Teresa present on rare occasions. The two lieutenants, Mario and Vinnie, handled drug trafficking and, at times, spare machinery parts to give police the impression they were legitimate salespeople of Emporium Machinery Imports P/L. From now on, Roberto was to be included in every meeting, regardless of its level of importance.

Mario and Vinnie sat at the table, casting a couple of concerned looks at Roberto. It was the first time in a long time. Dominic started the meeting once they all settled down.

'I've decided that Roberto will play a major role in the business. I'm getting too old for the intensity this work demands,' he said, clarifying that Roberto would take the reins.

'Both of you have been very loyal to the family, and I will never forget it.' Dominic implored the two to show the same loyalty to Roberto and help him in taking charge of everything that is happening and running this business. 'He has already started.'

'Boss, that is your decision, and I have no problem following your request,' Vinnie replied.

Both Mario and Vinnie were from the 'old school'. The Boss was not to be questioned, nor was his decision on such matters. Mario nodded in agreement with Vinnie's reply.

Vinnie stood and reached across the table to shake Roberto's hand. Mario followed suit.

'Roberto,' Dominic said, about to make a point. 'If you show even a hint of disrespect or think you're better than these two, you'll get a kick up the arse from me if I'm still around.'

Roberto's face was stern, as if to say, *Where did that come from?*

'These two men, Mario and Vinnie, have had my back so many times I've lost count,' Dominic continued. 'They looked after me, and I looked after them. They're like brothers, family.'

The two men smiled, and Roberto nodded approvingly. He could remember their coming to the house frequently and even staying for meals. His father was right. *They were family.*

'Now, down to business,' Dominic said. 'Roberto has just returned from China after visiting our suppliers, and he has some news.'

Roberto shuffled his chair closer and clasped his hands on the table.

'I must say it was an interesting trip,' he began. 'Our suppliers wanted to raise the cost of the product by ten percent across the board.' 'What! The thieving pricks!' Mario burst out.

'I negotiated a deal,' Roberto continued. 'I told them if the increase went ahead, we'd cut our quota by twenty-five per cent to keep prices steady for our clients.'

'What was their response to that?'

'They said an increase was necessary but ultimately settled for a smaller one. I said I was looking for an increase in supply, and a price increase would mean that it wouldn't be viable at a ten percent rise.

'I agreed to a two per cent rise this year and a further three percent next year only if they can increase their supply by ten percent to compensate for the increases. That means we can expand our market over time and still maintain a reasonable return by selling more products,' Roberto reported.

'An increase in supply may well balance out the rise in price,' Vinnie said. 'Some of my clients have asked for more product, so this may be a step in the right direction.'

'I also think with more product available, we can keep "intruders" at bay,' Roberto added. 'If we've got the stock at a fair price, we'll hold our clients.'

The others nodded in approval. They could see the long-term benefit of Roberto's deal. They had to protect their market share and deal with the intruders as they appeared, just like they had done in the past. An impromptu boat trip five kilometres offshore kept the competition at a minimum level. No one could swim back to shore with both hands tied and feet bound in cement.

'Have we had any incidents like that recently?' Dominic asked.

'I had one,' Mario replied. 'But I set him straight, and he left. Haven't seen him since he took the recommended boat trip.' 'When's the next shipment?' Vinnie asked.

'I pushed for three weeks from now,' Roberto replied, 'and with the increase in supply.'

'Do we have the funds available?' Mario asked.

'Yes,' Dominic replied. 'Mamma sorted it this morning.'

Mario and Vinnie leaned back with satisfied looks. Everything seemed on track.

'What have we done about that female lawyer poking her nose into our affairs?' Vinnie asked.

'I'll sort out that problem,' Dominic assured them. 'Once Sergio returns to town, I'll have him deal with it. Might even get his brother, Alexei, on the job.'

'Good, he's back then,' Vinnie replied approvingly. 'Anyway, how did she get involved with us?'

'One of our competitors who wanted to muscle in on our territory, the same one keeping the fish company five k's out to sea,' Dominic replied with a chuckle.

The other two chuckled as well, while Roberto could only smile. The way these problems appeared and were dealt with didn't impress him. Eliminating people in that manner could backfire and bring down the whole organisation. With Alexei back on the scene, they could tighten things up better than before.

'Do we need to contact our guys onboard to let them know a shipment is coming and needs to be intercepted?' Roberto asked, shifting the subject back to business.

'I'll do that once the ship leaves port. The shipment may face delays,' Dominic advised. 'It's good to see you thinking ahead. I like that. That's my boy. If you don't ask, you don't know.'

'Roberto, that end of the business you don't have to worry about,' Mario explained. 'I get told when the shipment is ready and onboard by text. Then I let our crew on the ship know to organise the drop-off before it docks. Simple.'

Roberto nodded to show he understood.

'Once the shipment has landed, it's my job to distribute the product,' Vinnie added. 'Just make sure when you pick it up, you tie a weight to it before heading back to shore.'

'What's the idea of that?' Roberto asked curiously.

'In case the water police try to intercept you. All you need to do is cut the line, and the product sinks to the bottom,' Vinnie explained.

'But it'll get lost,' Roberto complained.

'No, it won't. Plot the location on the GPS, and we'll dive for it later. The water's shallow out there, easy enough to retrieve,' Vinnie said.

Roberto seemed satisfied with that and asked no further questions. Dominic made a final round-the-table comment, and all were happy things were on track. Then he wrapped up the meeting.

'Good, I'll be off,' Roberto told them. 'I've got someone to meet.'

'Who is she?' Mario asked, presuming a girl was the reason for his haste.

'Give her one for me,' Vinnie added, and all had a hearty laugh.

'It's not like that yet. I've only just met her,' Roberto explained.

'Go on, boy, enjoy yourself,' Dominic said.

Roberto didn't need telling twice. He put on his jacket, got in his car, and drove off. He picked up Holly and took her dining at the Italian restaurant Pendolino on George Street. Roberto looked forward to getting to know her better. He was surprised she'd accepted, given she was studying for her final exams, but he wouldn't let the opportunity slip.

Roberto arrived at Holly's place and knocked. He could hear her inside, speaking to someone, likely on the phone. He knocked again, and a moment later, Holly answered the door. She wore an evening gown and accessorised it to complement her looks. Her long dark hair was shining and flowing past her shoulders. Roberto gasped for breath momentarily at this stunning woman standing in the doorway.

'Hello, you look fabulous,' he finally managed. 'Are you ready?'

'Thank you, I am,' Holly replied, accepting the compliment graciously. She turned and locked the door.

Roberto offered her his arm and escorted her to the car. He opened the door, and she slipped in carefully, making sure her gown didn't catch.

'I'm taking you to a fantastic Italian restaurant, Pendolino,' he announced, fastening his seat belt. 'Then we'll go to a nightclub, Club77.'

'Sounds great,' Holly replied, 'but I'm not dressed for a nightclub.'

'That's okay. We won't stay long, just enough to wind down after tea.'

Roberto dressed smartly in black trousers, a blue shirt and jacket, without a tie. Holly thought she might have over-dressed, but she felt comfortable, and that was what mattered. She was in high spirits too, having just finished her accounting degree, a fact she hadn't yet told Roberto.

'Oh, guess what?' she began. 'I've completed my degree.'

'Very good. That means we've a reason to celebrate,' Roberto said. 'Do you have work?'

'Yes, but only short-term where I trained. Now that it's over, I may have to look elsewhere.'

'You can work for us,' Roberto offered. 'We could use someone to handle accounts, if you're interested.'

Holly thought for a moment about the offer. Then, she considered it for a moment, inclined to accept, as she was told that her current role was ending soon regardless, so she was inclined to accept. Her boss had even told her.

'The experience you'd gain at another employer would be of benefit long term.' It was time to move on.

'Yes,' she replied, 'I'm interested.'

'Let me know when you're ready to start, and I'll tell my father tomorrow.'

Joanne Holland sat at a table in Club77, sipping a pina colada. She wasn't keen on dancing yet and had already told a couple of blokes to 'fuck off.' She wasn't in the mood for men gushing over her and expecting her to spread her legs just because they'd bought her a drink or two. The last one who asked got her middle finger, without eye contact or a word. He got the message.

The music was loud, and the DJ was doing a decent job, she thought. Joanne came only tonight because she wasn't tired enough to sleep. Maybe she'd meet a woman looking for feminine company. She didn't mind the occasional bloke either, but not tonight.

She noticed a man in black trousers, a blue shirt and jacket walk in with a lovely brunette in tow. The woman wore an evening gown with sparkles, classy for a nightclub. Maybe they were celebrating, and this was the last stop before heading home to screw. The brunette looked all right.

'Wouldn't mind playing with her between the sheets,' Joanne thought. 'Nice body.'

They took a table nearby, and he went to order drinks and headed for the bar to get the order. Joanne caught her eye, and both smiled at each other. It took a good ten minutes for her fellow to come back with the drinks. He motioned to the dance floor, and she shook her head firmly.

After a couple of sips, he stood and walked towards the door. Joanne noticed a man in blue jeans, T-shirt and a black jacket with a shaved head come into the club. Roberto immediately caught the man's attention, walked toward him, said a few words and both headed to the restroom.

'Kinky,' Joanne thought with a wry smirk. Then she made her move.

'Hi, my name's Joanne,' she said, introducing herself to Holly by speaking loudly and getting close to her ear to be heard above the music.

'Hi, I'm Holly,' was the reply.

'May I?' Joanne asked, pointing at the chair. Holly nodded in approval. 'Looks like he deserted you for a bloke.' Both Holly and Joanne chuckled.

'He'll be back shortly, he said,' Holly replied.

'Who was the skinhead he met up with?' Joanne asked.

'I don't know. I've never seen him before. To be honest, this is only the second time we've been out, so I know little about him,' Holly explained.

The music was deafening, and the crowd was dancing and jumping around on the floor. Smoke filled the air, even though there were 'no smoking' signs everywhere. Holly was starting to feel queasy in the stomach. Joanne quickly noticed her condition.

'Are you alright?' Joanne asked, concerned.

'I'm not feeling too good,' Holly admitted.

'Let's go out on the balcony and get some fresh air,' Joanne suggested.

'Yes, let's,' Holly agreed instantly.

Both women got up and stepped onto the balcony. Holly took a couple of deep breaths, and Joanne gently took her hand. Holly didn't pull away.

'That's better. There just seemed to be no ventilation in there,' Holly said. 'Maybe it was the meal we had at the restaurant.'

Joanne let go of Holly's hand, and their eyes met. Joanne caught a flicker of uncertainty, and Holly held the gaze until Joanne asked, 'Which restaurant did you go to?'

'Pendolino restaurant, the food may have been too rich for me.' 'The

food or the price?' Joanne teased.

Holly giggled before replying.

'The food, of course. It was lovely but spicy.'

The colour returned to Holly's face, and Joanne noticed a sparkle in her eyes. Just then, out of the corner of her eye, Holly saw Roberto approaching.

'Do you come here often?' Holly asked.

'Sometimes on weekends when I get bored and need some stimulation,' Joanne replied.

'Stimulation? Here?' Holly questioned.

'It works occasionally. You never know who you might run into, or who might introduce themselves.'

'Oh, he's back,' Holly announced as Roberto drew near.

'So there you are, and in the company of a beautiful woman,' Roberto observed.

Holly smiled, but Joanne refrained from replying. *Get a life,* she thought.

'Roberto, this is Joanne,' Holly introduced.

'It's a pleasure to meet you,' he said, taking her hand to kiss it.

Joanne pulled back slightly; she wasn't in the mood for the suave act he was trying to put on. She felt the sentiment wasn't meant for her, and she couldn't distance herself quickly enough from the 'slimy creep' she thought him to be. To her, he seemed strange.

'Well, I'll be off,' Joanne said. 'I'll leave you to it.'

'It's been nice meeting you, Joanne,' Roberto replied.

Joanne managed a smile and left them standing on the balcony.

Roberto watched her go, then asked Holly, 'Where do you know her from?'

'We just met. She saw me sitting alone and asked if she could join me,' Holly replied, a little uneasy at being questioned about Joanne.

'I think we should leave too,' Roberto said.

'Yes, sounds good to me,' Holly agreed.

Roberto led Holly to the car, glancing around the car park as if he, too, were looking for someone. He finally got in, and they drove off. Joanne, sitting in her car texting on the phone when she noticed Roberto and Holly leave the club. She followed for a short while but soon lost them in the traffic. She hoped she'd see Holly again.

After a short distance from the club, Roberto took a sudden turn down a street, and Holly wondered where they were going. Roberto must have heard her thoughts, as he said,

'I'll take you to my place. I think you'll like it.'

After circling the CBD, they drove north briefly before Roberto pulled into the driveway of a luxury penthouse complex. The estate was ten storeys high, not far from the city.

A remote opened the iron gates to the undercover parking area, and Roberto drove in.

'We're here,' he announced as he parked.

They stepped out and walked to the lift. Roberto pressed the button for it to come down. It was a matter of moments, and the doors opened, and two young blonde women got out of the elevator. They were 'done up to the nines,' and Roberto figured they were escorting girls who had just visited a client. They both got into a black, heavily tinted sedan.

He pressed the button for the sixth floor, and the lift whirred into life. It took less than a minute for it to reach the floor and open the doors.

A short way down the hallway, he stopped at 602 and unlocked the door.

 As they walked into the flat, Holly couldn't help but notice the magnificent view of Sydney Harbour, the Opera House in the distance, and the bridge, all framed by the glass panelling. The neighbouring flat block to the right caught Holly's attention, as it was relatively close and the shades still open, not drawn.

'So, what do you think?' Roberto asked.

'This is fantastic,' Holly said, setting her handbag on a lounge chair. 'The view is magnificent.'

Roberto came up behind her and wrapped his arms around her. She turned, and they embraced and kissed. His hand traced down her back, pulling her closer. They kissed again before he whispered.

'Are you staying the night, my darling?'

'Only if you want me to, and promise to love me as if I were a princess,' she replied softly.

'Your desire is my command.'

They embraced and kissed and finally made it to the bedroom, shedding clothes as they went.

# Chapter 7: A Night to Remember

A month had passed, and Joanne found herself at Club77 again. The club had a situation, and the police intervened, reprimanding the club for its handling of the incident. The police kicked the DJ out, threatening to charge him.

Joanne had spent time with a couple of girls, but that did little for her, so she was back on the prowl for some female talent. She sat in her usual spot, sipping her much-loved Piña colada, when a familiar face walked through the door. Spotting Joanne, she made a beeline for her.

'Holly! How are you, my dear?' Joanne greeted, standing to give her a big hug.

'Joanne, it's good to see you too. It's been far too long.'

'Yes, it has. Where's that boyfriend of yours?' Joanne asked, half expecting him to appear any moment.

'He's in Melbourne this week, sorting out business with a client who's purchasing some heavy machinery,' Holly explained.

'So, you are on your own, I take it,' Joanne presumed.

'You could say something like that,' Holly replied with a big smile.

'So how has it been between you two?' Joanne asked.

'We've had our moments,' She replied.

'Really? That doesn't sound very convincing.'

'Well, I feel like I'm just there as his plaything. At first, it was great, but then it became "wham, bang, thank you, ma'am", then he just rolls over and sleeps,' Holly explained.

'You need a bit of excitement,' Joanne replied. 'What do you want to drink? My shout.'

'I'll have a Bacardi and Coke, thanks.'

Joanne went to the bar to order. Holly watched her make her way through the crowd. The music was loud, the DJ spinning sixties and seventies tracks, and the crowd was getting into the swing. Holly had been thinking about her relationship with Roberto, and even though it was only a few weeks since they got together, the excitement of it all was ebbing away.

Joanne returned with the drinks.

'Let's go out on the balcony,' Holly suggested. 'It's quieter out there.'

They both picked up their glasses and headed out. Along the way, Joanne was propositioned twice, giving her standard reply: 'Fuck off!'

'Men!' she muttered once they reached the balcony. 'All they think about is bloody rooting. There's no such thing as love anymore,' she complained.

Holly looked at her for a moment, surprised at the bluntness of her opinion. It seemed there was some truth to it. Her own experience with Roberto wasn't exactly crash hot.

'How's the job going?' Joanne asked, shifting the subject.

'Yeah, it's going fine so far. Teresa, Robbie's mum, is showing me the ropes, and I'm getting a handle on how they want things done.'

'Is it a big operation?'

'Yes, it is. There's a lot to account for that keeps me on my toes,' Holly replied.

'All work and no play, huh?'

Holly smirked, recognising the implication. She had to agree.

'What if you come back to my place? We can snuggle up in front of the telly and watch a late-night movie,' Joanne suggested.

Holly looked at her eyes, the smile that always appeared when she expected something positive. Holly felt a comfortable warmth come over her. Joanne was a kind-hearted woman, tender in relationships with other females, but to men, she could be as brazen as an Amazon with some men.

'Sounds like the best offer I've had in a long time,' Holly replied.

Both got their bags and coats and left the club. Holly accompanied Joanne to her car, which was parked around the corner. She had caught a taxi to the club, which wasn't far from Roberto's flat, but not close enough to walk, especially at night.

Soon, Joanne pulled into the undercover parking of a block of flats on the other side of town from where Roberto's flat was. They took the elevator to the third floor. While they were in the elevator, Joanne reached out and slightly touched Holly's hand. Holly hesitated for a moment and then took hold of Joanne's hand firmly and smiled at her. Joanne felt a warm feeling welling inside of her. They both smiled at each other, and then the doors opened.

Walking down the hallway hand in hand, Joanne took out the keys and opened the door to her flat. The layout was like Roberto's, but the layout definitely had a woman's touch. Holly felt quite comfortable from the moment she entered. She put her bag and coat on the lounge, and Joanne scooped them up and hung the coat on a wall hook.

They stood in the centre of the room, waiting for someone to move first. Joanne knew what she wanted to do with her. Holly made the first move. She was checking Joanne's body language and made the first step. She approached Joanne, and when they touched, Joanne leaned in for a kiss. They gazed into each other's eyes, feeling the same intensity, warmth, and warming sensation, and the need for more. They kissed again and touched each other's bodies. Clothes were now being discarded as they made their way to the bedroom.

It was going to be a night to remember.

The container ship left Shanghai bound for Sydney with the precious cargo the Chinese suppliers had arranged with Roberto. There was an extra amount as agreed, though not quite the full ten percent. They couldn't make up for all the extra supply within the short time frame, so they discussed the shortfall and an arrangement to catch up.

No one had told Mario about the shortfall. All he knew was that the shipment was onboard and travelling the CA3 route to Sydney, a seventeen-day passage. Hanson, one of the four in league with the Rossetti's plan, had called on the other three members to meet in his cabin and discuss the handling of the shipment. They gathered after the evening meal.

'Styles, get on the computer and track down the container holding the shipment,' Hanson instructed. 'Once we know which one it is, Thomo and I will open it and retrieve the goods.' 'How heavy is it?' Thomo asked.

'Mario reckons about ten to twelve kilos,' Hanson replied. 'Jo here will do the drop as usual. This time it'll be further south, about five kilometres offshore. A boat will make the pickup after we've steamed past. The drop-off will take place at 0500, just before sunrise.

'When do you want me to search for the container?' Styles asked.

'As soon as you can, I don't want us rushing at the last minute,' Hanson said.

'Okay, I'll start checking the manifests tonight.'

'I'm on watch at 0200, so that'll be a good time to locate it,' Thomo added. 'That should give us plenty of leeway.'

'Good,' Hanson agreed. 'Let me know the moment you've got the serial number and location. Here are the container details and the manifest we need to match. Find it as quickly as possible.' 'Will do,' Styles replied, taking the note from Hanson.

The three of them, Styles, Thomo, and Jo, left Hanson's room and carried out their respective duties. Thomo and Jo went to their cabins, while Styles went to the communications room to use a computer to check the container log. He was friendly with the radio operator on duty at the time and had no problem accessing the container listing.

Thomo would need some time to locate the container among the three thousand-plus on the ship. He unfolded the note Hanson had given him and entered the details into the system. He had the port of departure, the loading platform, destination, and the receiving company's details. The system took a minute to display the information on the screen. Then he typed in the number.

'Are you looking for anything in particular?' the radio operator asked.

'I'm just checking on a container that's supposed to have some materials in it that need checking,' Styles replied.

'What, some sort of material?' the operator pressed.

'It's meant to be a chemical, and they're not even sure the container is on this ship.'

'Yeah, that sounds right. Dubious cargo goes missing or gets misplaced all the time,' the operator agreed. 'Hope you don't find it, if you know what I mean.'

The operator then put his headphones back on and listened to the chatter on the radio. Styles waited for the result, and finally it came on the screen. He hit the print key, and the printer printed out the information. The radio operated didn't hear the printer go into action. Styles grabbed the page, folded it, and tucked it into his pocket.

Styles stood and tapped the operator on the shoulder. That startled him, and he shot up out of his seat in a flash.

'Fuck!' he yelled. 'You nearly gave me a heart attack!'

Styles tried hard not to laugh but managed, 'Shit! Sorry. I was only going to tell you I'm done.'

'That's okay,' the operator replied. 'Find anything?'

'No, nothing to worry about for now. Thanks,' Styles reassured him. 'I'll need to log back in later to check something else. I just had to look at this one first to confirm it's here.'

With that, Styles left the communications room with the information Hanson wanted and made his way back to Hanson's cabin.

'Here's the information that's in the system. This one has the details we're looking for. Two more came up, but the departure details don't quite match,' Styles explained. 'The floor plan shows where it's located.'

'Good job. Thomo and I will check this container first,' Hanson replied, pointing to the one with the right details.

Styles left once his task was complete. All he needed to do was enter a note in the log once the container was located, opened, and resealed. Hanson now went to pay Thomo a visit in his cabin.

In the early hours of the morning, a catamaran slipped its mooring at Gosford and headed out to sea. Once it cleared the heads, it tracked in a southeasterly direction at a steady pace. The sea was calm, and the ship made good headway. A bright moon hung overhead.

Roberto tapped the GPS and radar screen, feeling a flicker of unease at the information he saw on both screens. Then he saw what he was looking for, a blip on the screen from a low-powered homing beacon that showed the location of the shipment Jo had dropped overboard earlier.

'Is that what we're looking for?' asked Vinnie, standing beside Roberto.

'Yep, that's our shipment. About five kilometres out,' Roberto replied.

'This is the first of the larger loads?' 'Yes,

and the price,' Roberto confirmed.

'Where's the container ship?' Vinnie asked.

'I'd say about ten kilometres to starboard,' Roberto replied.

'To where did you say?'

Roberto gave a bit of a laugh and realised Vinnie wasn't too nautically minded.

'On our right side, south of here. You're not too good with nautical terms, are you?'

'No,' Vinnie admitted. 'I only know boats float.'

Roberto shook his head and had a smirk on his face. He looked down at the radar. The blip was close now, so he throttled back.

'Vinnie, grab the gaff and get ready to haul it in,' he said with a grin. 'The gaff's the one with the hook on the end.'

'Yes, I figured as much,' Vinnie replied sheepishly.

In the moonlight, they spotted the package bobbing in the water. The horizon to the east was paling, showing that it was close to dawn.

'Pull it in and we'll tie it off to the side,' Roberto instructed. 'I'll add a weight in case we need to dump it.'

'I hope not, but it's a precaution if the water police decide to check us.'

'Exactly.'

Once Vinnie had secured and weighted the package, Roberto gunned the engine and made his way back to shore. He was aiming for a spot just south of Gosford on a section of beach that didn't attract too much attention. The sky was getting brighter by the minute.

'The sun will be up in twenty minutes. Let's get close to shore before then,' Roberto said.

The water was still reasonably calm, and he noticed a breeze was blowing. He increased the engine revs, and the boat sat up in the water and scooted along. As the morning light, Vinnie scanned for a dinghy near the beach. Just then, the two-way crackled.

'Cat 1, do you copy? Over,' came a voice.

It was Mario, waiting in a dinghy just offshore, far enough to avoid the breakers. The swell was rising.

'Roger, over,' Roberto replied. Cat 1 was their call sign for the run.

'Any news?' asked Mario.

'All's well here,' Roberto answered. 'We'll reach you in ten minutes.' As they neared the shore, they spotted a small craft in the distance. It turned towards them and would rendezvous with Roberto a little quicker. The sky was bright when they pulled alongside Mario's dinghy. Roberto released the rope, and the package dropped neatly into Mario's boat.

'Ok Mario, it's all yours,' Vinnie said.

Mario gave a thumbs up, sat down, twisted the outboard's hand throttle almost to full, and sped off back to shore. Roberto made sure he was far enough away to wheel the catamaran around and hit full throttle as well, and headed back to Gosford. The sun was just peeping over the horizon.

It took Roberto about fifteen minutes to return to the mooring in the boat pen. Activity in town was already picking up as people set off for work. After tying off the boat, the two men got into Roberto's car and began the drive back to Sydney.

'That all went rather smoothly, don't you think?' Vinnie remarked with a sigh.

'If it's planned properly, we shouldn't have any problems with the police along the way,' Roberto explained.

'We handled that quickly enough, I thought,' Vinnie agreed.

After a stretch of silence, Vinnie began making a few phone calls. He reached out to his major distributors, letting them know about the shipment and giving them the chance to place orders. By the time they reached Sydney, he had already sold nearly forty percent of the load, worth millions of dollars.

Vinnie asked to be dropped off in the city, while Roberto carried on to his flat. He looked forward to seeing Holly again. He believed that the connection they had with each other was getting stronger each day. There was some hope that he would marry her someday. Maybe she was the one.

Roberto arrived at his flat mid-morning. Holly was at work, so he had the rest of the day to himself. It was a chance to catch up on sleep, though he needed to call his father first about the shipment.

'Hello, Dad. Just letting you know it's all done.'

'Good job, my son. Any problems?' Dominic asked.

'None, it went smoothly,' Roberto replied. 'Vinnie came along this time.'

'Good. He said he wanted to see how the pickup worked,' Dominic said. 'Did Mario handle the shoreline transfer?'

'Yes, all went smoothly.'

'And what are you going to do now?'

'Get some sleep first, then wait for Holly to finish work. We might go out for tea again tonight,' Roberto told him.

'She's a fine woman. She knows her work, too. Mama was very pleased with how she helped here. You take good care of her.'

'I definitely will.'

'Very well. I'll see you tomorrow then. Enjoy tonight, both of you.'

Roberto hung up, took a quick shower, and climbed into bed. He was asleep almost as soon as his head hit the pillow.

# Chapter 8: Who Shot Her?

Holly finished work and went around to Roberto's flat. She had a hunch he'd be there waiting for her after his trip to Melbourne. She was hoping it had been a successful one.

Her duty, working for them, was paying the creditors and verifying invoices before proceeding with the payments. She was astounded at the cost of the parts and machinery, the company purchases, and the cash in their accounts. She knew nothing about the drug trade or the cash flow it was generating. Only a small portion of that trickled into the working account she was using to pay the bills.

Roberto was sitting at the table having a cup of coffee when Holly walked in. He was clean-shaven and neatly dressed.

'Hi, darling,' he said as soon as she entered. He got up and gave her a warm hug and a kiss.

'How was your trip?' she asked between kisses.

'Good, but it's better to be here with you,' he replied, kissing and groping more.

Holly enjoyed the attention and was getting aroused just as she did when Joanne touched her. The only difference was that she was being manhandled, and she felt the urge for him to be inside her now. With clothes peeled off, they moved into the bedroom. Their naked bodies became one. It was euphoric.

Roberto took Holly to a Chinese restaurant in Sydney's CBD. Fortune Village was a popular spot, and Roberto had only just booked a table for two. Holly dressed in an evening gown with all the accessories to match. The shopping spree she and Joanne went on the day before turned out to be perfect timing. She drew a few glances as she entered the restaurant, and even Roberto made an endearing comment before they'd left the flat. Roberto wore a suit and tie, and together they looked like a ritzy couple on the town.

'I never got around to asking. How was your day?' Roberto asked.

'You got side-tracked, didn't you?' Holly replied with a smile.

Both had smiles on their faces when the server brought them menus.

'I'll come back shortly after you've had a look,' she announced. 'I can tell you we have a special on satay dishes listed inside the menu.'

They chose two dishes to share, along with some fried rice. Nothing too elaborate, but filling. The wine server came by with the list and suggested one that would pair well with the meal. Roberto nodded in agreement.

'I had an interesting day. I achieved quite a bit, actually,' Holly said.

'That's good news. It sounds like you're settling in well,' Roberto presumed.

'I noticed some creditors can be real idiots,' Holly remarked. 'One in particular in Melbourne. I was close to giving you a ring, or getting you to visit them.'

'Yeah, you get those sorts of people now and then. Even some customers can be annoying,' Roberto replied, trying to console her.

The meal went down well and was enjoyable. After a bottle of wine, they decided not to linger. The night was still young. Roberto suggested returning to his flat, and Holly agreed it was a good idea.

That was the night things turned bad for Holly.

When they got back to the flat, both changed into casual clothes amidst more kissing, hugging, and groping. Roberto was working up to more fun, and Holly played along. Finally, he said,

'I've got something for you to try.'

'That sounds interesting. What is it?'

'Just give me a minute and you'll see,' he replied.

Roberto fetched a small plastic bag from his briefcase and emptied the contents onto the glass coffee table. He then took a plastic card from his wallet and divided the powder into four straight lines. Holly did not find what was about to happen impressive.

'All you need to do is sniff a line up your nose. It'll be magic.' 'I didn't think I would ever do this,' Holly said hesitantly.

'It won't cause you any grief. Just relax, it'll make you feel serene,' he coaxed.

'I'm not sure, Roberto,' she implored.

'Just try it. Once is enough.'

Roberto picked up the straw he had with him and sniffed up the first line. He hesitated once he finished and gave out an enormous sigh and rubbed his nose.

'You see? It's as easy as that.'

He kept urging Holly to try. He got a bit worked up towards the end. Holly relented and gave it a go. She reeled back on the first attempt, thinking for a moment she was seeing stars. Roberto sat on the floor, watching.

'How does it feel, darling?' he asked.

'I feel dizzy, it's hard to focus.'

'Just relax and let it work through your system. Give it a couple of minutes, then try some more,' he advised. 'Go on, give it another go.'

Holly knew this wasn't a good idea, but she felt Roberto would get cranky if she refused. She felt bullied into taking the drug and did some more anyway. The second lot was done, and she hallucinated. She tried to get up off the floor but only crawled to the lounge, pulled herself up and leant on the back of the lounge. Then she looked out the window.

Through the window of the neighbouring complex, Holly saw into a room on the same level. A man with a shaved head was pointing a gun at a woman. There was a heated exchange between them, and then the man fired.

'Roberto!' Holly yelled. 'Look!'

Roberto, more coherent now, joined her on the lounge. The woman staggered back against the wall, then slid out of sight. Roberto missed that part.

'What is it you want me to see?' he mumbled.

Just then, as a second man entered the room where the woman had been shot, Holly's heart sank. It was Dominic.

'Hey, there's Dad,' Roberto mumbled, and even waved.

Both Dominic and the gunman noticed Roberto and Holly watching. Dominic pointed at them and then drew the blinds.

'That guy shot a woman in that flat!' Holly said loudly, frowning.

'I saw nothing like that,' Roberto replied.

'It happened before you got here to the lounge.'

'So, what do you want me to do?' Roberto said aloud. 'You must be seeing things.'

Holly slumped down on the lounge with her head in her hands. She wasn't seeing things. Even with her head still spinning, she knew what she had witnessed was a murder. Suddenly, she realised the gunman looked like the same man Roberto had met at Club77. That was the same night she met Joanne. Roberto must have recognised him too but tried to act as if he either ignored him or hadn't seen him. He saw only his father.

Roberto was leaning over the coffee table and snorted the last of the coke that was laid out. He then slumped back on the floor against the lounge and closed his eyes. Holly stood up and found her head wasn't spinning as much as before. She decided she needed to get out of the flat.

She found her phone, searched for Joanne's number and called her. Joanne answered almost straightaway.

'Joanne? Can you come and pick me up from the flat?' Holly asked as clearly as she could.

'What's happened, Holly?' Joanne replied.

'Just get me, please,' Holly pleaded. 'I'll be in the foyer.'

'Sure thing, Holly, I'll only be a couple of minutes,' Joanne said and hung up.

Holly collected her handbag and a few belongings, then left. Roberto was out of it on the floor, still leaning against the lounge. She reached the elevator and pressed the button for the ground floor. She felt dizzy again but could cling to the rail inside the lift.

The doors opened on the ground floor, and she staggered out into the foyer. She found a seat and sat down. Passers-by looked at her bemused and kept walking. It wasn't long before she heard Joanne's voice.

'Holly, are you alright?' Joanne asked.

Holly looked at her with distant eyes, and Joanne instantly realised what had happened and why she had been called.

'You poor love,' Joanne said, trying to console her.

She helped Holly up and guided her to the car, then helped her inside. Joanne drove back to her complex and took Holly up to the flat. Holly cried, and Joanne held her close in her arms.

'Tell me what happened,' Joanne asked, worried about her state of mind.

'Robbie got me to sniff coke, I think,' Holly said, assuming it was coke.

'He got you to snort coke, not sniff,' Joanne corrected her.

'Yes.'

'Here, sit down. I'll make you a coffee,' Joanne offered. 'Then you lie down and sleep it off. That's the only answer.'

'I saw something I shouldn't have, and Robbie just ignored it,' Holly tried to explain.

Joanne went to the kitchen to make coffee. She was concerned about Holly and her relationship with Roberto, as it seemed the wheels were coming off.

'What did you see?' Joanne inquired.

'I saw a woman being shot in a flat in the next complex!'

Joanne almost dropped the cups of coffee in her hands. At the very least, some spilled.

'You saw what?' Joanne exclaimed.

'I saw a woman being shot?!'

'Who shot her? Where did it happen?' Joanne asked, now frantic.

'The man I saw shoot her is the same one Robbie met at Club77 that night I met you. Robbie's father was there as well.'

Joanne's eyes widened at Holly's revelation. She couldn't imagine Holly hallucinating about such a traumatic event. What was even more bizarre was that she knew the shooter and Roberto's father were both there.

They drank their coffee in silence for a while, collecting their thoughts. Then Joanne finally said,

'Going to the police is out of the question. By the time they got there, someone would have cleaned up everything.'

'I don't know what to do,' Holly bleated. 'I can't go back to Robbie's place.'

'Stay here tonight, and tomorrow we'll work out what to do next,' Joanne suggested.

Holly agreed but found it hard to sleep. Thoughts raced through her mind. What would Robbie say? Would his father make things difficult for her? Should she go to work tomorrow?

Her mind cleared as the effects of the coke slowly wore off. She welcomed Joanne's suggestion of staying the night. By the time Holly finally lay down, the spinning in her head had stopped, and she drifted off to sleep.

When morning came, Roberto was still on the floor in the foetal position. The sun poured onto his face, the shades still open. He blinked at the harsh sunlight and felt a throbbing in his head. He eventually managed to stand.

'Oh, fuck,' he muttered as he tried to get up. It felt like a classic hangover.

'Holly!' he yelled out, but there was no response. He finally got to his feet.

Entering the bathroom, he glanced at himself in the mirror. What he saw didn't impress him. He decided that a hot shower might brighten things up. It couldn't make it worse.

The phone rang as he was stepping out of the shower. Wrapping a towel around himself, he answered.

'Roberto,' Dominic said before he could speak. 'What are you doing?'

'I'm just finishing a shower. Why?' he replied, gathering his thoughts. The shower had refreshed him.

'Where is Holly? She hasn't turned up for work,' Dominic asked. 'I want you and her in my office now!'

'Hang on, what's going on?' Roberto asked, curious about the sudden demand.

'I want you both here within the hour!' Dominic snapped and hung up.

Roberto slammed the phone down and yelled, 'Fuck you too!'

Then got dressed and realised Holly wasn't in the flat. Picked up his phone and dialled her number, but it rang out. He finished getting ready to face his father, expecting the meeting to be unpleasant and feeling irritated by his father's heavy-handedness.

Holly and Joanne were sitting down having breakfast when Holly's phone rang. She picked it up and saw the incoming call was from Roberto. She put the phone back on the table and let it ring out.

'Roberto,' she said to Joanne.

'Why didn't you answer it?' Joanne asked.

'I'm not sure what to say to him,' Holly replied, tentative.

The phone rang again. This time she answered.

'Holly, it's Roberto. Can you come with me to work? I know it's a day off, but Father wants to talk,' he said. 'I can come and pick you up.'

'Okay, hang on,' Holly replied. She covered the phone with her hand and said to Joanne in a low voice,

'He wants to pick me up here. Can I give him the address?'

Joanne nodded. 'Yes, but don't give him my flat number.'

Holly nodded and gave Roberto the address, then hung up. She finished breakfast quickly, got dressed, and headed for the door. She hesitated as Joanne came up to her.

'See you later,' Joanne said, and they kissed. 'Call me when you're finished.'

Holly had to wait only a couple of minutes before Roberto pulled up outside in his car. She made her way out to him. Roberto was waiting on the footpath.

'Are you all right?' he asked, concerned. 'Who did you stay with?'

'I stayed with Joanne. I didn't know who else to call,' Holly replied, defending her actions.

'You could have stayed with me,' Roberto said.

'Robbie, you were out of it. I felt really sick.' 'I'm

sorry, that won't happen again,' he said.

Holly got into the car and shut the door. They drove to meet his father in silence. Holly felt used and uncomfortable. Even though she appreciated Joanne rescuing her, she couldn't stop thinking about Steph back in WA. Would she ever see her again? How was she doing? Maybe I should call her.

They arrived at the workplace to see Dominic. Holly felt apprehensive and worried about what was going to happen. She still had the vision in her brain of the woman being shot and collapsing against the wall kept replaying in her mind. She felt a chill as she and Roberto walked into Dominic's office.

'Holly, how are you, my dear?' Dominic greeted graciously. 'Roberto, my son, sit down, both of you.'

'Thank you,' Holly replied as she sat. 'I feel better this morning.'

'This won't take long,' Dominic began. 'There was an unfortunate incident you witnessed last night, Holly. Can you remember?'

Holly felt emotional. She remembered the incident clearly, even though she had been under the influence.

'Yes, I remember something awful happening,' she said, feeling choked.

'Please try to put it out of your mind,' Dominic begged, reaching across the table to pat her hand. 'That's not who we are.'

'I saw nothing of what Holly thought she saw,' Roberto put in.

'No, you couldn't,' Holly snapped at Roberto, accusing him of being stoned, unresponsive, and implying she was imagining it.

'What do you mean, stoned?' Dominic asked sternly, glaring at Roberto. 'You were doing drugs!?'

'It was just a small sample of our latest shipment,' Roberto answered, trying to sound plausible.

'Holly, my dear, could you leave us for a moment? I have something to discuss with Roberto that doesn't involve you,' Dominic said. 'See

Teresa and have a coffee with her for the moment.'

Holly left and closed the door behind her. Roberto's words echoed in her head: "the latest shipment." What shipment?

Dominic stared at Roberto for a moment.

'What am I going to do with you?' he snapped, raising his voice. 'It seems like I can't give you a simple task without you fucking everything up. And then you drag that innocent girl into your mess!'

Dominic stood and paced the room a couple of times.

'You don't deserve a woman like Holly. All she is to you is another bit of arse. Wake up, son. This is serious business. You did well negotiating with the Chinese and picking up the shipment, and then you fucked it up by "sampling the product". You're a fucking dickhead!'

'I didn't think it would have such an effect on her,' Roberto said in his defence.

'That's the problem. Sometimes you don't think, and eventually you're going to run this business!'

Roberto said nothing more; anything else would only anger his father further.

'You're lucky you're my son,' Dominic continued, looking out across Sydney Harbour. 'Someone else would take a one-way trip to the bottom of the sea.'

Roberto looked at his father, unsure of his place in the family after that outburst.

'Somehow, you're going to make that girl feel comfortable around us again. She shouldn't have witnessed the lawyer being shot. You know what Stromnikov is like. He doesn't like loose ends, and Holly is a loose end right now,' Dominic warned.

'He will not go after Holly!' Roberto shouted, standing up.

'No, not yet, and you better make sure it stays that way!' Dominic replied. 'If she goes to the cops, he'll snuff her without remorse.' Roberto virtually flopped back into his seat. He never thought that he'd put Holly in so much danger. The thought of letting her go wasn't an option. He would never let her leave.

'I'll have a talk with her and see what we can work out,' Roberto offered.

'That would be the best outcome for all of us,' Dominic said. 'Tell no one, not Mario, not Vinnie. They don't need to be dragged into this.'

Dominic turned back to the window, having said his piece and hoping Roberto would listen.

'Find your woman and start treating her with the respect she deserves for a change.'

Roberto didn't need telling twice. He left without another word.

# Chapter 9: Holly Was Lucky

Roberto left his father's office somewhat deflated. What made it worse was that he knew his father was correct in what he was saying. There was a strong possibility he had lost all credibility with Holly. He could kick himself for getting involved with drugs last night, even if it turned out to be a one-off. He found Holly sitting in reception.

'Why are you here? Did you come to see Mum?' he asked, concerned about her sitting alone.

'Your mother's gone out for the morning and will be back later,' Holly replied.

'I'm sorry, I didn't know.'

'That's okay,' she said. 'It gave me time to think.' 'What

about?' inquired Roberto.

'About us in particular,' came the reply Roberto was dreading.

'Let's go somewhere so we can talk,' suggested Roberto.

Holly rose without saying a word and followed him out to the car. She had grown cold at the idea of being with him and working with his family. He would have to come up with something good. They got into the car and sat there looking at each other.

'I've been an ass, and I want to apologise for getting you to try drugs,' he began. 'I messed up terribly. It didn't work out as I hoped, and I sincerely apologise for the negative impact it had on you.'

'Sorry, I didn't want to, but you kept on at me,' Holly replied. 'I don't want to be treated like that again, pushed into doing something I don't want to do.'

'All I can say is that it won't happen again,' Roberto said, trying to reassure her. 'Is that why you were thinking about us?'

'Yes, among other things.'

'Other things like what exactly?' he queried.

'That bloke that shot the woman? You saw him at Club77, didn't you?'

'Yes,' admitted Roberto, 'but he works for my father and I had to give him a message that night.'

'He saw us last night looking at him through the window after he....'

'Holly,' Roberto interrupted, 'don't worry about that anymore. Try to put it behind you. I'll sort it out.'

'Really? What will happen if you can't?'

'Father will tell him to back off and carry on business as usual,' Roberto replied.

Despite the reassurance Roberto was giving, Holly could not get the image out of her head. That traumatic event had shattered her view of life, and it would take some time to put it behind her, regardless of Roberto's attempts to console her.

Holly was thinking more and more about Steph. What would she do if she were here? Probably give them all a black eye for the hell of it. Holly smiled inwardly at that thought. She was convincing herself to visit her, but a phone call would have to do for now.

'Roberto, can you take me back to Joanne's place?' Holly asked.

'I thought we could go back to my flat?' he questioned.

'I have terrible memories from last night, so no.'

Roberto wasn't happy about Holly's request but tried to understand what she was going through. He hadn't seen the so-called shooting, so he wasn't able to comprehend Holly's demeanour at all. He reluctantly drove her back to Joanne's place.

'I'll give you a ring later,' he said as he pulled up outside the complex.

Holly got out of the car and didn't reply. She ignored him and hurried inside to the lift. Roberto drove off in a huff, frustrated at the turn of events that had plagued them since last night. Holly was growing distant, and that worried him.

## Holly, Joanne and Steph

Holly stepped out of the lift, walked down the hall, and knocked on Joanne's door.

'Just a minute,' came Joanne's voice. She was home. Then the door swung open, and Holly went straight into her arms.

'Hey, what happened, sweetheart?' Joanne asked, concerned at the way Holly entered the flat.

'Just hug me.'

Holly put her head on Joanne's shoulder and closed her eyes. This was the first time today she had felt warm, comfortable, and loved. No hidden issues, no excuses. Holly felt wanted, with just plain affection. After a minute in Joanne's arms, Holly slowly pulled away and said,

'I'm sorry.'

'What for, Holly? You have nothing to be sorry for in my eyes,' Joanne said softly. 'I'm here for you, for as long as you want. That's a promise.'

Holly had watery eyes now and knew in her heart that Joanne was the only person she could rely on, apart from Steph. She kissed her.

'Thank you,' Holly said.

'You're welcome, darling,' Joanne replied, feeling for her ordeal. 'Never think you can't reach out to me. I'm always here for you.'

Holly dried her eyes, smiled at Joanne, and held on to her hands.

'You're the best thing in my life so far,' Holly said. 'I'm ever so grateful you're here for me.' Her eyes watered again.

Joanne pulled her close, looked deep into her eyes, and with a soft voice only a woman could manage, said,

'I love you.'

They embraced and kissed again, but now sensually and lovingly. Holly felt the same inner warmth she had the first time she was with Joanne, and she realised her feelings for her were of love as well. 'What do you want to do for lunch?' Joanne finally asked. 'I don't want to break up the moment we were having just then, but I'm starving.'

Holly gave her usual amused giggle and, with some renewed vitality, said,

'Sounds like a radical idea to me.'

'I have very little in the fridge,' Joanne announced as she surveyed the contents. 'However, if you like, there's a small, quaint little cafe around the corner that dishes up some excellent meals.'

'I can handle that,' Holly replied with a smile, and at last a sparkle was back in her eyes.

They grabbed their bags and headed out. In the lift, Holly said to Joanne,

'I'll ring Steph later. I've been a bit of a bitch and haven't phoned her for a while.'

'She's your friend in WA?' Joanne confirmed.

'Yes, and a wonderful friend.'

'You should ring her and keep the contact,' Joanne agreed. 'How close were you?'

'Friends in high school and college, nothing more,' Holly replied. 'We had a lot of wonderful times together, though. I wouldn't mind going back to see her again. I'm sure you'll like her too.'

The elevator door opened, and they stepped out. They walked to the cafe almost next door to the apartment complex. They found a booth toward the rear and settled down.

'What do you fancy?' Joanne asked after perusing the menu.

'I might just have a fish and chip platter with salad,' Holly replied.

'Good. I'll order,' Joanne offered. 'You ring your friend Steph while I order and wait for our meals.'

Holly returned her smile of satisfaction. She was glad that Joanne wasn't making a fuss over her wanting to ring Steph. In fact, she was a little surprised Joanne didn't question her any further about her relationship with Steph. She thought that after admitting she was in love with her, some jealous tendencies might surface. Holly was glad they didn't. Roberto would most likely have given her the third degree in questioning her about their relationship.

Holly punched in Steph's number on her mobile. It rang twice before Steph picked up.

'Hello.' Steph's voice came over the phone.

'Hi Steph, it's Holly,' she replied.

'Oh my goodness, Holly,' came her eager voice. 'It's been a while since I've heard from you. How are you going?'

'I'm doing alright. Just a couple of hiccups, but nothing I can't handle.'

'How's your job? How are things with your boyfriend?' Steph asked curiously.

'It's hard to say where we're going relationship-wise, but the job's okay,' Holly replied.

'You don't sound very convincing. What's wrong?' Steph asked. She could sense from Holly's voice that things weren't all that good, and calling with a deflated tone meant matters weren't as bright as she was making out.

'I've met this friend who I'm stayed with from time to time. She's a gorgeous person and has helped me a lot. Her name's Joanne, and we've become close,' Holly explained.

Steph could sense a change in her tone to a lighter, happier one. That was of some comfort.

'That's excellent news, Holly. And you're not working today?' Steph asked, realising what time of day it was in Sydney.

'No, I wasn't feeling too good this morning, so I skipped work, and Joanne has two rostered days off, so we decided to do lunch together,' Holly explained.

'When will I see you again?' Steph asked.

'We have made no plans yet, but we've talked about a visit.'

'Good, I'm looking forward to it,' Steph replied. 'I'll be moving back to Geraldton in a couple of weeks and staying with my parents.'

'That's okay. We'll meet up there if you're not still in Perth by the time we visit.'

'Call me when you do and I'll let you know where I am,' Steph suggested.

'Yes, and I promise to ring more often,' Holly said. 'Lunch is ready and looks good.'

'Okay, Holly. I'll let you have your lunch,' Steph said. 'Catch you soon, alright?'

'Okay, bye.'

Joanne placed the meals on the table and sat down.

'That phone call was short and sweet,' Joanne remarked.

'Yeah, I know,' Holly admitted. 'I didn't want to tell her everything that went on in the last twenty-four hours. She'd only fret.'

'And with good reason, too,' Joanne agreed. 'Any friend would.'

They both ate their meals with no further conversation. Holly sipped her coffee and looked at Joanne eating hers. Joanne's blonde hair, her sparkling green eyes, and her beautiful smile were something to behold, Holly thought. She was so lucky to have met her and developed such a fantastic physical relationship. It would be hard to guess that Joanne worked as a security guard patrolling shopping centres during the day.

She was a lot like Steph when dealing with idiots and shoplifters. She could handle herself and had also undergone martial arts training. That was one reason she wasn't shy about telling blokes to 'fuck off' occasionally, 'especially when there was a woman around to be with,' as she'd put it.

Holly felt fortunate to have met Joanne.

Roberto was getting frustrated with Holly for not answering his text messages or her phone. He wanted to meet up with her and talk about any issues she had with him or the family business. She had been quite enthusiastic when she began working with his mum, Teresa, and took to it like a duck to water. But recent events had weighed on Holly, and that enthusiasm was waning quickly.

Roberto was putting some of the blame for Holly's mood on Joanne, and he was sure Holly had succumbed to her advances and lost all sense of reality. Even though he drank heavily and started hitting the drugs that one night, it didn't change the fact that he wanted Holly back. He still had feelings for her and would have her back in an instant if only he could talk to her, if only she'd answer her phone.

Holly's phone rang again for the fifth time that day.

'If that's Roberto again, answer it and put him out of his misery,' Joanne suggested.

Holly nodded in approval and had the intention of answering the phone this time, even if it was just a quick conversation with him.

'Hello, Robbie.'

'Holly, finally you picked up,' he replied. 'Can we talk, please?'

'Yes,' Holly said after a momentary pause. 'I think we need to clear the air.'

'I agree,' Roberto replied. 'How soon can you come over?'

'I could get Joanne to drop me off in the next hour,' Holly replied.

'That would be great. Come over as soon as you can.'

Holly ended the call and looked at Joanne with trepidation. She was worried. It was the tone of his voice that unsettled her.

'I won't rush over there,' Holly said. 'Will you take me when I'm ready?'

'Certainly, as long as you're sure,' Joanne replied. 'Ring me straight away if things go pear-shaped.'

Holly sat there for a while, pondering the situation. Holly sat there for a while, contemplating the situation of her relationship with Roberto reaching its breaking point. She wanted it to end.

'I'm going to tell him it's over,' Holly finally said. 'The only problem is that he might come here and start something with you.'

'I don't think he will. First, he doesn't know my flat number, and second, there's security downstairs.'

'Just the same, I wouldn't put it past him,' Holly opined. 'I'm ready when you are.'

'Are you sure about this?' Joanne asked, seeking reassurance that Holly wanted to go.

'Yes, I'll ring if I need to be picked up,' Holly confirmed.

They picked up their coats and handbags and took the lift to the underground car park. They went to Joanne's car and drove around to Roberto's flat complex. Holly got out, gave a short wave, and said,

'See you later.'

Joanne acknowledged and drove off after Holly walked into the complex. The thought of staying close to the apartment block in case Holly had to leave crossed her mind. She hoped Roberto wouldn't do something to Holly he would regret. Joanne continued back to her apartment.

Holly knocked on Roberto's door, and he answered in a flash. For all Holly knew, he had been waiting by the door for her to knock.

'Hi, beautiful, come in,' Roberto greeted her. 'Would you like a drink?'

'It seems like you've already started.'

'Sit down and make yourself comfortable,' he offered.

They both sat on the sofa, and Holly kept to one end, trying to stay at a distance. There was an atmosphere in the air that wasn't to her liking. She now realised it hadn't been the best idea to visit Roberto after all.

'So, how is it going with you and that lesbian bitch you're living with?' 'Robbie, that's not called for. Referring to her like that!'

'Well, what else is she then? Tell me?' he asked mockingly. 'That's right, Joanne's her name. I remember her now from the nightclub.'

Roberto got up and went into the bedroom. Holly thought it might be time to ring Joanne and ask her to come and get her. Shortly after, Roberto came back with a small plastic bag and began waving it at Holly.

'You want some of this? It will make you feel good.'

'No, thank you. I told you that's something I will never touch again,' replied Holly, recalling the last and only time she had ever snorted coke. Roberto put the powder on the glass-topped coffee table and took a line.

Holly was now on her guard as the feeling suddenly overtook her that this night would not end well. She should have listened to what Joanne was trying to tell her, while avoiding being too direct. Opening her bag, she felt tempted to ring Joanne to come and take her home. She reached in and pulled out her phone.

That was when the nightmare started.

'Who the fuck are you going to ring!' he shouted and slapped the phone out of Holly's hand.

Holly's mobile flew across the room and broke apart. The battery bounced off the wall and skidded across the room.

'Robbie!' Holly yelled. 'Stop it!'

Roberto got up and grabbed Holly by the lapels of the coat she still wore, pulling her up off the sofa with force. He was in her face and shouted.

'Who the fuck do you think you are, bitch, some fucking prima donna?'

He held her at arm's length and slapped Holly hard with his open hand and then again with the back of it. Holly reeled, and Roberto let her fall. She began crying not only from the slapping but from the betrayal of trust that was now glaringly obvious. He didn't love her at all. He just wanted sex and to treat her like a whore.

'Fuck you too!' she blurted out, but then came what she didn't expect.

Roberto threw her onto the floor and sat astride her, and began undoing his trousers. Holly lashed back and scratched his face, but that made him angrier. He struck her with his fist, punching her in the face. Holly saw stars and realised she had to act, fearing for her life.

He stood up, towering over Holly, looking down at her bloodied face and swollen eye. A trickle of blood came out of her nose and the corner of her mouth. She was still sobbing, at the very least. Holly mustered her strength and kicked at him, but missed. She was struggling to focus, having problems with seeing, now that one eye was partly closed from swelling.

Her kicking made Roberto retaliate with a kick into the side of Holly's rib cage, not once but twice. The excruciating pain made her grimace and cry out. She rolled onto her side, clutching her stomach. She thought her end was coming.

Roberto staggered back a little, trying to control his balance. The coke and the energy he had spent assaulting Holly impeded his self-control. Whether he realised how severe Holly's beating was at his hand might not have registered with him. Holly rolled onto her back again and saw Roberto's frame still standing over her, near her feet. She had one last chance, and she would not miss another opportunity.

Painful as it was, Holly bent both knees enough for one last strike. It was do or die. With both feet, she thrust them straight into Roberto's groin. She hit the mark, hard! He instantly doubled up in pain and collapsed onto the sofa, then rolled off onto the floor, moaning as he went, clutching the 'family jewels'.

'You fucking leso bitch! You're going to pay for this! Fuck you and your mate! You're dead meat, the pair of you!' he yelled as the pain coursed through him.

Holly even surprised herself at the impact her kick had. She knew this was an opportunity to get away from him for good. She struggled to her feet and picked up her bag and headed for the door. On the way, she dropped to her knees and retrieved the three pieces of her phone. The SIM card was still secured in the phone.

She shoved them into her bag and opened the door. She turned back and saw Roberto still on the floor, groaning and trying to gather his composure.

'Goodbye, you fucking arsehole!' Holly yelled, slamming the door behind her.

Holly staggered down the passage to the lift and repeatedly pressed the button. The doors finally opened, and she got in. No one else was inside. Taking one last look down the passage, there was no sign of Roberto. The doors closed. She was running on adrenaline, which was overriding her pain. Her right side was aching badly.

The lift doors opened on the ground floor to reveal four people waiting to go up. They all stepped back at the sight of Holly's mangled, bloody face. She stumbled forward and fell to the floor. A man caught her midway, stopping her from hitting the floor.

'My God, love, what happened to you?' he asked.

Holly's world started whirling, and she drifted into unconsciousness. The man helped her onto a settee and then shouted to a security guard who was in the foyer, talking to the desk clerk.

'Call an ambulance and the police. This woman needs medical attention!'

'The bastard belted me,' was Holly's weak reply to the earlier question.

'You'll be okay now. The ambulance is on its way,' came the reassurance.

'Tell Joanne what happened,' she managed.

Holly's world dimmed, and then the 'lights' went out.

Joanne was getting anxious, waiting for Holly's call to pick her up. She feared the worst, and this prompted her to go back to Roberto's flat to find out what was happening. She got into her car and drove to the complex. Joanne glimpsed an ambulance heading in the opposite direction but thought nothing of it.

She entered the front door amidst some activity in the foyer, a police car outside and two police officers inside talking to guests. One of the officers stopped Joanne as she approached the deck clerk.

'Are you a resident here, Miss......?' the officer asked.

'I'm Joanne Holland, and no, I'm not a resident.'

'What is your purpose here tonight, Miss Holland?' the officer asked.

'I'm here to pick up my friend. Why, what's wrong?'

'What's your friend's name?'

'Holly Jamieson. What's happened?'

'Can you describe your friend to me?' the officer persisted.

Joanne gave the officer a description of Holly. He wrote down the details and then said, 'There has been a brutal assault here on a woman, and we don't know the victim's name or who assaulted her. Just wait one moment, please.'

The officer then walked over to where the second officer was interviewing a man and a woman. He interrupted and asked the man something, showing him his notepad. The man nodded, and the officer returned to Joanne.

'Miss Holland, it appears your friend may be the victim of this assault. She told that gentleman over there before the ambulance came, "Tell Joanne what happened',' the officer informed her.

'An ambulance! Fuck. What happened?'

'Do you know who she was visiting here?'

'Yes, her arsehole ex-boyfriend, Roberto Rossetti,' was Joanne's stern reply, growing frantic. 'What hospital was she taken to?' 'St Vincent's, I believe,' the officer replied.

Joanne began walking towards the door. She was going to find Holly and see how she fared. The officer called out after her.

'Wait one minute, please, Miss Holland. I need your details in case we need to speak to you again,' he said, insisting on more information.

'Sorry, I want to catch up with my friend,' Joanne explained.

'She's a close friend, then?' inquired the officer.

'Yes, you could say she's my partner.'

'I see. Just your contact number will do for now, and you can go. I hope she's all right,' the officer said, showing some concern.

Joanne scribbled her number on his notepad and hurried back to her car. She hit the accelerator hard, did a U-turn and drove towards the hospital with tyres squealing.

'I should have stayed with her, even if only in the foyer,' she kept saying to herself.

For the first time in quite a while, tears welled in her eyes. She had to wipe them away so she could see where she was driving. Finally, she screeched to a halt in the hospital car park, got out, and ran to the emergency department. She flung open the doors and rushed to the nurse at the station near the entrance.

'I'm here to see Holly Jamieson,' she announced.

'I'm sorry, Miss. Who are you?' the nurse replied.

'I'm her partner! I want to know how she is.'

'If you would like to take a seat, I'll find out what is happening to her.'

'Please, I need to see her,' Joanne pleaded.

'I'm sorry, wait. The ER doctor is with her now,' was the reply.

Joanne reluctantly followed instructions and took a seat. She let out an enormous sigh. At least Holly was in the right place to be cared for. She just wanted to see her, hug her and promise she would never let her out of her sight again. All thoughts of things went flashing through her mind. 'I'll kill the mongrel, cut his balls off and shove them down his throat or something!'

Holly's idea of going back to WA and catching up with her friend Steph seemed like a plausible plan after this. Get out of Sydney and away from this element, especially with what Holly was supposed to have witnessed. Joanne realised she might not see Holly so soon. She settled back in the chair and watched the TV hanging from the ceiling.

She felt uncomfortable and tried to reposition herself. Just then, a medic in the standard green gown came down the corridor and spoke to the nurse at the desk. She then pointed in Joanne's direction, then came up to Joanne, and asked.

'Are you the person asking about our assault victim?'

'Yes, I'm Joanne Holland,' Joanne introduced herself and shook the medico's hand.

'I'm Doctor Tom Watson,' he replied. 'Do you know Miss Jamieson?'

'Yes, she is my partner.'

'The news is she will be okay,' he informed Joanne. 'The crazy part is that she has a fractured jawbone, two broken ribs and massive bruising on that side, plus some internal bleeding. It looks like a horse kicked her. We'll need to perform surgery to repair the jawbone once the swelling reduces.'

'Oh, my goodness!' exclaimed Joanne, a frightful look crossing her face.

How did she get away from Roberto alive and down in the lift?

'She will be in hospital for at least the next three to four days. We also need to examine her eye socket more closely once the swelling subsides in that area as well. I'm hoping it's not as bad as it looks.'

'Can I see her?'

'Yes, you can, but she is in an induced coma. She's been to hell and back, and we don't yet know the full extent of any other head injuries besides the fractured jaw,' the doctor added. 'I also have to tell you I am obliged to inform the police in cases such as these.'

'Yes, thank you. The police are already investigating,' Joanne replied.

The doctor nodded and then showed Joanne to Holly's ward. When she walked in, she was mortified to see the figure of a woman with bandages around her head, tubes in her mouth, and monitors illuminated with lights blinking like Christmas lights. Joanne wept openly at the sight. She kept telling herself she should have stopped Holly from seeing Roberto. She sat down next to Holly, took her hand, and said in a soft voice.

'I'm sorry, my love. I promise I'll do a better job of looking after you from here on.'

'Are you all right, Miss Holland?' the doctor asked from the doorway.

'Yes, thank you. I'll be fine as soon as Holly gets well again.'

'My dear, she's in expert hands, and she'll pull through,' the doctor reassured, feeling for Joanne's despair.

'I appreciate you sharing your prognosis. Thank you.'

'Have you two known each other for long?' he enquired.

'Just over a couple of months,' Joanne replied, wiping her tears with the wipes she had in her handbag.

'It appears you have a strong bond with her,' he observed, noticing how gently Joanne was hanging onto Holly's hand. 'She will need that from you to recover. It will be a long haul, but I can reassure you she appears to be in excellent hands.'

'Thank you,' Joanne replied, and the doctor left.

Joanne could see on Holly's face where she was bleeding from. She could see where Holly was bleeding from on her face. Her lips were swollen, and a blackish shade had formed around her uncovered eye. She could only imagine what the cover would look like. She guessed the fracture the doctor had mentioned was talking about caused the swelling on one side of Holly's jaw. Joanne continued to caress her hand.

Holly looked a pitiful sight.

'That mongrel will pay for this, big time!' she said to herself.

# Chapter 10: No One's Onboard

A Senior Constable arrived at the building complex where Holly was assaulted by Roberto. They gave him Roberto's room number on the sixth floor. He stood outside the door with one of the uniformed officers and knocked firmly.

'What do you want?' Roberto said in a loud voice as he swung open the door.

He was swaying about and then leant on the door to steady himself. The officer looked at him for a moment, trying to size up the person standing before him.

'Are you Roberto Rossetti?' the Senior Constable asked.

'Yeah, so what?' was the reply. 'Who's asking?'

'I'm Senior Constable Harris with the Parramatta Police. I believe there was an altercation here tonight, based on the report that I have here,' the Senior Constable replied.

'I don't know what you're talking about,' Roberto muttered, denying that anything had happened.

'Someone has made an allegation that a woman at the hospital visited you here a little earlier. Can you confirm that?'

'I'm not sure what you're on about. I'm just having a relaxing evening drinking Jacks,' Roberto replied casually.

'Do you mind if we step inside, sir?' the Senior Constable politely asked.

'I certainly do. Do you have a search warrant?'

'I shouldn't need one if you have nothing to hide,' answered the Senior Constable.

'Well, you'd best run along and get one,' Roberto snapped.

With that, Roberto virtually slammed the door in the officer's face. He stepped back and turned to the constable next to him, who was wide-eyed and surprised at Roberto's reaction.

'Let's get that search warrant, and we'll give him a surprise visit in the morning,' he said to the constable. 'Then he can also explain who gave him the scratch marks on his face.'

Joanne was still sitting next to Holly when a man entered the ward dressed in a suit with a trench coat over the top. The man smiled warmly and then introduced himself.

'I'm Detective Sergeant Parker.'

Joanne stood up, and the detective came to her and shook her hand firmly.

'I'm Joanne Holland.'

'Miss Holland, this lady here is a close friend of yours, I presume, correct?' he asked Joanne after seeing her holding Holly's hand as he came in.

'Yes, my partner, in fact,' Joanne said correctly to him.

'What can you tell me about the events this evening that led to Miss Jamieson being assaulted?' Parker asked, after fumbling through a notepad and finding Holly's name.

'I took her to visit her estranged boyfriend. He had been pestering her for some time to meet with him and sort out their differences,' Joanne explained calmly.

'Who was the boyfriend?' he asked.

He already knew the answer and was testing to see if Joanne was aware of who it allegedly was.

'Roberto Rossetti.'

'Ah, yes,' confirmed Parker. 'Someone mentioned that name earlier.'

'I should have stayed with her,' Joanne said, sitting down next to Holly again.

'Maybe so, but you might lie here alongside Miss Jamieson in a similar condition,' was Parker's response. 'Why did she see him?'

'She wanted to tell him it's over and that she wasn't into drugs like he is,' Joanne explained. 'The last time they were together, he got her to take some coke, and it reacted badly with her. She swore never to do that again, nor to go to his flat again.'

'Had she done drugs before?'

'No, she did nothing like that,' she replied. 'That's probably why I fell in love with her. She was innocent and vulnerable, and I wanted to protect her from all this shit.'

'That's very admirable of you,' he replied softly. 'It's unfortunate that she is lying here with the injuries she sustained.'

'Yes, you're right.'

'What did she have against going to his room? Did he sexually abuse her?'

'No, nothing like that,' Joanne replied quickly. 'She said she witnessed a woman being shot.'

'She said what?' Parker exclaimed in surprise. 'Who was shot?'

'She didn't know the person, but she witnessed who did it.'

'You know we are talking about a serious allegation here?'

'Yes, I do not doubt what Holly saw,' Joanne said firmly. 'She saw the man at Club 77 the night I met Holly for the first time. Roberto knew him too.'

'She saw a person being shot?' he probed further.

'Yes, she also said that Roberto's father came into the room after the shooting and saw her and Roberto looking at them through the window from the flat across the street. She was called into work the next day and told not to say anything about what she saw to anyone.'

'Well, now that is a revelation come true,' Parker finally said. 'Would Miss Jamieson be prepared to make a statement about what she saw and who was involved?'

'You'll have to ask her yourself when she's awake,' Joanne said softly.

'Miss Holland, when they realise that Miss Jamieson is hospitalised, they might conclude that she poses a threat to them, and possibly to you,' he informed her. 'I think it might be wise to place an officer outside this door.'

'Do you think we are both in danger?' asked Joanne, concerned about the detective's suspicion.

'I would prefer to be completely wrong about this, but I can't take the risk and ignore the possibility of an attempt. The Rossettis have a reputation for engaging in criminal activities, and anyone who has tried to provide evidence against them has faced threats, harassment, injuries, and even death. And if not killed, certainly gone missing, presumed dead,' Parker explained grimly.

Joanne's shock was apparent as she stood up, wide-eyed and with her mouth agape, staring at the detective without blinking. She was trying to process what had just been told to her, and then asked quietly,

'What should we do?'

'I'll arrange for Miss Jamieson to be taken to a more secure part of the hospital, and I suggest you stay as close as you can to her as well,' he said. 'Is your residence secure?'

'I live in an apartment complex, and it has security posted on duty every night,' Joanne informed him. 'I am also a security officer for the shopping centre in the CBD.'

'That may not be enough. I suggest you look at alternative accommodation for the time being,' he advised. 'Being a security guard yourself, I think you know what I'm alluding to.'

Joanne felt insecure and perplexed by the detective's revelation. She felt torn between not wanting to abandon her flat on a whim and not wanting to become a target for a drug dealer's revenge. She sat and held Holly's hand again, whispering softly;

'Get well soon, my darling.'

She got up and left the ward, only to find Parker talking to a police officer in the passageway.

'... And don't let anyone in unless they are hospital staff with the correct ID. Anyone else who tries anything, stop them immediately.' 'Do you think that is really necessary?' the officer queried.

'I don't know who will try to gain entry, do you?' Parker replied. 'Maybe nothing will happen, but there are no guarantees, and that's why you are here. I'll find you a partner as well.' 'Very well, sir,' the officer replied.

Joanne walked past them and heard the end of the conversation. The detective followed her and caught her at the duty desk.

'Have you thought about what I mentioned to you earlier?' he asked.

'Yes, I have, actually. As I said earlier, I work as a security guard, and I will see what measures I can take to ensure my safety. I don't like the idea of moving out,' Joanne replied. 'If I move, I will sell the place and leave for good.'

'That seems drastic,' was his reply, a bit surprised at Joanne's resolve.

'Holly and I were talking about visiting a close friend of hers in WA, and when we return, we might look at buying a house together,' Joanne informed him. 'It's all up in the air at present, but we all have dreams to chase, don't we?'

'Well, I wish Miss Jamieson a speedy recovery so we can sort out this mess once and for all,' the detective said. 'Can I have your contact details in case we talk again?'

'Yes, certainly.'

'Likewise, here is my card, in case you need to get in contact with me for any reason.'

Parker wrote Joanne's number in his notepad and then gave her his details. They both said their goodbyes and left.

Joanne grabbed something to eat at a cafe that was close by, within walking distance. She planned to return to sit with Holly for as long as she could, hopefully staying overnight as well. There was no harm in asking anyway.

Joanne had a quick meal and was back at the hospital within the hour. She asked the duty nurse if she could stay with Holly overnight.

'Unfortunately, we don't have anywhere for you to sleep, but we can give you a softer chair and blankets if you like. It won't be very comfortable,' the nurse explained.

After about ten minutes, the nurses provided Joanne with blankets and a pillow, and she settled herself as comfortably as she could in the chair. She would not leave Holly alone again. She looked towards the ward door and could just glimpse the officer outside. A second officer had just arrived as well.

She wriggled in the chair again, trying to find a bit more comfort. Closing her eyes, she slowly drifted off into a deep sleep.

Vinnie met up with Mario on the boat at the marina. He had the bookkeeper with him, who was protesting about going on a boat this late in the evening.

'I don't know what you're trying to do, but I'm not interested in any boat trips!' he protested. 'This could give the wrong impression, kidnapping!'

'I'd give it a rest if I were you,' Vinnie warned. 'You don't have a choice in the matter.'

'Why did you have to tie my hands like this, too? This is assault!'

Vinnie pushed him in the back to hurry him up and stop him from asking questions or making more remarks in protest. They reached the boat, and Vinnie pushed him onboard just as Mario came up from the galley.

'You're here at last. What took you so long?' Mario asked, sounding annoyed.

'I had some trouble convincing him he didn't have a say in whether he was going on a boat trip!' Vinnie explained, a little high-rated from the effort.

'What is going on, Mario?' the bookkeeper asked.

Mario didn't reply and raised his hand, bringing a batten down hard across the man's head. The bookkeeper buckled at the knees and fell to the floor of the boat. Mario then pushed him down the steps to the galley, and he tumbled to the bottom.

'Nice,' was Vinnie's remark.

'Well, at least that will shut him up for the time being,' Mario replied. 'We have to do this quickly and without being noticed on the way out by the water police.'

'Yeah, once we pass the Heads, we should be clear,' Vinnie agreed. 'We should go north after we've dumped him and sneak back in.'

'Yep, I agree.'

Mario gunned the engine, and the Catamaran cruised towards the Heads. Once out in the open sea, it would be a little rougher swellwise, but the weather forecast had it as quite manageable.

Vinnie looked down the steps and saw the bookkeeper still lying at the bottom where he'd fallen, still unconscious.

It took only another five minutes for the boat to hit open water. The sea wasn't too choppy, and the Cat handled it well.

'Go down and gag him, then bring him up so we can tie the weights around his feet,' Mario ordered. 'If he stirs, hit him again.'

Vinnie did as asked and brought him up the steps. Mario throttled the boat back a little and then gave Vinnie a hand with the bookkeeper. They dragged him onto the deck and tied the weights to his feet. Vinnie then double-checked that his hands were still securely tied behind his back. The gag stayed in his mouth.

'We're set to toss him over,' Vinnie reported.

'Good,' Mario acknowledged. 'We'll be out on the spot in about fifteen minutes.'

Mario was at the wheel and Vinnie beside him, both looking out to the front of the boat. They were swaying and knee bending with every rhythm of the Catamaran careering over the slight swell. Vinnie glanced at the bookkeeper twice to make sure he was still unconscious.

It didn't take long before Mario throttled back the engines, slowing the boat until it was almost still in the water.

'This is far enough, I think,' Mario announced. 'Throw him over.'

Vinnie immediately responded, and a groan came from the bookkeeper as he pushed him over the side. There was a splash as the body hit the water. Both Mario and Vinnie watched as the bookkeeper briefly regained consciousness and then Mario pushed him over the side of the boat, causing him to disappear in the ocean's darkness, never to surface again a small trail of bubbles followed, and Mario returned to the wheel of the boat and throttled up the engines.

'That sorts that out,' Vinnie said as he joined Mario at the wheel.

'Yep,' he replied. 'We might track north for a couple of kilometres before heading back in.'

'Okay, that's fine by me.'

Mario headed north for about ten minutes and then turned towards the West. Twenty minutes later, they passed through the Heads.

'Well, back home, none too soon after that trip,' Vinnie said.

'Yeah, those trips are always good to get out of the way quickly.'

They had just entered the bay when a siren, blue lights flashing and a searchlight, came from about half a kilometre to their left. The water police were going to stop them and check out the boat.

'Put on your life jacket,' Mario ordered as he slowed the boat.

The police boat pulled alongside the Catamaran, and one officer shouted out,

'Evening, I'm Constable Higgins, and this is Constable Johnston at the helm. Do we have permission to come aboard and carry out a licence check?'

'Yes, welcome aboard,' Mario replied politely.

He reached into the folder beside the console, retrieved the vessel's registration papers, and handed them to the constable.

'We saw you leaving the bay earlier and thought you might try your hand at fishing. Did you have any luck?' the constable enquired as he handed back the papers.

'That was the plan,' Vinnie confirmed. 'But we had equipment failure and called it a night.'

'Sorry to hear that. You wasted your time coming out,' the constable remarked. 'Do you have a current fishing licence and your skipper's ticket, please?'

Mario rummaged through the folder and gave the constable both documents. The constable checked the paperwork and returned it to him.

'This vessel can carry six people. You have one life jacket on. Do you have more for others onboard?'

'Yes, two in this cabinet and two in this one,' Mario answered as he opened both to show the constable.

'Do you have a flare gun and an EPIRB onboard?'

Mario opens the cabinet near the console again and produces both items. The constable looked happy at what he saw.

'I must thank you, gentlemen, for your cooperation. It's a pleasure to see that some people make the effort and get it right,' he said. 'Enjoy the rest of your evening.'

The police boat slowly pulled away as Mario and Vinnie watched it move off. It increased speed and had travelled some distance before Mario started the engines again.

'That wasn't so painful,' Vinnie observed.

'Maybe, but they know we were out here, right?' was Mario's questioning reply.

'What does that matter now?' Vinnie asked.

'The less the police know of our movements, the better off we are,' Mario explained. 'We can do without being in the limelight.'

Vinnie thought about Mario's response and realised what he meant. If their activities were revealed, the police had the boat's ID number, the time, and their location when they stopped them. As long as they covered their tracks, no one could point a finger at them.

They said nothing more until they moored the boat. Then Mario asked,

'Do you want to ring Dominic and tell him we've handled everything, or do you want me to?'

'No, I will,' he replied. 'There's something I need to see him about, something that could affect our trading arrangements.'

'What might that be?' Mario asked as they picked up their gear and left the boat.

Vinnie explained that some of his pushers had asked him several times about supplying meth. A lab blew up a week ago, a large one at that, and there is an increase in demand and short on supply. He planned to ask Dominic what he thought and whether they should go down that road as well.

'I can tell you this much, his reaction would be the same. Especially if there's money to be made, the Family is all for it,' Mario replied. 'The biggest hurdle is setting up a lab.'

They placed their gear in the back of the car, got in, and drove off. Little did they realise that a dark figure in the shadows was watching and heard snippets of their conversation. Once they were out of sight, the stranger took out his phone and speed-dialled a number.

'They're back, but only two of them,' he reported.

'Ok?' came the reply. 'Check the boat.'

The person walked down the gangway onto the boat and climbed aboard. He had a quick look around and then left. When he got back to the car park, he rang the number again.

'No one's onboard.'

'Okay, leave it with me.'

The stranger got into an SUV and drove off into the night.

Within the last seventy-two hours, the Rossetti family had taken the lives of three people, a private investigator, a lawyer, and a bookkeeper.

# Chapter 11: Hitman's Job

A week earlier, Tammy O'Lachlin had been poring over the pile of paperwork in front of her. The last bit of information she had gathered filled in the pieces of the puzzle she had been working on.

Tammy was working for a law firm in Melbourne when she received a call from a friend at McCormack & Sly to see if she was interested in doing some investigative work on the legal side for them.

It would be better than being stuck with the mundane pro-bono work she was doing in Melbourne and the occasional misdemeanour cases. The opportunity was too good to pass up, and Tammy moved to Sydney to advance her career further, as it was an opportunity too good to miss.

She found it difficult at first, but once she found her feet, it became a challenge and quite time-consuming. Tammy's job involved sifting through company structures, their business charters, and legal implications involved in transactions, as well as investigating any improprieties that could lead to illegal ramifications. The client base was broad and diverse.

A private investigator, Milton Clark, who was working for a client whose business partner had gone missing, gave her a report. The partner had simply disappeared off the face of the Earth. The police had investigated a missing person case and had nothing to show for their efforts in twelve months.

Clark came up with two strong leads. Both led to the door of a machinery import business owned by the Rossettis and a freight company. However, he could not establish a firm connection between the two businesses, at least not one that could be used as hard evidence. Most of what he learned comprised hearsay, rumours, and innuendo.

The authorities assigned Dominic Roberto Rossetti and Teresa Marie Rossetti to immigrate to Australia and establish a business on the east coast. This business would facilitate The Family in creating a crime syndicate focused on drugs, gambling, and money laundering. This would benefit the family back in Sicily and be a huge spin-off for the Rossetti family.

Emporium Machinery Imports set up operations focused on importing machinery from China as a classic ruse to conceal its activities, making them difficult to detect if executed properly. Their two sons, Dominic Jr. and Roberto, would eventually run the business when the time was right, while Dominic and Teresa would step back and play a lesser part in its operation.

Clark had circumstantial evidence, which wasn't enough to prompt the police into action or to search the premises for concrete proof.

'It would be a waste of time,' a senior police officer admitted to Clark. 'We need proof that will allow us to get a search warrant, and even then, the court would be reluctant to act if the evidence wasn't substantial.'

'I've got an inside man who might get the information we need,' Clark suggested.

'What would he be looking for?' the officer asked.

'Well, I've asked him to find transactions that show evidence of fraud, misappropriation, and bogus transactions, that sort of thing.'

'This informant of yours is an accountant?' the officer asked.

'No, he's a bookkeeper and has worked with them for some time,' Clark replied.

'What's the company's name?'

'I'd rather not say at this time in case I've got it all wrong. I'll let you know in due course if it looks dodgy.'

'Okay, but tread carefully when trying to bring these sorts of people to answer for their actions in court. It could turn nasty really quick,' the officer advised.

'Who would be an excellent solicitor to help with looking through the information once I have it?' Clark asked the officer.

'I'd give McCormack & Sly a go. They have some people there who can help with that sort of thing,' was the suggestion.

It took a couple of weeks for Clark to get the first bit of information he was looking for from the bookkeeper. The business had a new girl join the team, and the woman in charge of the office and the owner was paying attention to training the new girl. That allowed the bookkeeper to copy some records. Some dubious activities he found needed investigating.

'I'm not an accountant, Mr Clark, but I know enough to look at these transactions with scepticism. The new girl is an accountant and the son's new girlfriend, but I'm not sure what will happen to me,' he said with some concern.

'So what is the problem you're alluding to?' Clark asked.

'I don't know how the new girl will fit in or if I'm going to be out of a job. It worries me a little.'

'What's the new girl's name?' Clark asked him.

'Holly, I think, she was working in another office, and I only got briefly introduced to her in passing.'

'Let me take this to some legal people I know and see if they can uncover any dodgy dealings that are illegal and maybe get enough firm evidence for the police to act.'

'I'll see what else I can find. The new girl is recording the information in the accounts for the creditors. Teresa is keeping a close eye on her and explaining away any anomalies she's finding, putting her off the scent.'

'If she's any sort of accountant, she'll pick up on that soon enough.'
'That's why Teresa is monitoring her and limiting what she does.'

'So, what about you? Do you have access to all the files?' Clark asked.

'Most of them,' he replied. 'Probably about ninety per cent of all the business transactions, and that's why I already have these records.'

'You've done well. See if you can get as many files as possible,' Clark requested.

'I'll do what I can.'

Darryl McCormick and Gavin Sly were classmates during law school and struck up a close friendship throughout their college and university years. Once they qualified and there would be an admission to the bar, the next progression for them was to set up a law firm.

Over seven years, both made significant inroads into the legal profession and specialised in corporate law. They had to employ two solicitors within a short time to keep up with the demand for their services. Some corporate bodies were doubtful clients, yet others engaged their services contractually, with dedicated staff handling those key clients.

To represent a business in court, they were always the first to be called upon. Now the firm had grown to employ six full-time solicitors, along with four legal secretaries. Occasionally, they hired extra help when the workload became too heavy and to achieve an outcome within a reasonable timeframe.

Tammy started her employment six months ago and had a decent workload to begin with. She had received Milton Clark's file three days earlier and was currently engaged in determining how the transactions were calculated. Her background in accounting helped her in that process, but she needed more information.

Gavin poked his head through the door.

'Tammy, can you come to Darryl's office and bring Clark's file with you?'

Darryl and Milton Clark were standing in front of Darryl's desk discussing something when Gavin entered, closely followed by Tammy.

'Tammy, this is Milton Clark,' Darryl introduced.

'Hi Milton,' Tammy acknowledged, shaking his hand. 'How are you? I can now put a face to the name.'

'Likewise,' he replied. 'I'm doing well, and you?'

'Well enough, thank you.'

Once everyone sat down, Darryl began the discussion by asking Milton a question.

'Milton, have you received any further information from your source?'

'Yes, I have, and I believe there's more coming,' he replied.

'Tammy, how far have you gone with the information you have so far?' Darryl asked her.

'I have some queries about some periodic payments, but I haven't got the information about where the payments went,' she explained. 'It's quite a large amount, and I think it shouldn't have slipped through this easily.'

'So what are you saying?' Gavin asked.

'They're regular payments of ten thousand dollars plus, as if they were payoffs for services rendered by some unknown person or persons,' Tammy suggested.

'What are you thinking in legal terms?' Clark asked.

'Payments for inducements, fraudulent activity, maybe money laundering,' she replied. 'But we need cold, hard evidence.'

'I'm working on that, and hopefully this will help with that purpose,' Clark replied as he handed Tammy a folder with new information that Darryl had mentioned at the start of the meeting.

'I haven't been told who the client is you're investigating?' Tammy enquired.

'It's Emporium Machinery Imports, run by the Rossetti family,' Clark replied. 'They're a criminal organisation, and the police haven't yet had enough evidence to carry out warrant searches.'

Darryl informed Tammy that Milton was investigating the disappearance of a person who had vanished without a trace and used to work for them some time ago. That's why they were looking at monetary movements and hopefully can find evidence for a brief for further investigation by the police.'

There were another dozen pages of transactions and ledger entries, considerably more than the first batch. She quickly flipped through the pages and nodded occasionally as she finished perusing the pages.

'There's definitely a lot of money being moved around,' she finally said.

'In fact, plenty of movements with account numbers beside some transactions.'

'Do you have any idea yet as to the destination of the money?' Clark asked.

'I'll follow up on that with a couple of banks account numbers and see where it leads me,' Tammy said. 'Hopefully, I'll know the account locations by this afternoon.'

'That sounds encouraging,' Clark commented. 'It's unfortunate that as a PI, I have limited access to information like money movements, so I appreciate your help with this.'

'Well, there are limits for us as well, but asking the right people helps,' Darryl said, reassuring Milton Clark. 'Tammy will let you know how things go and any relevant information she uncovers.' 'That sounds good to me,' Clark replied.

'I'll call you as soon as I've found something,' Tammy confirmed. 'Oh, by the way, here's my new mobile number,' Clark said as he handed her a card. 'Someone smashed my car window and stole some stuff out of it, including my phone.'

'That's a pain,' Tammy replied. 'I hope you got it blocked?'

'I did, but that's not the important part,' Clark continued. 'It had some vital contact details on it. I just hope the block I requested overwrote the SIM card.'

'They usually do that on request, particularly for someone in your profession,' Darryl replied.

'Let's hope so.'

Clark said his goodbyes and left the office. Tammy also headed back to her office with renewed determination to investigate the accounts for Clark. She was hoping to have some information ready by the end of the day.

Stromnikov was five minutes early for his meeting with Dominic. He'd been told there was a job that needed to be handled, and he was the man for it. As he knocked on Dominic's office door, he opened it and stepped inside.

'Serge, come in and sit down,' Dominic greeted him.

Stromnikov, a man of few words, carried out tasks without hesitation, following instructions precisely. Dominic picked up the phone and pressed the intercom button.

'Roberto, we're ready.'

Roberto entered the office a minute later carrying a folder, followed by Vinnie. They both pulled up chairs and sat down after greeting Stromnikov.

'As Roberto and Vinnie are aware,' Dominic said, addressing Stromnikov, 'our bookkeeper has been leaking information to a private investigator concerning our transactions within our operation. Roberto has some details.'

Roberto sat up straight in his chair and handed Stromnikov the folder. 'We dealt with the bookkeeper last night, took him on a one-way boat trip to the five-mile ledge, 'But this man is of greater concern,'

Roberto explained, pointing to the folder. 'He's a private detective who's been snooping around, sticking his nose into our business.'

'What do you want me to do?' Stromnikov asked in a broad Russian accent.

'That's simple,' Dominic interjected. 'Take him out.'

The Russian nodded and looked at the photos more closely. There were three shots of Clark being handed a folder by the bookkeeper in a shopping mall.

'Who is this man?'

'Milton Clark,' Roberto answered. 'He's the one I mentioned the other night at Club77when I said he was a thorn in our side that needs to be removed.'

'When do you want this done?'

'As soon as you can,' Roberto replied. 'There may be another that needs to be removed. She works at a law firm in the city. We found her employer's details, and hers, on Clark's phone, which we had stolen from his car.'

'That was careless of him, leaving it in plain view, wasn't it?' Vinnie said with a wry smile on his face. 'I have some men I can call on for a job.'

'I have to identify the person he's been contacting at the law firm. Once I find out where she lives, I'll pass that information on to you as well,' Roberto told Stromnikov.

'I want to be there for that one. I want to find out how much she knows and what's happening with the information our bookkeeper passed on!' Dominic interjected and was getting angry at the redness on his face.

He looked straight at Stromnikov, who nodded in approval, then fixed his gaze on Roberto.

'I hope your new girlfriend isn't involved in this,' Dominic commented.

'I'm sure she's not. Mum's monitoring her and watching what she's doing,' Roberto replied. 'She's still learning the business as well.'

'I hope for both your sakes you're right,' Dominic said. 'That's all I wanted you for, so let's move ahead and make this happen.' They all got up and left without another word.

# Chapter 12: It Works Every Time

It was in the afternoon of the third day when Holly regained consciousness. The doctors believed that the longer she was under, the better her chances of recovering. Any movement could have caused severe pain and hampered her recovery in the initial stages of her treatment. Joanne was by her side, holding her hand when she woke.

'Hey, beautiful, welcome back,' she greeted with a smile.

Holly was still a bit dazed, and even though most of the swelling had subsided, she had to blink twice to focus properly. She turned her head towards Joanne and returned the smile.

'I know it's a silly question, but how are you feeling?' Joanne asked.

Holly hesitated for a moment as she tried to recollect what had happened.

'Alright, I guess,' she responded. 'Where am I?'

'You're in hospital, sweetheart,' Joanne replied. 'Can you remember what happened?'

Holly tried to straighten up in bed and grimaced with the pain that was still in her side from the broken ribs. Just then, a nurse walked in to check on her.

'Oh, you are awake,' the nurse observed, stating the obvious. 'You will still be sore, and it looks like you've been through the wringer.' The nurse checked her pulse and watched her breathing.

'You could say that,' agreed Holly, as she remembered what had happened at the hands of Roberto.

'I'll let the doctor know you're awake, and he'll be in to see you a bit later,' the nurse said as she scribbled some notes on Holly's chart, then left.

'He really did a number on me, didn't he?' Holly asked, tears welling in her eyes.

'Maybe you should have stayed away, but I didn't think he would do this either,' was Joanne's response. 'I knew he'd be a dick about it, but not to this extent.'

'So, I kicked the arsehole in the nuts and made my way out of there,' Holly informed her. 'I got to the elevator and from there on, I can't recall what happened next.'

'Some guests waiting for the elevator helped you after you collapsed in their arms,' Joanne replied, her own eyes watering. 'But you're okay now.'

'I don't think we'll be safe here anymore,' Holly suggested. 'We have to get out of town.'

'We'll worry about that later,' Joanne replied, inwardly agreeing. 'First, now that you're on the mend, getting you back on your feet.'

'How are you going with work if you're here?' Holly suddenly asked, concerned for Joanne.

'It's okay,' she replied. 'I got a couple of extra days off, but I have to go back to work tonight.'

Holly smiled again at Joanne, realising she had been here from day one. Her devotion was admirable, and Holly couldn't contemplate how to repay her. The love she felt for Joanne was going to endure.

'You're going to need some rest before you go to work,' Holly said, worried for Joanne's well-being.

'I'll be okay. I've been having naps here next to you,' Joanne replied with a big smile. Holly smiled, too.

'I'm going to leave you, sweetheart,' Joanne told her. 'I need to organise some things to get ready for work. There's a police officer outside making sure no "uninvited guests" get in here. Two, actually. We don't know whether Roberto wants to visit you.'

Holly looked a little surprised to learn two police officers were on guard outside her door. She didn't believe there was any immediate danger from Roberto, but then again, he might be vengeful and seek to harm her further. She had feared for her life during his brutal assault. It was something she would never forget or forgive.

Joanne gave Holly a soft kiss on her lips. She didn't want to press too hard and hurt her still slightly bruised mouth.

'I love you,' she whispered in Holly's ear.

'I love you too,' Holly replied, holding the side of her face.

She closed her eyes and fell asleep almost straight away. The TV was on at a low volume. Joanne picked up the remote and was about to turn it off just as a newsflash announcement appeared on screen; she slightly increased the volume. The bulletin startled her.

Police have confirmed the identity of a woman who was found shot dead at the side of the Princes Highway, opposite Flemington Racecourse. She was the missing woman Tammy O'Lachlin, a lawyer working with an investigation team into drug trafficking. Police suspect someone shot her at another location and then disposed of her body there within the last twenty-four hours. We urge anyone who has seen or heard anything concerning this matter to contact Crime Stoppers.

Joanne immediately thought about what Holly had said she witnessed that night while at Roberto's flat. Could it be the same person? Holly was still asleep. Joanne turned off the TV.

***

Joanne arrived at work a little earlier than usual to catch up on incident reports, any outcomes she had to be aware of and anything that would affect the usual security run. Because she'd taken a three-day break, she wasn't up to date with what had been going on. She signed in and collected her equipment to do her first run.

She also signed for her pistol, a Glock 19, which is the preferred weapon for many private and public security agencies. It's an ideal 9mm handgun for concealment and a good backup weapon. Her boss,

Jeremy, asked her to come to his office once she'd signed out the pistol. Tonight's news report was still at the back of her mind.

'Joanne, come in,' Jeremy greeted. 'How are you

travelling?' 'Better now, thanks,' Joanne replied. 'What

made you say that?' he asked.

'I have been visiting my partner in hospital,' Joanne explained. 'Some bloke from a dubious background beat her.'

'Oh,' Jeremy said, somewhat astonished. 'I'm sorry to hear that. Is she okay?'

'Yeah, she's on the mend.'

'Is that why you had the extra days off?' he asked.

'Yes,' Joanne replied, wondering at the questioning. 'Is anything wrong?'

'No, not at all,' he quickly replied. 'I just wanted to let you know your weapons proficiency qualification is due, and I was hoping to make a time for you on the range.'

'Oh, that time of year again.'

'Yes, I'm afraid so,' Jeremy replied. 'You can do the pistol tonight before you go on patrol and the rifle when you're on day shift.' 'Okay, that sounds good to me,' Joanne agreed.

'The pistol range is available to you tonight, and I've tentatively booked the rifle range for next Friday morning during your day shift,' Jeremy informed her. 'There will be three other officers doing the rifle with you as well.'

'Great, that sounds fine by me. Let's do it.'

'I'll meet you down at the pistol range in ten,' Jeremy said.

'Good, I'll see you there,' Joanne replied.

She went to the weapons officer and drew some more cartridges for the test. This let her complete a ten-round shoot and then two five-round rapid-fire sequences. Upon achieving a ninety percent strike rate in the vital area, the kill zone, to qualify at her level as a supervisor. In the past she'd had no problem qualifying, and especially with the new version of the Glock the shooting was even easier. In her opinion, it was a very versatile handgun.

By the time Jeremy got to the pistol range, Joanne had her ten rounds loaded, earmuffs and safety glasses on, ready to shoot. Jeremy saw she was prepared and stood behind her.

'I see you're ready,' Jeremy observed. 'Ten rounds to fire in your own time when you're ready.'

Joanne squeezed off the first round and hit the mark on the silhouette of a black target. The next nine rounds did the same, with a perfect score.

'Excellent,' Jeremy acknowledged. 'Now load five rounds of rapid fire on my mark.'

They retrieved the target and replaced it with a new one. Joanne put five rounds in the magazine, loaded the pistol, and waited for Jeremy to give the order.

'Once you've fired these five rounds, continue loading the next five and carry on shooting,' Jeremy ordered. 'Start firing... now.'

Joanne fired the first five rounds, hitting the mark dead centre in the heart. She dropped out the magazine, loaded the next five rounds, replaced it in the gun, and fired again, aiming for the head of the silhouette target, all within thirty millimetres of each other.

Jeremy said, 'Let's see the damage,' as they electronically retrieved the target.

'Well, well. That's pretty damn fine shooting, Joanne. Have you been practising?'

'I wish,' she replied with a note of disappointment.

'If I didn't know you better, I'd say you had someone in mind,' Jeremy opined.

'Who, me?' she replied with a smirk. 'I would never do that.'

'I'd say that's almost a perfect score,' he said as he assessed the target.

'That's harsh, boss,' Joanne replied with a laugh. 'It's a perfect score, just like me.'

'Yes, well, I might have to admit you're correct on both accounts,' Jeremy said with a smile. 'Maybe too perfect.'

'Thank you, I'll take that as a yes,' she replied with her typical smirk.

Joanne finished collecting the brass from the rounds, and both left the range to return to Jeremy's office. Once back, Joanne asked,

'How many holidays do I have left?'

'I'm not sure, but I'll check with Serena, who does the pay,' Jeremy replied. 'I'll catch up with you tomorrow. By the way, when you do the rifle, it'll be at four hundred metres.'

'Okay, that's fine.'

'Can I ask why you want holidays, apart from the obvious?' Jeremy enquired.

'Holly and I were thinking of going to WA for a bit to catch up with an old friend,' Joanne explained. 'Also, considering she had this run in with her so-called boyfriend, a change of scenery might do us both the world of good.'

'Sounds like it might be permanent.'

'I don't think it will be, but maybe a long break will be okay,' Joanne replied.

'I sincerely hope you don't leave us, Joanne,' Jeremy assured her. 'You're one of our top officers, and it would be hard to find a replacement.'

'First, let me know how much leave I have and I'll consider my options,' Joanne said. 'Thanks for your vote of confidence. I really appreciate it.'

'Not a problem. You're always welcome,' he replied. 'Have a good shift, and I'll see you tomorrow.'

Joanne left his office and went to the staff room. There were three officers sipping cups of coffee. She went to the noticeboard to check her roster and who she was partnering with tonight.

'Oh my goodness,' she exclaimed when she saw the listing. 'Marty, I'm with you tonight.'

'Yeah, and isn't that great,' Marty said, sitting with the other two officers, Rob and Johnno. 'It's about time I got some pleasant company to work with.'

'You think I'm pleasant?' Joanne said, playing along. 'You poor, disillusioned fool.'

'Oh, babe, I love it when you scold me,' Marty replied.

'You're a sick puppy, aren't you?' she jibed.

They all laughed, knowing it was harmless banter among work colleagues. Joanne turned back to the roster, and Marty joined her.

'So what's happening tonight?' she asked.

Marty began updating Joanne, pointing at a map, explaining that police had received reports of tenants in the light industrial area seeing a stranger supposedly casing the area.

'We already sent one patrol out and found nothing so far, even though there have been reports of undesirable activity happening at night in the southern area,' Marty said. 'We'll drive through in about half an hour.'

'No one knows what they were looking for?'

'No, nothing that made any sense, just the activity reports,' Marty replied.

Martin Smith had been in the security industry for at least ten or twelve years. The last six years were with Grey Night Security. He had been Joanne's instructor and mentor when she started in security five years ago, and they'd been close friends ever since.

About four years ago, just after Joanne qualified, Marty had a traumatic experience. His wife of thirty years was killed in a car accident one evening after dropping him off at work. Police reported that a young hoon, drugged up, ran a red light and crashed into the driver's side of her car. She passed away at the scene, and the hoon died the next day in hospital.

Joanne was there to lend a shoulder to cry on, and their friendship remained strictly platonic. It took some time for Marty to get over his loss. Joanne would visit, have a few drinks, talk rubbish, debate changing the world, and discuss why politicians couldn't solve the country's problems.

'The stuff that dreams are made of,' Marty once remarked.

Marty was in his fifties and didn't expect to find anyone else at this stage of life. Maybe, maybe not. Not just yet, anyway.

'You shouldn't give up. Just keep your options open,' Joanne told him. 'Sounds familiar, doesn't it? You said that to me a dozen times.'

Joanne had her fair share of disappointments with men, and when things went from bad to worse, Marty was there to pick her up, dust her off, and help her back on her feet. The last guy she dated thought that after wining and dining her, he could have his way. Joanne fought him off and, amid sustaining some hits and bruises, left him lying on the floor in pain. It felt like his balls had become lumps in his throat, or so it seemed, as he scrimmaged in pain and developed an uneasy cough. A knee to the groin ended that intended relationship in a flash. 'It works every time,' Joanne said to herself with a smirk.

They had time for each other during the hard times, working together and sometimes as shift partners, which cemented their bond. Some patrols tested them, and as colleagues, they had each other's backs. The bad guys came off second best every time. Joanne preferred this type of work to shopping-centre duties.

'We'll head off as soon as I finish my coffee,' Marty said. 'Do you want one?'

'No, I'm good, thanks,' Joanne replied, sitting down next to him.

Marty was the only person she would accept being called 'babe'. Anyone else would get a scolding, and sometimes a punch to the upper arm. Marty downed his coffee.

'Okay, I'm ready if you are,' he said.

'Yep, let's do this and see what we can find.'

# Chapter 13: There Was a Shooting

Vinnie received a phone call from one of his dealers that sounded urgent. Someone was muscling in on his territory, and he wasn't happy. It had become apparent that other drug syndicates were trying to corner the market on 'ice', and this was one reason Vinnie wanted to talk to Dominic for permission to set up a lab.

With the increase in cocaine shipments, the product had to be moved quickly and efficiently. Now that others were pushing 'ice', the cocaine had become a little harder to sell, and some users were switching to 'ice'. After losing one or two clients, the pusher was struggling to meet his quota for the month, hence the frantic phone call to Vinnie.

'Unfortunately, my friend, try harder,' Vinnie advised.

'But I've been trying and keep hitting a dead end,' he replied.

'Let's meet later when I'm ready, and we'll discuss the options,' Vinnie said. 'There's something I need to check first, and I'd rather not do this over the phone.'

'Okay,' he replied. 'I'll talk to you later.'

Vinnie ended the call and went to his car to drive to the location he had in mind for a meth lab. It was close to the industrial area, and he planned a nighttime recon to determine whether there was any activity that could jeopardise the project. The area is usually shut down at night, with workers milling around during the day, so daytime activity wouldn't attract attention. He phoned Mario.

'Mario, do you have an hour free?'

'Not really, I'm in the middle of something,' Mario replied. 'Why? What's going on?'

'I found a location for a meth lab and want to check it out tonight to see how well it would suit our purpose,' Vinnie explained.

'Tonight's not good for me.'

'That's fine, no problem,' Vinnie said. 'I'll do a quick check and see how it looks. At least then I'll have something to show Dominic.'

'Be careful down there,' Mario warned. 'The southern end of that area has seen some dangerous elements at night.'

'Yes, I've heard that too,' Vinnie replied. 'That's why I want to check it out at night.'

'So, be careful,' Mario said, ending the call.

Vinnie drove to the site he had been observing for a couple of days. At least he could present something to Dominic if the idea was favourable for the Family. As he arrived at the eastern end of the industrial area, he stopped when he saw a black BMW parked near a complex of buildings he was keen on. He watched for a moment to see what they were doing.

At the western end, Joanne and Marty drove into the area with their lights dimmed. They also saw a black vehicle at the northern end and noticed something being removed from the boot, wrapped in sheeting. It looked limp, suspiciously like a body. Just then, out of the dark, a muzzle flash and the crack of a rifle being fired.

'Holy shit!' exclaimed Marty. 'Call it in!'

'Mobile Four to base, shots fired! Repeat, shots fired at the southern end of the industrial area.'

'Receiving you, Mobile Four. Contacting the police now and dispatching backup.'

'They're not shooting at us,' Marty observed. 'Let's take cover near this building.'

An assailant targeted Vinnie with the first shot while he was still in his car. He saw the flash and the bullet pierce his windscreen. He grabbed his pistol, opened the door, and ducked for cover. As he did, a second bullet slammed through the open driver's door, just missing his head.

'Fucking hell, who are these wankers?' he muttered.

He moved to the rear of the car, and a third bullet ricocheted off the ground. Vinnie slowly poked his head out and fired back, hitting the BMW's passenger door. He heard a muffled yell of pain from inside the car. The rifleman shot at Vinnie again, missing by millimetres. He ducked back under cover.

Joanne and Marty watched the incident unfold, waiting for backup and the police to arrive. The men in the BMW, having finished their task, got back in and drove off. Vinnie broke cover and fired two more rounds at the BMW as it disappeared around the corner.

Out of the corner of his eye, he saw Joanne and Marty near a building not far from him. Fearing the worst and thinking they were part of the same gang, he fired two rounds in their direction and ducked back undercover. The first shot hit the building just above Joanne's head, who ducked instinctively. The second struck Marty in the left shoulder, dropping him in pain.

'Fucking hell, you bastard!' he yelled.

He looked around the building and saw Vinnie stand up as well. Marty took advantage of the moment to return fire, squeezing off one round. There was a loud report when the bullet hit, but to Joanne's amazement, Vinnie reeled backwards and fell to the ground. Then all went quiet.

'What just happened?' he asked, to no one in particular.

Joanne was still on her knees next to Marty, who had ducked down again, holding his wound.

'Why are you asking?' Joanne replied. 'Hold still while I check your shoulder.'

'I didn't shoot as straight as I thought, but he fell backwards as if hit,' Marty explained, still confused.

'Yes, I saw that too,' Joanne confirmed. 'Okay, the bullet went straight through the fleshy part of your shoulder. I can't feel any bone damage.' Just then, the siren of the police car grew louder. Joanne stood up to flag it down. She looked towards where Vinnie lay and saw he hadn't moved. He might be dead.

The police saw Joanne wave, and the car skidded to a halt. A backup car did the same. The occupants of both vehicles came over to Joanne and Marty.

'What happened here?' a police officer asked. Seeing Marty's bleeding shoulder, he yelled to his companion, 'Call an ambulance. We have an injured person here.'

'Marty, are you alright?' Rod, one of the backup security officers, asked.

'Thank fuck it's only a flesh wound,' Marty replied. 'It hurts like hell, though.'

'Can you tell me what happened?' the police officer asked.

His companion carefully walked over to where Vinnie lay and checked for a pulse. Vinnie was dead. He saw Vinnie's gun lying nearby, gingerly picked it up by the barrel, and placed it in a plastic zip-lock bag. Then he returned to the first officer, who was talking with Marty.

Joanne began explaining, 'The police had asked us to patrol this area after receiving reports about a stranger frequenting it over the last couple of days. Within a minute of our arrival, we heard gunshots, which we promptly reported on the two-way.'

'Base believed we would immediately report to the police,' she added.

'Yes, we got the call,' the officer replied. 'We weren't far away on patrol ourselves. Who was doing the shooting?'

'We observed two occupants of a black BMW lifting something from the boot, and another shooting at this man over here,' Joanne continued, pointing to Vinnie's body. 'We heard a commotion from the BMW; they all got back in and drove off. This person here fired two shots after the car.'

'Did he hit anyone?' the officer asked.

'Not sure. We can't confirm that,' Joanne answered. 'Then he turned the gun on us and fired two rounds, one struck Marty. He returned fire, and the gunman fell to the ground.'

'He must be an excellent shot to do that with a shoulder wound,' the officer remarked. 'You say you saw them taking something from the BMW?'

'Yes. We think it might have been a body,' Joanne replied. 'Over there, at the far end of that building.'

'Okay, we'll check it out.'

The two police officers headed towards the building, their torches sweeping the ground as they went. Marty was sitting on a crate next to the building, flanked by Rob and Johnno. In the distance came more sirens, and it didn't take long for another police car to arrive, followed by an ambulance. They stopped alongside each other, behind the second security car. The ambulance paramedics immediately went to Marty and began treating his wound.

Two detectives stepped out of the police car and approached Joanne, surveying the scene as they came closer. She knew the first detective.

'Ah, Miss Holland,' he said, recognising her and surprised to see her in a security uniform. 'Fancy seeing you here.'

'Senior Detective Parker,' she responded. 'And a good evening to you.'

'Likewise,' he replied. 'What have you been up to?'

'Persons unknown at this stage caught Marty and me in some gunfire,' Joanne replied.

'I see,' Parker said, scanning the area. 'By the way, this is Detective Ashcroft.'

'Detective,' Joanne acknowledged.

'I see you have a deceased person over here,' Parker observed. 'Do you know who it is?'

'No, I don't. I haven't been over there yet to see if I recognise him,' Joanne said.

The detectives walked over to Vinnie's body, and Joanne followed. Marty was in the ambulance, ready to be taken to the hospital. Rob and Johnno followed Joanne to the body. Parker recognised it immediately.

'Well, well. Vincenso Sattorri, aka Vinnie,' Parker announced. 'What were you doing here?'

'It sounds like you know him,' Joanne observed.

'Indeed,' Parker replied. 'You're going to be surprised to know that Vinnie held the position of lieutenant in the Rossetti family.'

Joanne caught her breath. Her thoughts went straight to Holly and Roberto. This was too awkward, and she wasn't comfortable with the situation. If Roberto found out she had been involved in the shooting, he might mark her too and hunt her down. That wasn't the outcome she was looking for.

'Shit!' she muttered under her breath, just loud enough for Parker to hear.

'That changes the playing field a bit, wouldn't it?' Parker commented. 'The Rossettis won't be happy once they learn who killed him.' 'If

you're trying to scare me, you've succeeded,' Joanne replied.

'What's going on?' Rob asked.

'Best you not know,' Parker replied. 'It doesn't concern you.' Rob and Johnno started back to their car.

'Joanne, we'll see you back at base,' Rob yelled out.

'Okay, see you there.'

Parker knelt down to inspect the body and then asked Joanne,

'How many shots did your partner, Marty, fire?'

'One shot, that's all he could get off, just the one,' Joanne replied, puzzled by the question.

'There are two holes in his chest. One went through the heart and the other into the shoulder near the collarbone,' Parker determined. 'You didn't fire one?'

'No, I had my gun out, but never discharged it.'

One of the uniformed police officers returned from around the building just as the detectives' radio received an incoming call. Ashcroft went back to take the call, and the police officer announced they had found another body, wrapped in a linen sheet.

Parker accompanied the officer back to the discovery. She was a young woman, with most of her clothes torn off and badly bruised. Joanne had a flashback to seeing Holly after her ordeal at the hands of Roberto.

The young woman appeared to be in her early twenties, with red hair and fair skin. She was very pale; no one could have guessed how long she had been dead. Parker knelt on one knee, inspecting the body as best he could.

'Unfortunately, she's a substance user,' he said. 'Needle marks on both arms, the left being the worst.'

Just then, Ashcroft returned in a bit of a hurry.

'Traffic police have found a black BMW with a bullet hole in the passenger door and a lot of blood inside, about three kilometres from here,' he informed the group.

Parker turned to the two officers and then to Joanne.

'I'll contact forensics, and you two preserve the scene as best you can. Joanne, you're free to go, and I may catch up with you later for a statement. How's your friend in hospital? Sorry, partner.'

'She's conscious and doing alright,' Joanne replied. 'Thank you for asking.'

'I hope you realise I'll need to interview her when she's ready,' Parker said.

'Yes, I understand,' Joanne confirmed.

'We'll catch up later,' Parker reminded her as he got in the car and drove off.

Joanne got into her car and drove back to base. Rob and Johnno reported Marty had been taken to hospital and that they would wait for the results of his injury after a doctor treated him. Joanne couldn't understand how Vinnie had received fatal wounds from Marty's single hasty shot, which may not have directly hit him.

By now, the forensic officers should have cordoned off the scene, and a report should be pending. The discovery of the young woman was a surprise. How she died, where she died, and who dumped the body might not become clear for some time.

Joanne compiled her report of the incident, printed it off, and reviewed it twice more before signing it. She handed it to the night shift supervisor, Allan.

'Thanks, Joanne. I'll leave this on Jeremy's desk, and it has to be filed tomorrow,' Allan told her. 'He'll most likely wait for Marty to countersign it in due course, so it's official.'

'Yeah, no problem,' Joanne replied. 'The police will probably want a copy too.'

'Yes, no doubt,' he replied. 'Jeremy can handle that as well.'

'I guess all I can do now is paperwork?' Joanne tentatively asked. 'I need a partner for routine patrols.'

'Yes, that's right,' Allan confirmed. 'Could be a boring night for you.'

Just then, Rob and Johnno came into the staff room and headed straight for the coffee machine. Joanne and Allan heard them come in and joined them.

'How's Marty getting on?' Joanne asked.

'He's doing fine,' Rob replied. 'They're doing an X-ray to see if there's any bone damage, but apart from that, a couple of stitches and he'll be right.'

'Oh, and Jeremy's with him as well,' Johnno added. 'He told us to come back here.'

'Jeremy?' Joanne queried. 'He went home before Marty and I went on patrol.'

'I rang him and told him there was a shooting,' Allan said. 'You need to let me know about incidents like this.'

'Yes, quite right.'

'He didn't waste any time getting there,' Joanne said. 'Which is encouraging, as it shows he genuinely cares for our well-being.'

'He's always said that, and I agree with Joanne,' Johnno added. 'He's got my respect as a manager.'

'What else was on your schedule for tonight, Joanne?' Allan asked.

'We were to patrol the rest of the light industrial area, up to the marshalling yards, a couple of shopping centres, and around the wharf,' Joanne explained.

'Johnno and I can do that. We're doing a drive-by on some centres as well, and down to Jervis Bay,' Rob replied. 'We can cover those on our way.'

'That sounds like a plan,' Allan approved. 'When you've finished your coffee, you can make a start.'

'Yep, work's for me,' Rob said.

Rob and Johnno went out on their extended patrol, indicating they'd be back in a few hours. Joanne and Allan chatted for a while, then got to some paperwork that needed tidying. Jeremy phoned in to say that Marty was okay. There was no bone damage to be found on the X-ray. He received a few stitches to close the wound and then was taken home.

'Joanne made out a report, and we need Marty to countersign it when he's ready,' Allan informed him.

'He'll probably come in tomorrow to collect his gear and sign it then,' Jeremy said. 'The doctor has given him a week of sick leave, so he'll need to fill out these forms as well.'

'That is enough, especially for him,' Allan replied. 'Fortunate, I'd say.'

'He sure is,' Jeremy agreed. 'How's Joanne coping?'

'She's a little upset about having to do paperwork, but she'll manage,' Allan responded.

Both chuckled at his remark.

'Okay, I'll catch up with you in the morning,' Jeremy said. 'Night.'

'Night, Jeremy.'

# Chapter 14: Plans Of Mice And Men

Once again, Roberto's father called him to the office, and he wasn't happy about it. He was a bit put out, as it felt like a case of the headteacher summoning a student for unacceptable behaviour, destined for detention or, worse yet, the cane.

He could already hear his father ranting from down the corridor, his Italian accent thickening as his temper rose. What was going on now?

'You were told time and time again to have his back!' his father yelled at Mario as Roberto opened the door. 'What the fuck was he doing down there on his own?'

Roberto got halfway across to Dominic's desk when he was yelled at as well.

'Did you know someone shot Vinnie?' Dominic shouted.

'No, I didn't,' Roberto replied, now standing in front of his father. 'Is he alright?'

'Is he alright!?' Dominic repeated sarcastically. 'No! He's fucking dead! Shot the other night, and I only got told this morning!'

Roberto went white in disbelief and couldn't respond right then and there. He stepped backwards, dropped himself into a nearby chair, and stared vacantly at the floor. As he looked around, he saw the same blank look of shock on Mario's face. Then he noticed Stromnikov standing by the far wall, wearing that normal, unnerving, cold steely look that was his trademark. It was obvious from his presence that an order to kill was forthcoming.

'And now that you're here,' Dominic said, staring straight at Roberto. 'Where do you fucking get off belting women?'

Roberto sat there, still saying nothing.

'Do you know you put her in hospital with a broken jaw and cracked ribs? What the fuck has gotten into you?' Dominic was furious. 'That's the third woman you've bashed! Now I have to order a hit on her to stop her from blabbing to the cops!'

'No, you don't have to do that,' Roberto said, defending her. 'She knows not to talk.'

'And you can guarantee that, can you?' replied Dominic. 'She's already spoken to detectives, and God knows what she's been telling them.'

'I told you she won't talk!' Roberto fired an angry retort back at his father.

'Don't you dare talk to me like that!' Dominic snapped. 'The last girl you bashed, Rebecca, went running to the cops, and the thing for us is, it was Fleming she went to.'

Roberto shifted uneasily in his chair. He had long forgotten Rebecca. It had been at least twelve months since she'd broken up with him and complained about being drugged and then raped. Luckily for him, she'd sought help from Fleming, who was bribed to turn a blind eye to their illicit dealings. He was a crooked cop who fed information to the Rossettis when requested.

Rebecca had been a stunning redhead with a temper to match. She'd blabbed a lot of information to Fleming about the Rossettis, venturing into dangerous territory by doing so. She was the first female to take the one-way, five-kilometre sea trip out of Sydney. He hoped that wouldn't happen to Holly.

'Mario,' Dominic said, catching his attention. 'I want you to find out who shot Vinnie and why he was out there in the first place.'

'Yes, I'll see what I can find out,' Mario replied, somewhat subdued by Dominic's rage and the way he was ranting and raving.

'If it was a gang, I want their names! I want them dead, their parents, their sisters and brothers, their kids, the fucking entire family, dead!' Dominic was thumping the table with his fists, his face red with anger. The Sicilian heritage was coming out in him.

The way his father was carrying on mortified Roberto. He had never seen him this angry and overwrought before. The shooting of Vinnie had made him blow his fuse big time. Even Mario took a step back from the desk. Stromnikov, still steadfast, was watching the proceedings without flinching once. He was Russian mafia-trained and as dangerous as they come.

Dominic sat down and rested his head in his hands for a moment, then said,

'What am I supposed to do with all this shit going down?'

There wasn't an answer from any of them. They all looked bewildered and unsure of their next move, or even what to say.

'Stromnikov,' Dominic finally said, 'I want you to find out which hospital that woman's in and shut her up for good when you can.'

Stromnikov straightened up and acknowledged Dominic's order. Roberto looked stunned by his father's request. He knew Stromnikov would carry it out without compromise or remorse.

'Do you think she really needs to be killed?' Roberto pleaded as he stood up.

'You haven't given me any choice.'

'Oh, so it's my fault now,' Roberto shot back, irritated by the insinuation.

'Yes, it is,' Dominic replied. 'I didn't bash her and put her in hospital. I'm expecting the cops any day now to come looking for you to charge you with assault.'

Roberto sat back down and had to admit to himself that, yes, he'd fucked up again.

'Right,' Dominic said, bringing everyone to attention. 'Mario, find out who killed Vinnie and give the information to me. Stromnikov, you know what your job is?'

'Yes,' came the bitter reply from the Russian.

'Oh, and there's another thing,' Dominic continued. 'One of our girls has gone missing. I've asked around, and no one's seen her for some

time, which is another thing that's pissed me off. I want her found.'
'Who's that?' Mario asked.

'The girl Roberto used to screw,' Dominic replied, motioning to his son. 'Emily Spain.'

'Okay, I'll see what I can find out,' Mario replied.

Mario and Stromnikov left the office. Roberto was told to stay back to talk with his father.

'Do you really think it's necessary to eliminate Holly?' he asked again.

'I can't take the chance of her telling the cops what she learned about the business while she was working here,' Dominic explained. 'As you know, if the cops snoop around, it could mean the end of our operation.'

'We can talk to Fleming and get him to throw them off the track,' Roberto suggested.

'Seriously? You think so?' Dominic questioned. 'He can only do so much before he draws attention to himself, and it could all turn to shit quickly.'

'I don't think we should kill Holly.'

'Get it through your thick head!' Dominic snapped, his anger flaring again. 'That night you bashed her, you should have killed her, but letting her live only gave her a death sentence, anyway.'

Roberto finally realised it was pointless trying to make his father change his mind about Holly. He didn't know which hospital she was in, but then again, what would he do if he visited her? She'd probably have him thrown out and barred from seeing her.

Joanne and Holly were both glad to be home together again, and none too soon. Holly had 'mended' really well and was eager to visit Steph in WA. She had to ring and let her know that she and Joanne were coming over for a visit. Holly spent a couple of days at home in Joanne's flat 'convalescing', as she put it, and rightfully so. Joanne had two night shifts left before her leave kicked in.

The rest in Joanne's apartment had done Holly a world of good. She could make herself something to eat whenever she wanted and have a shower rather than follow the hospital routine. The nurses had done a fantastic job, and she was grateful for their efforts. She had even packed some of her things for the trip and was glad there was virtually no more pain in her ribs while packing, only the occasional twinge now and then.

Joanne had packed as well and was working on a list. A lot of thought went into what she did, and she was more organised than Holly. She showed herself to be proactive and well-prepared, something Holly had found difficult to manage lately. She referred to Robbie bashing her as a painful, near-death experience and was glad to have come out the other side, warier of men.

The four or five months she had spent with Joanne were exhilarating, an experience she had only ever read about in *Mills & Boon*. She had thought it was all just storytelling, not something one would experience in real life. Sleeping with Joanne, the hugs, the kisses, and the occasional orgasm, was beyond her wildest dreams.

She could never feel like that with a man, certainly not with Roberto. He would be inside her, pumping her crotch relentlessly until the job was done, and then roll over and go to sleep. Then there was his mess, which she had to put up with afterwards. The mess she made when she orgasmed was hers, no one else's, and it felt exceptional. Just thinking about it made her feel horny.

'Joanne, where are you?' she asked herself. 'Mm, time for a cup of coffee, I think.'

She got up and made herself a cup of coffee. Joanne was on the early night shift and would be home just after midnight. It was already 10:00 pm, only 8:00 pm in WA, and time to ring Steph. She picked up the phone and dialled her number.

'Hello.'

'Hi Steph, this is Holly.'

## Holly, Joanne and Steph

'Holly! My goodness, how are you?' came the eager reply from Steph.

'I'm doing okay now, and you?' Holly replied.

'Fine,' said Steph. 'Nice to hear from you again. What's been happening?'

'Nothing much, really,' Holly replied, trying not to say too much over the phone. 'I'm not working anymore, so we'll pay you a visit.'

'That sounds great,' Steph replied. 'We have a lot of catching up to do. Are you coming with your boyfriend?'

'No, we've broken up, and consequently, I've given up my job.'

'Oh, that's not good. What happened?'

'I'll tell you the gory details when we see you, hopefully by the end of the week.'

'We, you said?'

'Yes,' Holly replied. 'I'm coming with my partner, Joanne.' 'Joanne's your partner?' Steph queried.

'Yes, I've known for a month, and we're now living together in her flat.'

'It sounds like you're in love?'

'Yes, we are, and it feels wonderful,' Holly replied confidently.

'Well, lucky you,' Steph said. 'I'm glad you've found someone. You sound a bit more cheerful than the last time we spoke. Good for you.'

'Thank you, Steph,' Holly replied as a tear welled in her eye. 'You don't know how much it means to me to hear you say that.'

'It's up to you to decide what you do in your life and who you're with,' Steph replied, supporting her choice. 'As long as it works for you and you're happy, that's all that matters to me.'

'I'm sure you'll like Joanne,' Holly said. 'She reminds me of you. A straight talker, takes no shit from anyone, and stands her ground.'

'That sounds like my type of woman,' Steph replied, and both chuckled at the comment.

'She's very loving and so tender when we're together,' Holly explained. 'It's something I've never experienced with a bloke. I really love her.'

'I'm thrilled for you, Holly, and it sounds like she loves you too,' Steph said. 'When are you flying out?'

'Tomorrow evening, after Joanne comes home from work,' Holly confirmed. 'We'll be in Perth for a couple of days and then drive up to Geraldton.'

'Excellent,' Steph replied. 'I can hardly wait to see you again.'

'Me too,' Holly said. 'By the way, is there a place you can recommend for us to stay?'

'I'd love to have you stay here with me at Mum's, but she's only got three bedrooms,' Steph replied. 'You're welcome to put a mattress on the floor, though.'

'Thank you, Steph. I really appreciate the offer, but I think we'd prefer to stay at a motel.'

'That's fine,' said Steph. 'The offer's there if you need it. Otherwise, I'd check with the Ocean Centre. They've got a restaurant and a bar as well.'

'Oh, hang on, there's someone at the door,' Holly suddenly announced.

Steph waited while Holly went to answer it and could hear voices in the background. Then Holly came back to the phone.

'It's only Joanne. She finished early tonight. I'll put you on speakerphone.'

'Okay,' replied Steph.

'Hello, Steph,' Joanne called out from the background.

'Hello to you as well,' Steph replied. 'Nice to meet you, even if it's only by voice for now.'

'No problem, Steph,' Joanne replied. 'That'll change in a couple of days, at least by the weekend.'

'I'm looking forward to seeing you both,' Steph said.

'Okay, I'll talk to you again later, Steph,' Holly said. 'We're going to do some more packing before turning in. Catch you later. Bye.'

'Bye, Holly,' Steph replied. 'And you as well, Joanne.' 'Bye,

Steph,' Joanne called back.

Holly ended the call and said to Joanne,

'You're home early, Babe.'

'I couldn't stay away from you any longer,' Joanne replied jokingly, with a smile on her face.

'That's sweet,' Holly said with a big, cheesy grin. 'It makes me all warm and fuzzy inside.'

They both laughed for a moment, then hugged and kissed.

'It's good you rang, Steph,' Joanne said. 'She sounds okay.'

'That woman's a cool chick,' Holly confirmed. 'And an excellent friend.'

Joanne made herself a cup of coffee and offered one to Holly.

'I've still got this one,' Holly replied. 'Thanks.'

Joanne grabbed a snack from the fridge and put it in the microwave.

'Have you eaten, Holly?'

'Yes.'

'After I've finished this snack, we'll do some more packing,' Joanne suggested. 'I've got to go to work early tomorrow, but there'll be plenty of time to get to the airport.'

'It's hard to believe we're finally going,' Holly said, excitement in her voice. 'It seems like a long time coming.'

'I'm glad you spoke to Steph,' Joanne said. 'At least she knows we're coming and we won't just lob up on her doorstep.'

'I asked about accommodation, and she gave me a motel to try.'

'Good,' Joanne said. 'I've booked the Perth one for two nights, and you can book the Geraldton one if you like.'

'I'll go online now and book it,' Holly suggested. 'That way, everything's sorted and paid for.'

'Sounds good,' Joanne agreed. 'While you do that, I'll do some more packing. We shouldn't need to take too much.'

At last, they had everything organised for the trip to WA. Within the next twenty-four hours, they would wing their way across the country and, hopefully, leave behind the drama they'd both been through over the past month or two. They could do with a well-earned rest and a chance to stay out of harm's way.

'Such are the plans of mice and men.'

# **Chapter 15: Three Eliminated**

The lunchtime traffic gets extremely busy on Sydney's main street. It's always like that anyway, but the midday traffic just seems to double, if that's even possible. A white Commodore Captiva pulls up at the red traffic lights and stops first in line. Traffic flows in front of it in a continuous stream from both left and right.

Up ahead, neither the drivers nor the pedestrians noticed a brief flash of something bright that vanished as quickly as it appeared. Then, chaos erupts. The Captiva slowly creeps forward into the line of flowing traffic. Cars screech to a halt, people are yelling, and some are screaming.

The Captiva is T-boned on the driver's side by a car braking heavily. As the impact hit with some force, even though some of the speed had already been washed off. The driver of the Captiva slumps forward over the steering wheel, covered in blood. Those who rush to help quickly step back at the sight inside the Captiva.

'Has anyone rung the police and ambulance yet?' someone yells.

'Already done,' comes the reply.

All traffic grinds to a halt in that lane, and drivers down the line are getting impatient, unaware of what's happened ahead. It takes almost ten minutes before the police and ambulance finally make it through the congestion. A police officer looks inside the Captiva from the passenger side and pulls the driver back from the steering wheel.

'Oh, fuck,' is all the officer can mutter under his breath.

He's joined by a second officer, who reacts much the same. Blood covers the driver's face, lap, steering wheel, and the back of his neck, streaming from a hole in the centre of his forehead and a gaping exit wound at the back of his head. The windscreen has a clean bullet hole in the driver's side.

The intersection is closed off to keep people away while paramedics attend to the other driver, who has only minor cuts and bruises from the seatbelt. They wrap him in a blanket and monitor him for delayed shock.

Detective Sergeant Parker is now on the scene, scanning up and down the street. The body is finally removed from the car and placed in a body bag. The detective searches through the deceased's pockets to find some ID before zipping the bag closed. He finds a wallet and opens it. The driver's licence identifies him as Milton Clark. There's also a private investigator's card inside.

The first responders zip up the body bag and load it into a second ambulance that's arrived on the scene. The detective walks over to the first ambulance, where the driver of the second vehicle is now up and moving.

'I'm Detective Sergeant Parker,' he introduces himself. 'And you are?'

'I'm Joe Morrison,' the driver replies.

'Mr Morrison, did you see anything apart from the vehicle pulling out in front of you?' the detective asks.

'No,' he replies. 'I was following the traffic, about two or three car lengths behind, when that car suddenly pulled out.'

'Did you see the driver before you hit him?'

'Yes. He caught me by surprise. I think he was slumped over the steering wheel,' he explains. 'I didn't have time to react as quickly as I should've, and unfortunately, I hit him.'

'How are you feeling at the moment?' the detective asks.

'A bit shaken, to say the least,' he replies. 'I just couldn't react fast enough to avoid the collision.'

'Where were you heading?'

'I was meeting my wife for lunch up there, at that cafe on the next block,' he says, pointing up the street. 'She'll be getting frantic about my being late.'

'Alright, I'll take care of that,' the detective says, calling over a police officer. 'This gentleman was meeting his wife at the cafe in the next block. Can you find her and bring her here?'

'Sure thing. What's her name?' 'Fiona,'

the man replies.

It takes only about ten minutes before the officer returns with a frantic woman at his side. As soon as she sees her husband's car, and him wrapped in a blanket, she rushes forward.

'Oh, my dear!' she exclaims. 'Are you alright?'

There's no need to question the driver any further. The accident was unavoidable. No one is to blame except the person who fired the shot. Parker scans further down the street, looking for a vantage point from which the shooter might have taken aim, but nothing obvious stands out.

There are some two-storey buildings, a hotel with a top-floor balcony, and a few high-rise apartments further down the street. A uniformed officer might manage identifying where the shot came from.

Figuring out who shot him will be a challenge. There are no visible clues or evidence in the car, though forensics will go through it once it's impounded.

Parker wonders if this is the start of a crime gang's hit. Could it be a drug syndicate trying to stay out of the spotlight of an investigation, or a bikie gang silencing an investigator who's digging too close into their business, drugs, shootings or gambling rackets? Or maybe just a case of mistaken identity. The latter seems unlikely, and he dismisses it, leaving only the two other possibilities.

A bikie gang doing a shooting in broad daylight doesn't seem probable either, it's not their usual style, especially not in town. That leaves only one reasonable theory that holds water: the drug gang. But which one would be this brazen?

Dominic's phone rang, and he quickly answered it.

'Yes?' he said.

'Dad, I've got the information about the law firm person looking into the information that Clark was providing,' Roberto informed him. 'She is Tammy O'Lachlin and lives in the flat complex next to mine on the sixth floor. She's been away for a week and has only just returned.'

'That's good, son, that's very good,' Dominic replied. 'Seeing she's that close to your flat complex, Stromnikov and I will handle this one. I want to question her first.'

'That's okay. When are you planning to see her?' Roberto asked.

'I'm uncertain, but I have to organise a time with Stromnikov,' he replied. 'Sometime soon. Thank you, Roberto, you did well.'

Both hung up the phone without further comment, and Roberto went back to his flat and rang Holly. He was planning to make it up to her and take her out for tea.

Dominic rang the Russian and said that he had the information he needed and wanted to take care of her once and for all, before things went horribly wrong. The police he was paying might get exposed, and that could unravel everything. He didn't want to wait.

He met Stromnikov that night at the complex around teatime, when some were indoors and perhaps most had gone out to restaurants for a meal. Dominic made a phone call to the complex and asked to be put through to Tammy's room. It was a bogus call.

'Hello, this is Tammy,' she said when she answered the call.

'Hi, can I speak to Vanessa?'

'I'm sorry, there is no one here by that name,' she replied. 'This has been my flat for some time.'

'Oh, I am so sorry to disturb you. Thank you.'

After putting his mobile back in his pocket, Dominic let the Russian know everything was in place. She was at home, and the job was to be done tonight. It was time to pay her a visit.

Dominic arrived first and gave the clerk a story that he was her father.

'Could you ring upstairs and let my daughter know her father is here to see her? She's on the sixth floor.' He spoke to the clerk.

'Yes, what's her name?'

'Tammy, Tammy O'Lachlin,' he replied.

The clerk looked through the register, picked up the phone, and was about to hit the house-call key when Dominic stopped him.

'Actually, wait a minute,' he began. 'She's been away for a little time, and she'd tried to catch up with me before. Unfortunately, I missed her, so this will be a surprise. What's her room number?'

'I'm sorry, sir. I can't give out that information,' the clerk objected.

'That's a pity,' Dominic complained, 'because we will lose the element of surprise. If you must, then ring.'

'Three years, you say? You'll have some catching up to do,' the clerk remarked.

'Yes, quite true.'

'I guess this one time won't hurt,' the clerk relented. 'It's 609 on the east wing.'

'Why, thank you so much,' Dominic replied, playing the sympathy card like a well-rehearsed actor. He smiled at the clerk and walked toward the lift. Stromnikov had come into the foyer earlier, unnoticed while Dominic was talking to the clerk. He was waiting in the lift for Dominic.

They got out on the sixth floor, headed down the passageway and found flat 609. A loud knock on the door produced a response from inside.

'Just a minute,' came the female voice. Tammy opened the door to the two men standing there.

'Miss O'Lachlin?' Dominic questioned.

'Yes, what can I do for you?'

'May we come in?' Dominic asked politely.

'I'm not sure. What do you want?' Tammy asked.

'We want to ask you some questions, and it's best if we come in to do that.'

'Tell me what you want to ask me,' Tammy insisted.

'I wasn't asking for your permission the second time. Only to tell you we are coming in,' was Dominic's stern reply, and with that he pushed his way past Tammy. Stromnikov drew out his gun, and Tammy reeled back in fright at the sight of it.

'What the hell do you think you are doing?' Tammy complained. 'You are trespassing!'

'Sit down and shut the fuck up!' Dominic shouted at her. 'Now listen carefully. We can do this the easy way or the hard way!'

Tammy almost fell into her lounge chair, having a weird feeling about the whole situation. Stromnikov stood near the closed door with the gun in his hand. Dominic now stood in front of her, glaring down at her.

'What do you know about the Emporium Machinery Imports business and its owners?' he asked in a raised voice.

'Nothing at all. Why do you ask? Who are you?' Tammy asked, her mind racing.

'That's not what I've heard. How do you know Milton Clark?'

'I don't know him.'

'You are a liar, and I'm short on patience. So tell me what I want to know!'

'I know nothing about what you are asking,' Tammy repeated.

'I'm sorry, my dear, you know more than you are telling me,' Dominic said impatiently. 'So the sooner you tell me, the sooner we'll be out of here.'

'I've got nothing to say,' Tammy said, standing her ground.

'So you must have some paperwork here. It's there in your bedroom, isn't it?' Dominic surmised, and slowly headed for the bedroom.

Tammy stood up, and Dominic stopped his advance toward her bedroom. That was a sign there was something in the bedroom that was important.

'If you have something in that room, then I suggest you get it for me,' Dominic said.

Tammy hesitated for a moment and realised that denying her involvement was fruitless. She made her way past Dominic, and he nodded his head to Stromnikov, who followed her to the bedroom, the gun in his hand now with a silencer hanging by his side. There was a scream of 'No, no', then a dull thud and then silence.

Dominic went into the room and saw that Tammy had fallen to the floor, bleeding from a wound in the centre of her forehead. Stromnikov was unscrewing the silencer and put it back in his pocket. Dominic looked up and out the window where he saw a woman staring at them from the other complex. It was Holly, and Roberto also popped up in the window. Dominic pointed a finger at them, and both disappeared from view like two scolded children caught with their hands in the biscuit jar. Stromnikov flashed a look at Dominic and left the room. Dominic saw a buff folder on the dresser with some paperwork inside, and a quick look was enough to see it was the information she had denied having. He took it with him.

'I'll deal with them,' Dominic assured him. The Russian nodded in approval.

They both left the flat and went back down to the lift. The clerk who was at the desk was now a different person from the one Dominic had seen on the way in. The clerk bid them goodnight as they left the complex.

Someone had murdered the bookkeeper, a private investigator, and a lawyer within the last twenty-four hours.

# Chapter 16: Body in the Freezer

The next morning, Ashcroft visited the main branches of the four big banks in Sydney to see if he could find any banking details for Emily Spain. Parker felt it was important to establish her last movements through her bank accounts, hoping it could give a timeframe to work with. Determining when she was killed would be a vital step in the right direction for finding the killer. The discovery of her body was all over the news as well.

Forensics reported they had recovered blood type and DNA from the black BMW, but they hadn't been able to match them with any current records. There were no clues regarding the identity of the person who was shot or the occupants of the black BMW. DNA and hair follicles recovered from Tammy O'Lachlin's flat yielded the same result. No records existed to match the samples recovered.

Similarly, the shot that killed Milton Clark had the same consequence. At best, they guessed the trajectory angle, and the shot could have come from one of three positions. The police searched all three areas and came up with nothing that could conclusively pinpoint the site.

Parker would have to try another approach and hope that more video from the industrial site might help, or that the information in Emily Spain's accounts might provide a solid clue. For the time being, however, the killer, or killers, were free.

Parker shuffled through the paperwork on the killings, the evidence, and the notes both he and Ashcroft had taken, looking for clues, anything that could be used as a lead. What had they missed? What evidence had a grey cloud hanging over it?

The phone rang while he was deep in thought, startling him.

'Hello, this is Detective-Sergeant Parker,' he answered.

'Hi,' the voice replied. 'I'm Liam Bell, and I believe you're looking for information on Emily Spain?'

'Yes, we are,' Parker said, a little surprised that someone had called about Emily.

'I was her boyfriend for a while until about three weeks ago, and I saw the news about her. I might be able to help with some information,' Liam advised.

'By all means, yes,' Parker replied enthusiastically. 'I would appreciate any information.'

'I finish work early today, so I can come in then if you like,' Liam suggested.

'Yes, please do, Mr Bell,' Parker replied without hesitation. 'I look forward to our meeting.'

'Okay, see you at about 3:30 pm,' he replied and ended the call.

Parker sat back in his chair with a sigh of relief. He hoped this might present the lead he was looking for.

Meanwhile, Ashcroft was having some luck at last. He found the bank that Emily was a customer of, but was reluctant to provide any information. At his insistence, he could meet with the manager.

'We normally don't give out customer information,' the manager said. 'I'm afraid that's our policy.'

'I think you can appreciate that this is a murder investigation and that account activities may help us with our enquiries,' Ashcroft replied.

'As you can well appreciate, the bank rules are there to protect our customers...'

'Stop right there,' Ashcroft interjected, getting a bit annoyed with the man's arrogance. 'We can do this the easy way or the hard way.'

'What do you mean?'

'You can give me the information I'm requesting, or I can come back tomorrow with a court order to close the branch for the day so we can find what we are looking for,' Ashcroft advised. 'And the other thing is, I can have you charged for obstructing a homicide investigation.'

'Now that you've put it like that, I think it's in the bank's best interests to assist the police with their enquiries to the best we can,' the manager replied, a complete turnaround. 'What was the young lady's name again?'

'The person's name is Emily Spain,' Ashcroft replied, trying hard to hide his smirk.

The manager tapped away on his keyboard and waited for the computer to show a result. He then keyed in some more information and said,

'Miss Emily Spain has a credit card and a savings account, which she uses as a working account with us.'

'Could I trouble you for a printout of the last six months' worth of activity on both accounts?' Ashcroft requested politely.

The manager obliged and had the information printed in a couple of minutes. The credit card statement showed that Emily had nearly maxed out her card. She purchased clothing, haircare, fuel for her car, some repairs, jewellery, and so on. There wasn't anything out of the ordinary. She made her last purchase two weeks ago at a shoe shop.

The so-called working account presented a different picture. It had sizeable sums of money deposited one week and then removed the following week. The amounts were consistently between seven and eight thousand dollars. Outgoings were between four and six hundred dollars at a time. Other amounts of around one thousand dollars each week were her wages from work being deposited. The activity also stopped two weeks ago.

'Do you think the money flowing through this account is unusual for someone like Miss Spain?' Ashcroft asked.

'No, not at all,' the manager replied. 'We have customers with far more funds going in and out of their accounts.'

'How far back does this account go?'

'Three years,' he replied. 'She started with a thousand-dollar deposit to set up the account.'

'Can you tell me where these amounts are going and the name of the receiver?' Ashcroft asked. 'I would also like the full printout of her account.'

He keyed in the command, and the statements came out of the printer. There were close to forty statements covering the account. While printing, the manager was busy at the keyboard, trying to find more information for Ashcroft. The account that the funds were intended for was displayed in the final print.

Ashcroft raised his eyebrows when he read the name: Vincenso Sattorri.

'Does this man have an account here?'

'No, that BSB number is for the bank across the road, the Merchant Bank,' replied the manager.

'Well, I have to thank you very much for your help. I hope there's no further need to call upon your services again in this matter,' Ashcroft said, shaking his hand.

He headed back to see Parker and give him the heads-up about what he had found. The money activity suggested it was being laundered, and Emily was getting a spin-off. All deposits were in cash.

'Money laundering,' Ashcroft announced as he walked into Parker's office.

'Really?' Parker replied, with a contented look on his face.

Ashcroft informed him that Vincenzo Sattorri is the one who moves the money that is withdrawn via online banking. Parker looked at the statements going back three years in Emily Spain's name, right from the day she opened the account.

'Cash deposits, I see,' Parker observed. 'Drug money, I'm guessing.'

'Yes, I have to agree with you on that score,' Ashcroft replied in support.

'I also see that she stopped using her credit card about two weeks ago, and the same with transferring money to Vinnie's account. Someone is still putting money into her account regularly, though. There are over sixty thousand dollars in there!'

'If she wasn't there to transfer the money out, that would suggest that someone killed her two weeks ago and put her on ice,' Ashcroft said.

'Yes, and that connection with Rossetti's through Vinnie is intriguing. But who killed her, and why?'

They pondered the question for a moment, and then Parker asked,

'What's the time?'

'It's just gone 3:00 pm. Why?'

'I had a phone call from a Liam Bell, who is Emily Spain's ex-boyfriend. He is coming here of his own free will to offer us some information.'

'Nice,' replied Ashcroft. 'Looks like things are coming our way for a change.'

'Yes, you could say that,' Parker agreed. 'We'll talk with him in the interview room.'

'Okay, I'll set it up.'

Parker got comfortable in his chair and began inspecting the statements from Emily's account. By calculating quickly, it was determined that about one million dollars' worth of money had gone through that account in just under four months since it was opened. Emily would have earned about sixty thousand dollars. That equates to about nine million dollars over the three years the account has been open.

Ashcroft came back in and said,

'Your man, Liam, has just arrived.'

'Good,' said Parker. 'Let's see what he has for us.'

They went to the interview room and formally introduced themselves to Liam, sitting opposite each other.

'So, what would you like to tell us?' Parker asked.

'Well, first,' he began, 'I'm surprised to learn that people here believe she is dead, but her body is still missing.'

'Did you know her for long?' Ashcroft asked. 'We haven't confirmed that she is dead with anybody yet, so this speculation is at best tentative for now.'

'Oh, I see. I've known her for about three years,' Liam answered.

'Let's start at the beginning,' Ashcroft suggested. 'Tell us what you know about Miss Spain.'

'We met by chance at the Gay Mardi Graz about three years ago. Not that we were that way inclined. We were just spectators enjoying the glitzy parade,' he began. 'We discussed the floats, the work that was put into them, and several of the costumes. She then agreed to go for a drink, and we began seeing each other regularly.'

'Things were going well until about three weeks ago. She mentioned that there were some problems at work and that she wanted to quit. I didn't get to find out what the problems were, but she wasn't the bubbly person I met. I think someone was giving her a hard time. Then, suddenly, one day she said we were through and not to contact her again.'

'You've got no idea why the sudden change in her?' Parker asked. 'Was it work-related?'

'No,' Liam replied. 'All I know is that she got involved in something and wasn't willing to share.'

'Where did she work?'

'She worked at the Westfield supermarket in Parramatta,' Liam answered. 'She works behind the deli. Second in charge.'

'What about you? Where do you work?'

'I'm a mechanic at an Isuzu dealership in Harris Park.'

'Do you think her workmates know anything?' Ashcroft asked.

'I spoke to a mate who works there as a trolley boy, and he reckons some bloke was giving her grief,' he answered.

'What sort of bloke?'

'Some Chinese git, apparently. No one knew where he was from or what he was talking to Emily about, but it seemed to upset her,' Liam explained. 'That was also about the same time she broke up with me. We talked once about getting hitched, but that obviously turned to shit too.'

'How long ago did you notice the change in her?' Parker asked.

'About three weeks ago, I guess,' he replied. 'It was only a week after that when she told me to get lost. It was a complete change of character.'

'Was she taking drugs?'

'Not as far as I'm aware,' Liam said. 'I know for a fact she hated them and even swore she would never do drugs.' 'And you believed her?' Ashcroft asked.

'Absolutely, without a doubt.'

'Well, let me thank you for volunteering your information about Miss Spain,' Parker said. 'If there's anything else you remember, please get back to us.'

'Okay, sure, I certainly will,' Liam confirmed.

'Oh, one last thing,' Ashcroft began. 'Did you see any Chinese hanging around the shopping centre?'

'No, but my mate saw them twice,' Liam replied. 'He gets his lunch there.'

'Them? You mean there's more than one was hanging around?' Ashcroft tried to confirm.

'Yes, my mate said there were three of them in a dark BMW.'

'We'll have to look into that,' Ashcroft replied. 'Thanks again for your help.'

'No problem,' Liam replied. 'I hope you catch the mongrel that took her.'

'So do we, Liam,' Parker agreed. 'So do we.'

Liam left the interview room, leaving Parker and Ashcroft staring at each other. Now, with Liam's information, the money transfers into Vinnie's account, and the dark BMW blokes harassing Emily after taunting her at work were making the pieces of the jigsaw puzzle come together.

'You're deep in thought, Ashcroft. What do you make of all this?' Parker asked.

'Well, I'm trying to tie some of this together and make sense of it,' he began. 'Emily and Liam had been dating for nearly two years. Both had jobs, and everything appeared fine. Then these so-called Chinese blokes pay her a visit and everything goes pear-shaped. She suddenly breaks it off with her boyfriend, fiancée, and disappears a week later. All her accounts stopped being used. Where is the body if someone killed her? Have the Chinese dumped it somewhere? They're involved somehow, I'm sure of it.'

'Yes, agreed,' Parker responded. 'Then you have the supposedly "accidental" shooting of Vincenzo Sattorri, but the question is...'

'Why was he there in the first place? You also have the mystery man watching some of what happened from the shadows. That is only hearsay for now.'

'Is Emily dead, or just missing? Scarpered in fright. And where is her body if she's been dead for two weeks?' Ashcroft added. 'Who killed her and hid her body?'

'There is a pattern emerging, but it's only us supposing what the outcome may be,' Parker said.

'What are you thinking?' Ashcroft asked.

'We know the Chinese are trying to muscle into the drug trade if our sources are correct,' Parker speculated. 'Why not find out where the money from a particular drug dealer is going and stop the flow of money to the importer? No money, no more product coming in, and there is an opening to muscle in.'

'Okay, so can we tie in the murders of Milton Clark and Tammy O'Lachlin into this hypothetical?' Ashcroft asked.

'I like the way you think,' Parker applauded his colleague's train of thought. 'What if Milton Clark had been investigating the dealings of the Rossettis?'

'Someone within the organisation, specifically the discovered and now missing bookkeeper, gave Clark information.'

'But how much of the information ended up with Tammy O'Lachlin?' Ashcroft posed.

Just then, the door opened, and the Superintendent came in.

'I'm just letting you know that the boys have some video footage of your mystery man at the shooting from last night,' he informed Parker and Ashcroft. 'They've put together footage from a couple of cameras and it's waiting for you in the viewing room.' 'Very good, Sir, thank you,' Parker replied.

Parker and Ashcroft made their way to the viewing room, where a constable had set up the footage on a computer. It didn't need to be projected onto a screen, as they only needed a clear image of the person in question. Parker nodded to the constable to roll the footage.

There was a figure at the corner of the building, seen in the previous footage, watching the first shots being fired. Two gun flashes reflected off the surrounding buildings, and the man ran from the scene. Another camera caught him running around another building and out of sight. The video continued, taken from another camera with better lighting, capturing a clear facial image of the unidentified man.

'Stop there!' Parker ordered. 'Well, I'll be damned, I know him.' 'You know him from where?' Ashcroft asked, a little surprised.

'Darren Cole,' Parker replied. 'He polices a drug pusher, and law enforcement has charged him several times, but he's always avoided conviction.'

'Could this have been a sting gone wrong?' Ashcroft suggested.

'No, I don't think so,' Parker said. 'I think he was to meet with Vinnie and ran into the Chinese by mistake.'

'If you're right, is he the one depositing money in Miss Spain's account?' Ashcroft theorised. 'He had planned to meet with Vinnie because the flow of drugs had stopped, and they didn't know she had been murdered days earlier, weeks, in fact.'

'Does putting the body in a freezer stop it from deteriorating?' Parker asked the obvious.

'I'll get a uniform to bring in Darren Cole for questioning,' Ashcroft said.

# Chapter 17: Do You Have a Solicitor?

As planned, Joanne came home early from work after completing the rifle proficiency test. Jeremy could see she wanted to head home sooner rather than later. She had picked up a day shift for one of the other guards and would return the favour when she got back, if she got back.

Joanne had an easy shift patrolling a shopping centre in the CBD with five other guards. The primary task was to watch out for shoplifters and any signs of undesirable elements causing a nuisance in the shopping precinct. Apart from some kids trying to be quicker with their hands than the eye could see, and getting caught, it was a relatively quiet morning.

Her stint at the shopping centre lasted only four hours, after which she returned to base to fill out a report of the morning's proceedings. It was just after noon when Joanne finished.

'How was the morning?' Jeremy asked as she walked in.

'Apart from a couple of kids getting a kick up the arse for shoplifting, it was quiet,' Joanne replied.

'You didn't kick anyone up the bum?' Jeremy asked, a bit concerned about the legality of kicking anyone up the arse.

'No, but some of the bloody little shits need it,' Joanne replied, putting his mind at ease. 'Makes you wonder what the kids' screwed-up parents have taught them.'

'Yes, I know what you mean,' Jeremy said. 'My wife is a primary school teacher, and she often wonders what happens to them as they progress from Year One to Year Six and then high school. She notices the change in their character, their attitude, and their respect for others. She reckons it's all downhill from here for most of them.'

'Yep, I guess she feels powerless to do anything,' Joanne said in support.

'Oh, by the way, once you've done your report, we'll head to the rifle range for your proficiency,' Jeremy told her.

'Thanks, Boss,' Joanne responded with a thumbs-up. 'Your wish is my command.'

They both smiled at each other, and Jeremy returned to his office while Joanne sat down at a table to fill out her shift report. It took her about twenty minutes to finish, and she even completed two incident reports for the young shoplifters she caught red-handed. She had just finished the last report when Marty walked in.

'Hey, Marty,' she said, a little surprised, 'fancy seeing you here. How's your shoulder coming along?'

Marty's arm was still in a sling but looked good despite the ordeal of being shot. People said that even after the wound heals, the mind holds onto the trauma for some time. Despite not being life-threatening, Marty might have experienced it that way.

'I'm doing okay, really,' Marty replied. 'The doctor reckons the bandages will come off in the next couple of weeks, and I'm to move the arm to exercise it. I'll probably need a six-week physio program to iron out any muscular issues, but all looks good.'

'That's good news,' Jeremy said, leaning against his office door when he heard Marty talking to Joanne. 'So when did the doctor say you could come back to work?'

'Now,' he replied mockingly. 'I need to get out of the house. I'm over watching the midday shows and B-rated movies.'

'You can help with some paperwork now that bossy-boots here is going on eight weeks' leave,' Jeremy jibed.

'Hey!' Joanne fired back. 'Enough of the bossy-boots stuff.'

'Seeing you're going away shortly on leave, I just want to get in some last-minute ribbing before you go.'

The three of them laughed at each other's remarks. It was reminiscent of good-hearted, friendly office banter. The more serious questions came as Marty sat down next to Joanne. Jeremy was still at his office door.

'How are you going?' Joanne asked. 'I'm not talking about the physical side of things.'

'Honestly, I think getting back to work will help,' Marty replied. 'When I lie down, the first thing I see is a muzzle flash from the gun and then pain in the shoulder.'

'You think coming back to work will help?' Joanne asked, concerned about Marty's state of mind. She wondered how she would react if it happened to her.

'Have you told the doctor this?' Jeremy asked, also concerned for Marty's mindset. 'He could recommend some help.'

'Yes, I have told him, and he recommended someone,' Marty replied, 'particularly if the visions don't ease up.'

'Have they eased up?' Joanne asked, putting her hand on his arm.

'Yes, somewhat,' he replied. 'I haven't woken up in the middle of the night feeling like a rabbit caught in a spotlight over the last two nights.'

Marty got up and made himself a cup of coffee. Jeremy came over and said,

'Hey, buddy. I'm here if you need my help.'

Marty turned and hugged Jeremy. Jeremy hesitated for a moment, surprised, but quickly embraced him, realising it felt like Marty was reaching out for support.

Joanne got up as well and did the same once Jeremy had finished. She kissed him on the cheek.

'As Jeremy said, we're here to help,' Joanne acknowledged. 'If I hear differently when I come back, I'll give a kick up the arse, so don't be shy to talk about it either.'

'Yes, bossy-boots,' he replied with a smirk.

'Hey, what's with the bossy-boots stuff? Where did that come from?' Joanne replied with a smirk. 'I know what it is. You need me to keep you all in line.'

There was more laughter, and Marty seemed to be in happier spirits. Maybe it was time for him to come back to work after all. Joanne handed her report to Jeremy and said,

'Well, boys, I'll be off. Make sure you look after the place. Jeremy, monitor all of them.'

'Yes, Miss bossy-boots,' Jeremy replied with a smile. 'Have some lunch, then we'll head to the rifle range.'

'Okay,' Joanne said as she reached the door. She turned, winked at them, gave a thumbs-up, and was gone.

Marty turned to Jeremy and asked,

'When can I start?'

'Come back in the morning and I'll see what I can do,' Jeremy confirmed. 'It might just be paperwork first and maybe running some errands.'

'Sounds good to me,' Marty replied. 'I'll see you in the morning.'

Marty also left, and Jeremy returned to the pile of paperwork on his desk. It was unceasing, or so it seemed.

Jeremy had his sandwich for lunch and then headed to the armoury in the basement, signing out a Heckler & Koch HK33SG/1 rifle and twenty rounds of .308 ammunition.

It was an hour's drive to the range, and Joanne was already there when Jeremy arrived. She took the mat from the vehicle and laid it on the ground where she would shoot, then took the magazine and bullets to load.

'We'll only shoot twelve rounds, so just load the magazine as required,' Jeremy instructed.

After loading the magazine, Joanne equipped herself with earmuffs and safety glasses and awaited further instructions.

'Joanne,' Jeremy started, 'this is a Heckler & Koch HK33 with telescopic sights and a modified trigger mechanism. You are to shoot two sighting rounds followed by ten rounds that will count towards your score. Are you ready?' 'Yes,' she replied.

'Take your position and load the rifle.'

Joanne lay down on the mound, got comfortable, and loaded the rifle. She pressed it into her shoulder and waited.

'Fire one round,' Jeremy instructed.

Joanne placed the crosshairs in the centre of the target and squeezed the trigger. The first round fired from the high-velocity rifle sent up swirling dust in front of her.

'High and slightly right in the eight zone at two o'clock,' Jeremy called, noting the shot.

Joanne adjusted the sights a couple of clicks, then fired the second round.

'Nice shot,' Jeremy reported. 'Twelve o'clock in the nine zone.'

With a couple more clicks to adjust the sights, Joanne was ready to shoot the next ten rounds.

'These next ten rounds count towards your score,' Jeremy informed her. 'We've taken your previous score into account and set a target of ninety for you to qualify as an Elite Rifleman.'

Joanne took a deep breath a couple of times, setting her sights on the target.

'When you're ready, in your own time, begin firing,' Jeremy ordered. 'I can call your shots if you like.' 'Yes,'

was all Joanne said.

She concentrated on the next shot and fired.

'High nine.'

The next three shots went off at a steady rate, all tens.

'Nice shooting, Joanne,' Jeremy acknowledged.

Squeezing off the next six shots at the same pace, Joanne impressed Jeremy.

'I think you shot a ninety-seven,' Jeremy said with excitement. 'Where did you learn to shoot like that, and at four hundred metres?'

'I'm a Queensland farm girl from a cattle and sheep station,' she answered. 'I've shot the occasional fox, feral pig, and water buffalo at similar distances.'

'Well, I can say this much, you can have my back anytime.'

They packed up the rifle and equipment, collected the spent brass, and headed back to base. Joanne was waiting in Jeremy's office after he had returned the firearm to the armoury.

'Well, that display of marksmanship earns you an Elite Rifleman badge, or should I say rifle person?' Jeremy said. 'Doesn't sound quite right, does it?'

They both smirked.

'Well, now you're officially on holiday,' Jeremy informed her. 'Since you're on leave, they brought the rifle proficiency test forward. It was originally scheduled for you in two weeks.' 'That's fine, I understand,' she replied.

'Now get out of here. Enjoy your break.'

'Thank you. I'll see you in eight weeks.'

Joanne made good time getting home. She parked in her allocated spot in the underground car park, locked the car, and headed up to her flat. She found Holly all spruced up and ready to go somewhere.

'Yahoo!' Holly shouted as Joanne entered. She was skipping about and came over, giving Joanne a big hug. Joanne returned the affection, and both kissed.

'Looks like we're going somewhere?' Joanne casually observed, eyeing the three stacked luggage bags.

'Yes, yes, and yes,' Holly replied, giggling like a schoolgirl.

'Sweetheart, what are you on?'

'There's nothing I can't handle,' Holly replied, fluttering her eyelashes.

'Great to see you in high spirits, my love,' Joanne replied. 'I'll have a quick shower, and then we'll head off. Call a taxi to take us to the airport while I'm in the shower.'

Joanne went for a shower, and Holly rang the taxi. It would be about twenty minutes before it arrived, plenty of time for Joanne to get ready and both to go down to the lobby and wait. Joanne didn't take long to complete some final packing, and then they were ready.

'Did you print out our tickets?' Joanne asked.

'Yep,' Holly replied, pulling them from her bag. 'They're right here.'

'Good,' Joanne replied. 'We're out of here.'

They turned off the lights, carried the luggage outside, and locked the door. In the lobby, Joanne told the clerk they were leaving for a holiday and asked him to keep watch over her vehicle and flat. The clerk agreed. Joanne handed him her car and flat keys.

They only had to wait another five minutes before the taxi arrived, driven by an Indian man wearing his traditional headwear.

They loaded the luggage into the boot and climbed in, ready to depart for the airport. Holly was beaming with excitement, and Joanne felt a brief flutter in her stomach as well. It had been quite some time since she had flown, and it was her first trip to WA. Evening traffic was heavy, with red lights holding them up occasionally.

Joanne looked around, something she seldom did when driving herself, but could enjoy as a passenger. She noticed a tall, middle-aged man with a shaved head walking down the footpath towards her flat complex. She recognised him, but from where?

Then it suddenly hit her as the lights turned green and the taxi took off. It was the bloke who had met with Roberto the night she introduced herself to Holly. She squeezed Holly's hand and smiled at her. Holly was busy looking around as well. The streetlights were coming on, and the neon signs lit up the surroundings.

Joanne glanced back to see if she was right about who she had seen, but he was no longer in sight. On second thought, she considered it might have been a case of mistaken identity, but she didn't think so. He had looked straight at her, but since they had never been introduced, he didn't know who she was, just another passenger in a taxi going somewhere.

The taxi made its way through the Sydney traffic, down Botany Rd, and finally pulled into the airport for departing passengers.

'Who are you flying with today?' he asked in a wonderful, mellow accent.

'Virgin,' Joanne replied.

'Okay, I'll drop you off at their entrance,' he offered.

'Thank you,' Joanne said.

He pulled into a loading bay. Joanne paid the fare. He got out to help with their luggage, and Holly thanked him.

'You're most welcome, ladies,' he replied. 'Enjoy your flight.'

Both waved briefly in acknowledgement and entered the terminal. They went over to the line-up at the check-in counter, which seemed quite busy. Once they had checked in their luggage, Joanne suggested they find somewhere to eat.

'That's an excellent idea,' Holly agreed. 'I'm feeling a little peckish as well.'

It took about ten minutes to check in their luggage, and in no time they were through security and up in the departure lounge. Once they located their gate, they noticed an eatery nearby. They ordered something to eat and drink, and Holly used her credit card to pay. They found a table and sat down with about forty minutes to wait before boarding.

***

Stromnikov rang Dominic, asking to meet him. He had something to report but would not do so over the phone, so they met at his office with Mario and Roberto as well at about 10:00 pm. The matter couldn't wait until the next day. He arrived to find them already there.

'What is it that couldn't wait?' Dominic asked as he entered the office.

'I haven't been able to find the girl in the hospital,' he informed them in his Russian accent. He explained that the hospital had discharged the girl two days before.

'Do you know where she is?' Roberto asked.

'You don't need to know that!' Dominic snapped at Roberto. 'You want to bash her some more, hey?'

'No, I'm just curious.'

'I don't know where she is,' Sergei replied.

'Maybe she's with her friend at the Merriton Suites complex on Kent Street?' Dominic suggested. 'You said you met her once at Club 77, Roberto.'

'Yes,' he confirmed. 'It was Joanne something. Joanne Holland.'

'Have you looked there, Sergei?' Dominic pressed.

'Yes,' he replied, 'I asked the desk clerk, and he said the woman I described as Holly left with a blonde woman on a holiday.'

'She did what?!' Dominic retorted. 'She went on a bloody holiday!'

'That's what I was told,' Sergei confirmed.

'I have to get hold of Fleming for some help,' Dominic told them as he dialled the phone number. It rang a couple of times before someone picked up.

'Hello,' came the reply.

'Fleming,' Dominic said. 'I want you to do something for me in the morning, and it's urgent.'

'Well, hello Dominic,' Fleming replied. 'It must be important if you're calling at this time of night.'

'It is very important.'

'What do you need?' Fleming asked.

Senior Detective Anthony Fleming had been on the force for some time. He had been promoted early in his career but had never seemed to rise further. Some said it was his attitude; others said he was just hard to get along with. Some speculated he needed to drop the old-school ways and adapt to twenty-first century policing. He could hide the fact that he was on the take, and no one suspected him.

'I want you to do two things for me,' Dominic began. 'I want you to find out the credit card activity of Holly Jamieson and Joanne Holland as soon as possible. Second, find out how much is in Vinnie's account and how we can get access to it.'

'Why do you need that information?'

'That's my secret for now,' Dominic replied. 'All I can tell you is that this Jamieson woman worked for us and has some records with her I need to retrieve. It's all business.'

'That must be important information, then,' Fleming suggested. 'I'll be sticking my neck out for you again.'

'Yes, and you do that for the Family,' Dominic reminded him. 'You also get paid well, right?'

'Yes, right,' Fleming confirmed.

'Then contact me tomorrow morning as soon as you have the info,' Dominic instructed, then hung up.

'Now, Mario,' Dominic continued. 'Check Vinnie's list of contacts and find out the amount of money in his account. I calculate it should be about two hundred and fifty thousand dollars.'

'Wow,' sighed Roberto. 'That's a lot just sitting there.'

'Yes, thank you, Mr Intelligence,' Dominic said mockingly. 'You need to get smarter in the way you handle things as well.' 'What are you talking about?' Roberto said, annoyed.

'The women, for a start. You can't stay away from the ones we employ,' Dominic replied loudly. 'With the bookkeeper gone and now Holly, your mother is beside herself trying to keep on top of it all!'

Roberto looked dejected again, like a scolded schoolboy. In his mind, one day that would have to change.

'I'll see what I can find out from the pushers,' Mario said.

'Make sure no more money goes into Vinnie's account but into the Teresa-May account,' Dominic instructed. 'Get hold of the launderers first thing tomorrow.'

'How many are there?' Mario asked.

'Here's a list of those transferring money into Vinnie's account,' Dominic said, handing him the list. 'It's in order of the daily transfers, starting on Monday. The new account number is at the bottom.'

'Okay, I'll get on that straight away,' Mario said. 'I can even ring some tonight.'

'Yes, that would be best,' Dominic agreed.

Mario said his goodbyes and left. He had to ensure that transfers scheduled for early Monday morning were diverted to the new account. Teresa-May's account was bogus, and Dominic had access to it himself.

'Sergio,' Dominic said, 'as soon as I find out where these two are going, I'll get you to follow them. I'll tell you later what to do.'

'Okay,' he replied. 'I'll be waiting for your instructions.' Sergio left as well.

'Roberto, I want you to help your mother with some paperwork tomorrow and with the accounts,' Dominic told him. 'She needs help to keep on top of everything.'

'Alright, I'll come in early and make a start,' Roberto replied.

'You make sure you do.'

Roberto bid him goodnight and left. On his way home, his thoughts wandered to Holly, and he grew frustrated, acknowledging his father's correctness in the way he treated women. He regretted it all, especially with Holly. She was by far his favourite, and he had messed that up too.

Maybe there will be a next time?

***

Uniform police picked up Darren Cole, one of Vinnie's drug pushers and the mystery man in the video, early the next day. When Parker arrived at the station, he found him waiting in the interview room, and Ashcroft greeted him and informed him.

'He's in the interview room.'

'Good, let's talk to him.'

They went in and sat down opposite Cole.

'Darren Cole, I'm Detective Sergeant Parker and this is Detective Ashcroft,' Parker introduced them. 'This interview is being recorded and, for the record, is your name Darren Cole?'

'Yes, it is.'

'Mr Cole, look at the monitor for me, please,' Parker requested. 'You will observe security footage from the light industrial area recorded a couple of nights ago where a shooting took place. Is that you in the top frame on the right near that building?' 'I don't think so,' Cole replied.

'Are you certain of that, Mr Cole?'

'Why would I be present at a shooting, if that's what it was?' Cole questioned.

'Yes indeed, I asked that question as well,' Parker replied. 'You see, the next piece of footage shows a man who looks like you running from the scene.'

Cole didn't reply. He just watched the monitor, and the clarity of being caught on camera surprised him.

'You don't have an identical twin, do you?'

'No.'

'Then clearly that person running is you, is it not?' Parker suggested.

'Yes, it is,' Cole reluctantly admitted.

'What were you doing there?' Ashcroft asked. 'Waiting for someone?'

'I was to meet someone there that I had arranged with earlier in the day,' Cole confirmed.

'Look, let's cut the bullshit here!' Parker said, getting agitated with the short answers. 'Either you give us the complete account without hesitation, or we will charge you with being connected to the murder!'

'I didn't kill anyone, and I didn't know that Vinnie was going to be shot,' Cole babbled faster than his brain could process.

'Vinnie who?' asked Ashcroft.

Cole suddenly realised he had named someone he shouldn't have. After a moment, he took a deep breath and answered.

'Vinnie Sattorri.'

'Do you mean Vincenzo Sattorri?' Ashcroft asked to ensure the correct name was recorded.

'Yes, that's who I mean,' Cole confirmed. 'Do I need a solicitor?'

'I don't know, Mr Cole,' Parker replied. 'Have you done something wrong that warrants a solicitor being present?'

'I have done some things that might get me in trouble with the law,' Cole admitted.

'Like what sort of things?' Ashcroft asked.

'Selling drugs and things like that.'

'That's your call if you think a solicitor should be present,' Ashcroft replied.

'Okay. Vinnie rang me about the money not going into his account as quickly as we had organised. After calling him back, I asked if we should meet and recommended the industrial site,' Cole elaborated. 'When the security people pulled up, I wasn't sure what was going down. I didn't see Vinnie, but I heard the gunshots. There was no reason to hang around.'

'What about the money? What was the schedule for depositing it?'

'I was a little surprised by Vinnie's question. I always banked the cash every Friday without fail into the designated accounts,' Cole continued.

'How many accounts are there?' Parker asked.

'Five that I know of,' Cole replied.

'Do you know the names of these accounts?' Ashcroft asked.

'No, I only have the account numbers,' Cole replied.

'Would one of those five accounts be Vinnie's?' Ashcroft asked.

'I'm not sure. I couldn't honestly say.'

'How much do you bank every week into each account?'

'Close to two thousand dollars into those five accounts,' Cole replied.

'That's ten thousand a week. It works out at half a million dollars a year,' Parker calculated. 'How many pushers like you would Vinnie have?'

'There are five or six, I think, but I'm not sure,' Cole said.

'Well, I'll fuck me!' Parker exclaimed. 'That's upwards of six million dollars a year.'

'Would you know who might have been in the black BMW that started the shooting?' Ashcroft asked.

'Yes, the Chinese guys,' Cole explained. 'They are moving into our territory, and that was one thing I was going to mention to Vinnie. They have no scruples and are unsympathetic about what they have to do to get a piece of the action.'

'Since when do criminals have scruples?' Parker asked. 'Anyway, you know you're risking being charged with drug possession and trafficking?'

'Yes, I know, but I'm not prepared to risk being killed for it either by the Chinese out there,' Cole said. 'So if you lock me up, I don't care.' 'Do you have a solicitor who can advise you?' Ashcroft asked.

'No, I don't have one,' Cole replied.

'The court can appoint one for you when you first appear before the magistrate,' Parker advised. 'We can keep you in custody for twenty-four hours without charging you.'

'Okay, I'm ready for that,' Cole said. 'I don't want to go back out on the street.'

'We'll hold you in remand for tonight, and we'll determine what charges to prefer in the morning,' Parker advised.

'Sounds fine to me.'

Parker called in a constable to take Cole to the lock-up overnight. Ashcroft wondered what the outcome would be with the information they had just received.

'Cole didn't hold back once he started,' Ashcroft said once Cole was gone.

'No, he didn't,' Parker agreed. 'He was quite forthcoming, and that changes things a little in our favour.'

'How so?'

'We can now confiscate the funds in both Emily Spain and Vinnie's accounts. We can also get a search warrant for Vinnie's residence and see if we find any drugs. That also puts the Rossetti family in the spotlight.'

'What about the other accounts Cole was depositing money into?'

'The same thing applies. We confiscate the funds,' Parker replied. 'First move would be to freeze Vinnie's account, hopefully today.' 'I

can get that done,' Ashcroft offered.

'Let me get the Boss up to speed, and I'll let you know the decision before jumping ahead of ourselves,' Parker suggested. 'This could be the break we've been waiting for. I don't want to blow it.' 'I agree,' Ashcroft replied.

# Chapter 18: Joanne Buys a Car

Fleming made an early start by checking Holly and Joanne's credit card activity. The bank opened at 9:30 am, and he was the first customer. He showed his ID to the staff member at the front desk, who directed him to the manager. Fleming made his request and got the information without any difficulty. Apart from retrieving the two girls' information, he also asked for and received Vinnie's account details.

When he got back to his car, he rang Dominic and told him he had the information he wanted about the girls and Vinnie. Twenty minutes later, he walked into Dominic's office.

'Here are the printouts of Miss Joanne Holland and Miss Holly Jamieson's account activity, plus Vinnie's account,' Fleming informed Dominic as he laid them on the table.

'Well, well,' Dominic replied. 'You've been busy, my friend, and early too.'

Dominic looked at the documents and saw Holly's account activity. Two transactions stood out: one for accommodation in Perth for two nights, and a meal at Sydney Airport. Joanne's account revealed accommodation booked at the Ocean Centre Hotel in Geraldton for seven nights.

'This is valuable information,' Dominic said. 'Thank you.'

'Not a problem,' Fleming replied. 'I'd better get back to the office.'

Fleming left, leaving Dominic poring over the reports. Vinnie's account held an astonishing one hundred thousand dollars. He would have to get Teresa to transfer it out this afternoon when she returned from the markets. Roberto didn't have the login information to access the account. Dominic then rang Stromnikov.

'I have a job for you,' Dominic informed him. 'Meet me in my office as soon as you can.'

Stromnikov didn't reply. He simply ended the call. Dominic knew he would be on his way in response to the request. Twenty minutes later, he arrived at Dominic's office.

'I want you to fly to WA and go to a place called Geraldton,' Dominic began. 'Your mission is to locate Holly Jamieson with her blonde-haired friend and eliminate them both.'

'Do you have a picture of the women?'

'I have one of Miss Jamieson, but not of the blonde woman,' Dominic explained. 'They've booked a room at the Ocean Centre Hotel. That's all I know.'

'Good, that will do for a start,' Stromnikov replied. 'I'll find out the details when I get there. When do I leave?'

'The earliest flight we can get is tomorrow night to Perth,' Dominic advised. 'There's a four-hour wait in Perth for the connecting flight to Geraldton. Hire a car at the airport when you get there.'

'Okay, I'll come up with a plan to eliminate them,' Stromnikov said.

'Yes, that's right,' Dominic agreed. 'But you're a resourceful man. I'm certain you'll have a plan by the time you arrive.'

Stromnikov was a man of few words, but not on this occasion. He made sure his intentions met Dominic's approval as he accepted the job.

'Come by tomorrow around noon,' Dominic said. 'I'll have your tickets and everything ready for you.' 'Okay,' he said and left the office.

Dominic looked at Vinnie's account details, feeling annoyed at seeing so much money left there. Vinnie was usually on top of transferring money regularly, so it was unusual for so much to remain. Unfortunately, they would never know his reasoning. All Dominic had to do now was ask Teresa to make the transfer sooner rather than later.

***

Detective Sergeant Parker explained to the Inspector what had come to light in the investigation into the shooting at the industrial area. He also explained the voluntary testimony given by Darren Cole.

'I think it's sufficient evidence for us to act and have those accounts frozen,' Parker suggested. 'That will at least stop some flow of money from drug dealers.'

'Are you sure the Rossettis are involved in this?' the Inspector asked.

'It points that way, Sir,' Parker replied. According to the informant, Sattorri had the job of meeting with the drug pusher we have in the lock-up. The scheduled meeting at the industrial site was to explain that someone was muscling in on their territory, and the Rossettis needed to be aware of that.

'What about the woman someone found there? Have you established a connection to the Rossettis?'

'Only that she connected her transaction account to Sattorri's account via regular transfers, and we have the bank's printout to support that.'

'Okay then,' the Inspector said. 'Get Ashcroft to go by the courthouse and pick up the court order. I'll ring through a request to freeze all accounts feeding into Sattorri's account and his account as well. We'll soon see what reaction we get.'

'Thank you, Sir,' Parker replied with gratitude. 'We've set the wheels in motion.'

'Yes, we have,' agreed the Inspector. 'At least now we have evidence to act on.'

Parker left the Inspector's office with a big grin. He found Ashcroft at his desk and said,

'How would you like to freeze a couple of bank accounts?' 'What, are you for real?' Ashcroft asked, surprised.

'The Inspector has approved it,' Parker replied. 'Swing past the courthouse and pick up the order. Freeze Vinnie's account first, then all the others feeding into it.'

'You beauty,' Ashcroft said with glee as he got up and grabbed his coat. 'See you when I get back.'

Parker nodded, and Ashcroft left without further encouragement. The day of reckoning for the Rossettis, though perhaps still a way off, was about to begin.

Ashcroft went to the courthouse to pick up the court order. A magistrate, who was between hearings, signed it. Everything went like clockwork. Once Ashcroft had the paperwork, he went to the bank that held Vinnie's account. It took very little time to meet the manager.

'You blokes acted quickly on this one,' the manager said.

'What do you mean?' Ashcroft asked.

'Well, it was only earlier this morning when one of your colleagues collected information about this account and two credit card accounts belonging to two ladies,' the assistant manager replied in his English accent.

'Yes, well, when the information is overwhelming like this, we have to act,' Ashcroft replied, playing along.

He didn't want to make it obvious that he knew nothing about a 'colleague' doing anything. After a couple of minutes, the manager finished tapping on his keyboard and said,

'That's all done, plus two accounts that regularly transfer money into that first account.'

'What about the other three accounts?' Ashcroft queried.

'They won't be able to transfer any money from them to here, but you'll have to see the bank across the road for those two accounts, and the Merchant Bank in the next block for the last one,' the manager advised.

'Are you able to give me those account numbers?' Ashcroft asked. 'It'll save me time.'

'Yes, I can give you the account numbers, but not the BSB numbers,' the manager advised. 'That shouldn't be a problem once you're at the respective branches.'

He wrote the numbers down on the notepad and handed the note to Ashcroft.

'Thank you so much for all your help,' Ashcroft said.

'I had little choice with a court order, did I?'

'No, none, but thank you anyway,' Ashcroft acknowledged.

'You have a good day, detective,' the assistant manager bade him.

'Oh, by the way, who was the detective that came in earlier?' Ashcroft asked.

'Fleming, I think. Yes, Senior Detective Fleming,' the manager replied, a little puzzled. 'I would have thought you would have known?'

'Yes, I do. It's just that we have several of us working on the same case, and you can lose track of who is doing what,' Ashcroft explained, trying to justify the question.

'Okay, I best let you get on with it then,' the manager replied with a smile.

Ashcroft went to the bank across the road and froze two more accounts. He also managed to freeze the last account at the Merchant Bank, then returned to the station and went straight to Parker's office with news about Fleming.

Ashcroft confirmed they had frozen or deactivated all accounts.

'Do you know Senior Detective Fleming?'

'Mitch Fleming,' Parker repeated. 'Yes, I know him. He works at the Parramatta station. Why?'

'According to the manager, Fleming came and got information on Vinnie's account and two credit card accounts belonging to two female customers of the bank,' Ashcroft explained.

'Why would Fleming be asking about those accounts, I wonder?' Parker asked no one in particular.

'Can't we just ask him?' Ashcroft asked.

'No, he outranks me, and I haven't got the authority to press the matter with him,' Parker explained. 'But the inspector can.'

Parker and Ashcroft visited the Inspector's office to update him on the latest information. Ashcroft recounted the meeting with the bank manager.

'You are absolutely certain of this?' the Inspector pressed Ashcroft.

'Absolutely, Sir, without a doubt,' Ashcroft responded. 'I purposely asked him for the name as I was leaving the manager's office. He responded straightaway.'

'Well, well. Fleming, of all people,' the Inspector said in deep thought. 'If he's been feeding information to a criminal organisation, then that being a crime in itself means jail time if convicted.'

'If he's done this now, what else has he leaked before?' Ashcroft asked speculatively.

'Detective, that is the sixty-four million dollar question I'd hate to answer,' the Inspector replied. 'Let's just keep this under our hats for the moment. I'll have some colleagues I can trust ask the relevant questions and see what I can do.' 'Yes, Sir,' Ashcroft replied.

'Also, make sure you put that in your report,' the Inspector advised. 'I don't aspire to being caught out by someone saying it's hearsay. Let's make absolutely sure we play this one by the book. I'd hate it to bite us in the arse by some sleazy lawyer.'

'Yes, Sir. I'll make sure my report is here this afternoon,' Ashcroft confirmed.

'Put your report in the case file and give me a copy as well.' 'Yes, Sir,' Ashcroft replied.

'Ashcroft, good work,' the Inspector said as he saw them both to the door.

Parker and Ashcroft returned to Parker's office, and both sat down, looking at each other.

'Do you know who the two women are that Fleming inquired about regarding their credit card activities?' Parker asked Ashcroft.

'I think I do.'

'I'm not sure, but didn't someone bash and hospitalise one girl?' Ashcroft surmised.

'Yes, excellent call,' replied Parker. 'Miss Holly Jamieson and her partner,
Miss Joanne Holland.'

'Why would Fleming be interested in those two?'

'I know Fleming well enough to suspect him of giving vital info to the Rossettis,' Parker replied. 'I'll also say he has been tipping them off on raids and searches for drugs on their premises.'

'But there is no information to support that line of thinking,' Ashcroft said.

'There is nothing concrete yet, but the way things are revealing themselves, it won't take long before this case blows the lid off,' Parker predicted.

'I hope you're right,' Ashcroft replied.

'Okay, let's follow the sequence of events,' Parker recounted. 'Roberto Rossetti bashes Miss Holly Jamieson near to death, and is yet to make an official statement. Darren Cole gives us enough information voluntarily to close several drug money accounts. Yet the body of Emily Spain is still missing, and she has a connection to drug money. Then, Vinnie Sattorri is killed in a shootout with the Chinese and security guards. Now, Milton Clark and Tammy O'Lachlin are shot while investigating the Rossetti family for fraudulent behaviour. These are circumstances that are pointing in one direction and building up to something big.'

'You mentioned Clark and O'Lachlin,' Ashcroft queried. 'Any connection found to link their shootings to the Rossettis?'

'Not yet,' Parker replied, 'but I'm hoping something will show up to connect with them. If only we could get a search warrant.'

'Yes,' Ashcroft agreed, 'and find something that will light the fuse for the big bang.'

'I think the fuse is already lit,' Parker replied. 'It's just a bloody long one.'

'The Chinese have been sticking their noses in as well and making a move,' Ashcroft opined.

'Well, there's another angle that we need to pursue,' Parker said, reflecting on the situation. 'We need to find Emily Spain's body. My guess is that someone murdered her and then dumped her in a freezer somewhere. Hopefully, we can also capture those culprits.'

Ashcroft recounted the report, stating that the reports they received showed that they had stolen the black BMW from interstate.

'I have some reliable contacts in Chinatown that may help us in that direction.'

'That sounds like an excellent suggestion,' Parker agreed. 'See what you can find out.'

***

Holly and Joanne's flight went smoothly, as expected. They watched a movie, had a snack or two, chatted for a while, and even had a nap before landing just before midnight in Perth. Once they had collected their luggage, they made their way to the taxi stand outside the airport terminal and caught a taxi into the city.

'Where would you like to go?' the taxi driver asked.

'Travelodge Motel on Hay Street, please,' Joanne requested.

It took about twenty minutes to reach the motel and carry their luggage into the reception area. They found the reservation and entered the final booking details. Once Joanne and Holly received the key, they made their way up to their room. They had a room on the fourth floor at the rear of the motel, which overlooked Langley Park and the Swan River beyond.

'This is quite nice and has a magnificent view,' Holly observed.

'Yes, and it's nearly as good as my flat in Sydney,' Joanne tentatively agreed.

'It's too early for breakfast,' Holly said. 'I might take a shower to freshen up a bit. Then maybe order a midnight snack.'

'A snack sounds good. I might come in the shower with you,' Joanne announced. 'Is the shower big enough?'

Holly followed Joanne to the bathroom and looked inside. They both turned to each other and almost said the same thing simultaneously.

'There's plenty of room.' They both laughed.

Holly already had her toiletries and gown with her and was first in the shower. Joanne wasn't far behind her. She stayed in the bathroom, stripped naked, and stepped into the shower with Holly. They embraced and kissed as the warm water splashed on their heads and trickled down their bodies. Holly then took the soap from the holder and began washing Joanne's back and around to her breasts and down to her thighs. Then she turned around, and Joanne did the same for her.

They got out of the shower and dried themselves off. Holly dried her hair, and it got all frizzy. Joanne's blond hair hung down to her shoulders like rat tails. Once she had combed her hair, it looked tidier and a lot neater. Both laughed at each other as they tried to change their hairstyles by combing it one way, then the other. Joanne used hers as a pretend moustache, looking in the mirror this way and then that. Both laughed at the pretence.

Holly made her way to the bed. Joanne did the same. It was dark outside and probably three or four hours before daylight. Both snuggled in bed together, embraced and kissed, with their hands running up and down each other's bodies. Holly was really getting into the kissing routine and gently massaging Joanne's full, round breasts and erect nipples. Joanne responded and reached down to Holly's thighs as she rolled on her back and put her hands between her thighs. Holly squeezed her bum cheeks together as her expectations rose. She cupped her other hand against her face and sensuously continued kissing her. Both finally reached a high.

They now both lay facing each other with smiles of satisfaction and calmness. Arm in arm and with legs entwined, they drifted off into a deep sleep. It didn't seem long enough when the alarm clock went off and Holly awoke, still in the arms of Joanne. She stirred as well, and the morning light was creeping into the room. So much for a midnight snack.

It was 7:30 am, and both had slept in. In Sydney, it was 9:30 am, and both would be well and truly at work by now. But breakfast was there, and they were on holiday!

'We deserved a well-earned rest, and we can sleep all day,' Holly announced.

'Yeah!' Joanne replied, lying in bed and watching Holly skip around the room naked and without a care in the world. Joanne smiled and wished that this day would never end, even last for all eternity. She'd never seen Holly this eager. It was a revelation in terms.

'Hey!' Joanne said out loud.

Holly stopped dead in her tracks as if she had hit a brick wall.

'Why did you shout 'hey' to me?' Holly replied, trying not to appear startled.

'I want the beautiful woman who is prancing around my room in the nude to come here and let me kiss that gorgeous babe.'

'Damn, you make it hard to resist you,' Holly replied as she came over to the bed.

'Do you want to resist?'

'Never, never, never,' Holly replied, jumping into the bed.

There was more laughter than silence as their lips met time and time again. Holly rolled over on her side, and Joanne embraced her from behind and cupped her hands around her breasts, slowly drawing her closer. Then she whispered,

'Holly Jamieson, I love you so much. I never want to let you go.' Holly put her arms over Joanne's and pulled her even closer.

'I feel the same way about you too, Miss Holland.'

Both giggled and wriggled around in the bed for a moment, and then Holly said,

'I'm starving. Breakfast would go down well right now.'

They both got out of bed and went to the bathroom to freshen up, got dressed, applied a bit of make-up, and then went down in the elevator and across to the dining room. It was only at half its capacity, but the buffet breakfast of bacon, eggs, toast and so on wafted through the room, making stomachs scream for food. They each took a plate and helped themselves to a warm breakfast and percolated coffee.

'What are we doing today?' Holly asked.

'I think the first thing we do is look for a hire car,' Joanne suggested. 'I'm thinking of buying one that we can always sell before we fly back to Sydney.'

'Wouldn't that cost too much just for our stay here?' Holly asked in surprise.

'I've been thinking that if we hire a car for eight weeks, fifty-six days, it will cost us about four thousand dollars for the privilege, plus insurance costs for the period. But if we buy a car for a third of that as a deposit, or buy one for that amount in cash, then we can sell it later,' Joanne explained. 'We should get a decent unit for that price.' Holly looked at Joanne for a moment and then nodded.

'I think you might be right,' she agreed. 'It will save us some money in the long run.'

They finished breakfast and went back out to the reception desk in the lobby. There, Joanne asked the clerk at the desk,

'Where is the closest car yard?'

'There are quite a few areas, but the closest ones I think, and the best, are in Vic Park just over the causeway,' the girl replied.

'Okay, that's where we'll start then,' Joanne replied. 'Can you call us a taxi?'

'Yes, no problem,' the girl replied and picked up the phone and dialled the number.

They had to wait only about ten minutes, and a taxi arrived at the front of the motel. Joanne requested the taxi to take them to the first car yard over the causeway as they were looking to buy a second-hand car. The taxi driver agreed that Vic Park was an excellent choice unless you were looking for a particular make of car. They arrived at the first car yard, and Holly paid the taxi fare as they got out.

The first car yard had a vast range of cars, but nothing suited Joanne or caught her fancy. She noticed a salesperson get out of his chair in the office through the huge glass panelling, and she urged Holly to move on. She wasn't interested in anything, and a salesperson 'pouring' his spiel over to persuade her otherwise wasn't for her. Besides, she had nearly all day to find a car she liked, unless one caught her eye in the meantime.

They quickly left that car yard and moved on to the next. She had a quick look along the first row of cars and then Holly said,

'What about a BMW? Would you be interested in one of those?'

'Where did you see that?' Joanne replied, trying to see where Holly was looking.

'In the last row at the back,' Holly replied, 'a red sedan.'

'Oh yes, I see it now,' Joanne acknowledged. 'Let's have a closer look.'

As they approached the car, a salesperson coming out of the office met them. Dressed in a fancy suit with nicely polished black shoes, the salesperson exuded arrogance that Joanne picked up on right away, without the bloke even uttering a word.

'Morning, ladies,' he greeted. 'Pleasant morning, isn't it?'

Joanne ignored him for a moment. His questioning had confirmed her assumption of him to a T.

'What's the best price you can do on this car?' Joanne asked without looking at him.

'Well, this car is quite good, low k's for its age and...'

'Spare me the sales pitch,' Joanne interjected. 'How much for this? I'm offering cash.'

The salesperson's eyes widened, and he became unable to speak at that moment. He checked the price tag and said,

'Just a minute. I'll confirm the price for you,' he replied and disappeared into the office. He returned a moment later and said,

'The best I can do is seven thousand two hundred and fifty dollars plus on-road costs.'

'Make it an even seven thousand. You may have yourself a deal,' Joanne replied.

Holly gave Joanne a quick look and then noticed the astonished look on the salesperson's face. She guessed he hadn't expected a woman like Joanne to be this pushy so early in the morning and to know how to barter as well.

'Better still, an even seven thousand dollars and no on-road costs. You've got a deal,' Joanne offered.

'I don't think I can do that, sorry,' was the reply.

Joanne responded, 'I'm sorry as well. Let's go to the next car yard.'

The salesperson suddenly realised he was losing the sale and tried one more attempt to comply with Joanne's offer.

'Excuse me, Miss, before you leave,' he offered Joanne. 'Will you allow me to put this last offer to the manager? Hopefully, I can persuade him to accept your offer?'

'I hope you're not wasting my time,' Joanne replied. 'We have things to do and we need a car, either that one from here or from another sales yard somewhere down the road.'

The salesperson didn't hesitate any longer. He virtually spun on his heels and disappeared back into the office to see the manager. Joanne watched him disappear into another office from where she was standing. It wasn't the same office or person he had spoken to earlier. He may have been 'misleading' her with his first offer and never seen the manager at all.

This time he was gone a little longer than before as well. He returned with a smile on his face.

'The manager has agreed to your offer of seven thousand dollars even, no more to pay.'

It almost sounded like a line from a TV commercial, and she had a bit of a chuckle to herself. 'Got you nicely.' With success in hand, Joanne turned on the charm.

'Well thank you, I'm now glad that we stopped and took our time to view the car,' she said. 'Let's do some paperwork.'

## Holly, Joanne and Steph

They all went inside, and the salesperson introduced them to the accountant, who was responsible for signing and organising finance, or completing transactions in cash. While this was going on, the salesperson took the car to a service station close by and filled the fuel tank for them. The deal had been completed by the time he returned. Joanne and Holly got into the car, waved goodbye and drove away.

'Holly, my sweet,' Joanne said as they drove away. 'That's how you negotiate a deal when buying a car.'

Both were beaming with smiles on their faces.

The rest of the day to visit a couple of shopping centres, some cafes for lunch and snacks, and even watching a movie. They returned to the motel for a rest from the day's activities and to prepare for tea. Holly gave Steph a call.

'Hi Steph, it's Holly,' she said when Steph answered the phone. 'How are you?'

'I'm fine, and you?'

'We're in Perth and plan to travel up in the morning sometime,' Holly informed her. 'We can finally catch up tomorrow.'

'That is great news,' Steph replied. 'I'm looking forward to catching up.'

'Me too. It's been a long time since we've been together,' she replied. 'I'm looking forward to it.'

'What time do you intend to leave Perth?' Steph asked.

'We haven't made a time yet, but we have to be out of here by ten. We were going to have lunch somewhere, probably a Swan Valley eatery, and then drive up.'

'Okay, it's just that I'm on the late shift the next couple of days, but I'll make time to catch up and do lunch or something before work,' Steph suggested.

'That sounds like a plan,' Holly agreed. 'It will be fun, and you'll meet Joanne, too.'

'I'm looking forward to it, Holly.'

'Okay then,' Holly replied. 'We're going to finish packing, not that there's much to do, and then have an early night.'

'You take care driving up,' Steph replied. 'Hope to see you sometime tomorrow.'

'Okay, bye for now,' Holly said.

'Bye, Holly.'

Steph was feeling a little more excited now that Holly was actually in WA and only a day away from seeing her. She had often wanted to travel to Sydney and see Holly over there, but work had restricted that from happening. Now Holly would be here to see her at long last.

Little did anyone expect Holly to plunge to her death within the next forty-eight hours.

# Chapter 19: She's Disappeared

Teresa Marie Rossetti was punching away at the keyboard, trying to sort an account online. Whether it was to do with her age, her Sicilian upbringing, or just the simple fact the drug trade had taken its toll on her patience with having to deal with idiot drug pushers, it didn't help that Holly never came back or even said goodbye, leaving her in the lurch. The bookkeeper never came back to give his notice, either. He just didn't come to work one morning.

Regardless of the reason, she wasn't happy with having 'access denied' come up on the screen when she tried to get into Vinnie's account. She had already made three attempts and was trying one more time, with the same result. She got off the chair so quickly in frustration that it almost toppled over, then stormed off to Dominic's office.

'Dominic,' she said in a raised voice as she entered his office. 'Do you know what is going on with Vinnie's account?'

'No, what do you mean?'

'I can't get access to the account anymore,' Teresa announced. 'I want to transfer the money as you asked me to.'

'Ring the bank and find out what is going on,' Dominic suggested. 'There was no sign this morning that there were any issues. Fleming mentioned no.'

'Fleming?'

'Yes, I convinced him to find out the details of the deposits and the balance of the account,' Dominic informed her.

'I'll ring the bank then,' she replied.

She left the office in a bit of a huff, firmly slamming the door closed behind her. The company hadn't planned for things to be late because sales of the product had slowed and the front of selling machinery had stalled for a couple of months. That was putting a strain on many areas of the business. The Chinese exporter had also emailed her, as the next shipment was already fifty percent complete and would call for an advance payment shortly.

She got to her desk and rang the bank.

'Hello, this is Mrs Rossetti,' she said when someone answered the phone. 'I would like to speak to the manager.'

'May I ask what it is a reference to?' the receptionist inquired.

'It is an account of mine,' she replied.

'What type of account would that be?'

'Just put me through to the manager. I'm not in the mood for your twenty-twenty questions at the moment, and I have more important things than being grilled over the phone!' Teresa replied, getting angry as well.

'I'll see if he's available,' the receptionist replied.

A moment later, the manager answered the phone.

'Mrs Rossetti, what can I do for you?'

'Inform me why my Sattorri's account comes up with 'access denied' when I try to log in?' she asked straight out.

'I'm sorry to inform you that a court order delivered to me early this morning has frozen some of your accounts,' he explained.

'What! Why did that happen?' Teresa asked, uncertain about what was happening.

'I cannot say why,' the manager replied. 'All I had was a court order, and I had to act on it immediately.'

'You said some accounts are on hold. Could you tell me how many accounts are inaccessible?'

The manager responded;
'I'm afraid I cannot reveal that information, Mrs Rossetti. I'm truly sorry that I can't help you any more than that.' Teresa slammed down the phone without even saying 'goodbye' to the manager. She was

thinking about the manager's attitude and evasiveness in answering her questions. There was a feeling in her gut that her worst fears were being realised. She got up and virtually ran to Dominic's office and flung open the door. Dominic almost jumped out of his seat as she burst in.

'The banks are freezing our accounts!'

'What!' exclaimed Dominic in surprise. 'What reason did they give?'

'It's a court order that was given to them this morning,' she replied. 'He said he couldn't tell me anymore or give any details. We are to ring the police if we want more information.'

'I might give Fleming a ring to see what he can find out,' Dominic suggested.

'What is going on, Dominic?' Teresa asked as her anger was giving way to fear. 'I don't understand anymore!'

'OK, ok,' Dominic replied, trying to reassure her. 'Like I said, I'll give Fleming a ring and get it sorted out.'

Teresa didn't say another word. With just a moment's glance at Dominic, she accepted his reassurance that everything would be fine. She then returned to her little office and sat down at her desk, not knowing what to do next. She would pray that Dominic could sort it out, and quickly.

Dominic rang Fleming as soon as Teresa left his office. The sudden change of events, along with Vinnie's account. Sure, unfortunately, he was dead, but was that a reason to stop the account so quickly, especially when there is a second person with credentials to use the account?

'Hello, this is Detective Fleming,' he said, answering the phone.

'Fleming, it's Dominic here. I need you to do me a favour, urgently.'

'What is it that is so urgent?' he replied.

Dominic told him he had investigated the Sattorri account that morning and that it was currently frozen.

'Have you rung the bank to find out why?'

'Yes, and all he could say was it was a court order, and he had to abide by it,' Dominic replied. 'If we want more information, we need to ring the police.'

'Did he mention the officer's name that brought the court order?' Fleming asked.

'No, he didn't, and I don't think Teresa would think to ask.'

'Okay, I'll see what I can find out and get back to you.' 'Do

it soon too,' Dominic implored him.

'I will.'

Dominic hung up the phone and tried to work out why someone had frozen the account so quickly, who had organised it, and what the real reason was. He always covered his tracks and left no evidence for the police to find a reason to act like they had this time. Teresa was right to become worried. He wondered whether Mario was aware of anything out of the ordinary and whether he had found Emily Spain yet. He dialled his phone number.

'Hello,' Mario answered.

'Mario, how have you progressed with looking into who shot Vinnie?'

'I spoke to some people and said it was a security guard who shot him accidentally,' Mario replied.

'How can you shoot someone accidentally?' Dominic replied. 'This is not a bloody joke!'

'It seems there are some Chinese guys involved in the shooting,' Mario said. 'The bullet that got Vinnie ricocheted off a steel structure.' 'Bullshit!' replied Dominic.

'I haven't found Emily either. She's disappeared.'

***

They parked the Leeman's Road Traffic Patrol car at the junction of Brand Hwy and Ocean Drive, hoping to entice Stromnikov to follow the Brand Hwy. The intention was to wait there until Stromnikov drove past and confirm that to the road patrol, following him from Dongara.

It was only a brief wait of about twenty minutes when Stromnikov's vehicle drove past the junction and down the Brand Hwy.

'The suspect just drove by, and down the Brand,' the officer reported.

'I'll radio Geraldton and let the detectives know,' was the reply from the Dongara patrol car.

'We'll begin diverting traffic down Ocean Drive.'

It seemed like the trap to catch Stromnikov was coming together. PolAir had made preparations and was ready to leave Geraldton at a moment's notice. As soon as Detectives Ralph and Matt received the information about Stromnikov, they headed off to the airport to board PolAir. It would take an hour to reach the pre-determined blockade a couple of kilometres north of Eneabba.

Stromnikov was to be arrested before he reached the bridge, which spanned a fifty-metre 'creek' rather than a river. It was just a 'overpass' construction crossing the creek. Once you crossed from the north side of the crossing, you could take the easterly road that would take you into farming country and hundreds of 'side' roads as well. Keeping on the highway was a better option management-wise.

A patrol car blocked the bridge over the creek on the north side and was well lit with flashing lights to encourage Stromnikov to stop as he approached. Another patrol car was south of the town and diverting traffic west towards Ocean Drive via Leeman Road. Everything was now in place to catch the fugitive, and now, the waiting game.

PolAir had left Geraldton with Ralph and Matt. Their ETA was fifty minutes to the blockade. The plan was to land on the west side of the highway and behind the old train tracks. There was a two-metre-high mound of ballast that would screen them from the activity on the road. Matt had a rifle with him should it be required to capture Stromnikov during the blockade.

PolAir was fifteen minutes out when one of the patrol cars radioed the other car.

'We have the vehicle in sight,' was the report, 'and it's slowing down.' This was the Eneabba patrol car 2.

'Confirming we are gaining on the suspect's vehicle,' the Dongara car one replied.

Ralph's pulse was about to speed up. He was certain that they would apprehend Stromnikov shortly.

'For communication, Dongara is Group One and Eneabba is Group Two,' Ralph advised. Both groups responded with 'affirmative.' The next lot of radio chatter was a concern for Ralph and Matt.

'Shots fired! Repeat, rifle fired!'

'He's leaning up against the rear wheel and is loading a rifle,' was the response from Dongara's Group One.

'How long before we land?' Matt asked the pilot through the intercom.

'Less than ten minutes. Look down there,' the pilot replied.

Ralph and Matt saw the two patrol cars and maybe Stromnikov's vehicle parked at the side of the road. There was some movement near the rear of the vehicle, as the Dongara officers reported, but they couldn't see exactly what was happening. Ralph then saw someone draw up the rifle and observed the weapon being fired. PolAir was descending at that moment and was behind the rail line mound. The radio revealed what had happened.

'Officer down!' was the next transmission from Group One.

Ralph and Matt stared at each other. This guy would not give up easily, if at all.

'The officer is okay. He's wearing a jacket.'

Ralph sighed with relief.

PolAir landed, and both detectives virtually jumped out onto the ground. Both made their way to the rail line mound and peered over the top towards the vehicle where the fugitive sat. He was on the other side of the vehicle, at the rear from Ralph and Matt's position.

Ralph grabbed his handheld two-way and spoke into it.

'This is Senior Detective Ralph,' he introduced. 'What is the current status of the fugitive?'

'Our man is okay but has a large bruise on his chest. The fugitive has a handgun and a rifle. We have returned no fire at this stage.' Just then, more shots rang out, this time from a handgun.

'We are being fired upon,' the Eneabba officers reported.

'Reposition yourselves if needed and return fire,' Ralph ordered. 'Make sure the Dongara guys aren't in your line of fire.'

'Confirming we are taking the precautions.'

'Good, proceed with your action.'

A rifle shot rang out, but this time not from Stromnikov.

'I think someone hit him,' Matt reported as he looked through his binoculars. He could see under the vehicle, and it appeared as if the fugitive's right hand had completely loosened the grip on the handgun. 'Group One, how is your man who was shot?' Ralph asked.

'All appears good, Detective. I think he'll have a nice bruise, though.'

'Very good,' Ralph replied. 'I'll get you to move towards the vehicle. We believe the fugitive may have suffered fatal wounds. Make sure you keep the vehicle between him and you as you approach. Matt and I will do likewise from our position.'

'Understood,' was Group One's reply.

'Group Two, maintain a keen eye and cover our approach,' Ralph requested.

'Will do, Detective,' they replied.

Ralph and Matt broke their cover and advanced toward Stromnikov's vehicle with handguns raised. Group One officers were also advancing and would reach the vehicle first. Two of the officers stopped a short distance away while the other two continued to the vehicle. All had their weapons at the ready.

The first officer slowly walked around the vehicle from the rear to get a full view of Stromnikov. He was motionless and slightly slumped forward, with his chin almost resting on his chest. The copious amount of blood trickling down his left leg had soaked through his jeans and the bottom half of his shirt. He was wearing Asics, and these also had blood on them. He had bled out after being shot with the rifle by the Eneabba officer.

'Clear!' the officer yelled as he moved around the fugitive and kicked away the handgun. All officers converged on the scene. Ralph took control.

'Let's process the body when it's back in Geraldton,' Ralph requested. 'Is there an ambulance available?'

'Yes, Eneabba has one standing by,' one of the Group Two officers replied.

'Let's get him off for a full examination. I want DNA and fingerprints recorded.'

'I'll organise that now,' volunteered the officer.

The ambulance arrived quickly, almost as if it was waiting up the road for the drama to end.

After securing Stromnikov's body, the ambulance returned to Dongara.

Senior Detective Ralph asked the senior officer from Dongara to organise having Stromnikov's vehicle taken to Geraldton and impounded for forensics to inspect. Ralph and Matt then returned to the PolAir helicopter to head back to Geraldton. He asked the officers to have the area cleaned up as best they could and to get traffic flowing again. Stromnikov's vehicle was the top priority.

Once the ambulance arrived with the body, the staff processed it almost immediately. It wasn't until the next day that Ralph and Matt received the report they had requested. Ralph asked Matt to enter the details into the main national system, along with the DNA and fingerprints. Once Matt had entered the last pieces of information, the system began to 'light up' with alerts and warnings, all in the Sydney area.

*** 

The police in Sydney, particularly in Parramatta, were a little shocked to see new information entered the system from the other side of the country and to have alerts trigger so quickly. Reports were being printed off, and detectives gathered around to see what the fuss was about.

'Well, I'll be fucked!' Senior Detective Parker exclaimed. 'We have the person's ID from the DNA found at our recent crime scenes.'

Parker flicked through the paperwork, a wry smile forming on his face.

'Gentlemen,' he began. 'We have just received reports from the boys in WA about the key evidence to start warrants on the Rossetti operation. They have identified the DNA of Stromnikov, a hitman for the Rossettis, at the murder scene of the lawyer. Also, uniformed officers used DNA evidence to confirm the location from which they believe the shot that killed the private investigator was fired.'

There was silence in the room as Parker read out the information. Even Superintendent Clive Warren was leaning against the door as Parker continued. They had matched fingerprints from a couple of other crime scenes they had been working on, with little result until now.

'The only problem is the suspect, unfortunately, met his demise in a shootout with the Geraldton police,' Parker informed them. 'But it gives us reason to collect more evidence from Dominic Rossetti, like his DNA and fingerprints, and his son, Roberto.'

'Detective Parker,' the Superintendent interjected, 'when you've finished your briefing, I would like to see you in my office.' 'As you wish, Sir,' Parker replied.

'So, if you don't have any important pending cases,' Parker continued, 'let's go through these reports and come up with a plan to dismantle this mob completely. You can start the process.'

Parker left and headed for the Superintendent's office. He did not know why he wanted to see him. He knocked on the door.

'Ah, Parker,' the Superintendent greeted him. 'Come in and sit down. Close the door behind you.'

Parker closed the door and took a seat. The Superintendent was looking over some paperwork in front of him.

'This is a revelation, having this info sent through from the WA Police,' he started.

'Yes,' Parker agreed. 'Absolutely.'

'Do you know the events that led up to the capture of this info?'

'Not yet, Sir, but I was planning on ringing Geraldton to find out more details,' Parker suggested.

'Good, make the call and keep me informed,' Warren requested. 'If we issue warrants, we need to act quickly.'

'Yes, definitely,' Parker agreed. 'I'll make the call.'

He got up, left Warren's office, and returned to his own. He rang the WA Police, and after several minutes could get through to the Geraldton police and speak to Senior Detective Ralph. Parker and

Ralph spoke on the phone for over half an hour. Ralph gave Parker all the relevant information and also mentioned that the case notes would be available online within the next twenty-four hours on the police net.

Ralph wasn't surprised that Stromnikov's DNA and fingerprints had caused an intriguing situation. They had found his fingerprints, which tied him to several crime scenes in the east. The saga of the Rossetti family was soon to reach a climactic conclusion. The wheels were definitely in motion.

# Chapter 20: Wrong Side of the Law

Joanne was planning on returning to Sydney as soon as possible and had finally booked a flight online out of Perth. She packed her bags and was ready to go. Attending to unfinished business in Sydney was her priority. She wanted to see Steph first before leaving, so she strolled into the Regional Hospital and asked the nurse on duty at reception where she could find Steph.

'Visiting hours are nearly over,' Joanne was told. 'Are you a relative?'

'Yes, she's my partner,' Joanne replied sternly.

Her response took the receptionist aback. 'She is in Ward G, Room 11,' she said.

Joanne turned in the direction the receptionist was pointing and headed down the corridor.

'Now wasn't that easy?' she muttered to herself as she looked for Steph's room.

Joanne found the room and walked in. It was a three-bed ward, and she recognised Steph at the far end, sitting up and reading a book. Steph looked up as Joanne approached the bed.

Steph recognised her as the woman who had nearly bumped into her when she was on her way to see Holly at the Ocean Centre. She also remembered her quick departure in the red BMW.

'Hi Stephanie, I'm Joanne,' she said, introducing herself.

'You're Holly's best friend,' Steph quickly replied.

'I would like to think of us as being partners,' Joanne responded.

'Sure, I remember Holly mentioning you frequently during our phone calls,' Steph said. 'She was very fond of you, and a friend of mine, if I can put it like that.'

'Agreed. You could say we had a very close relationship, one we both cherished,' Joanne replied.

'I should thank you for looking after her like you did while in Sydney,' Steph said. 'She needed some looking after.'

'I have to admit that we got on well once she got away from her so-called boyfriend, Roberto,' Joanne complained. 'He bashed her on a couple of occasions. I wanted to do the same to him so badly that, hopefully, I may get my chance.'

'It never crossed my mind that things weren't going so well. Holly never mentioned it,' Steph said.

'I encouraged her to stand up for herself. I believe she did,' Joanne replied, 'much to her boyfriend's surprise.' 'Is that right?' Steph asked.

'Yeah, a kick in the balls works wonders,' Joanne said. 'Definitely an attention-getter.'

'You can say that again,' Steph replied with a smirk.

'I have something to tell you about what happened with this hit-and run,' Joanne began. 'I think you were mistaken for me.'

Steph looked a little perplexed but began thinking along the same lines. She had not recognised the man and had only had a brief glimpse of him. It had all happened so quickly.

'We both have blonde hair, a similar build, and I think he mistook you for me,' Joanne opined. 'He possibly knew that Holly had a 'blonde' companion, and marked her as well.'

'You think he was here to kill both you and Holly?' Steph asked, somewhat concerned.

'Yes, I do, and I'm going to set things right.'

'How are you going to do that?' Steph asked.

'I'll go back to Sydney and sort things out there,' Joanne replied.

'Are you going to come back?' Steph asked.

'Yes,' she replied. 'I like what I've seen of the place so far. Put aside Holly's mishap and add to that I found someone I like. I'll be back. You and I should get along okay as well.'

Steph smiled. If anything, she was friends with someone who had taken care of Holly for a time and pried her away from the mess with Roberto. Joanne would be good company as well in the future.

'So, when are you planning on leaving?' Steph asked.

'I'll drive to Perth after Holly's funeral tomorrow,' she replied. 'I've got a midnight flight booked to Sydney already.'

'Is that all that's taking you back to Sydney?'

'I have a flat there I want to check, plus there's a loose end I want to tidy up,' Joanne replied, giving Steph the impression that the loose end wasn't a topic for discussion.

'Sounds sinister,' Steph remarked.

'It could be, but I'll need to play it safe and with caution,' Joanne said, a wry smile on her face. She had worked out a plan, and it was going to be set into motion as soon as she touched down in Sydney. Steph noticed her smile and surmised that she wasn't to be messed with or you would face the consequences.

'I'll be off and let you rest,' Joanne finally said.

'It's good of you to call in and see me,' Steph replied. 'All the best for your trip to Sydney.'

'Thank you. See you in about a week's time, if not sooner.'

With that, Joanne left and headed to the car park. Steph seemed a good sort, and she now understood why Holly had been so determined to see her again. The unfortunate thing was, it never happened. Other influences had seen to that.

Joanne was in revenge 'mode' and was going to attend to Roberto for what he did to Holly. She was also sure he had ordered the hit on Holly and herself, and she would not lie down for anyone. Regardless of her plans, she wasn't aware of what was unfolding in Sydney at the moment.

***

It would have been a tedious trip driving to Perth. Hence, she had booked a plane flight. 11:45 pm wasn't a way to spend a full day on her feet at the airport. She had trouble sleeping on a plane, but this time it was manageable. Ten minutes into the onboard movie, she dozed off. Joanne woke when she heard the refreshment trolley being wheeled up the aisle. Some passengers were awake and opted for tea or coffee, a couple of biscuits or fruit cake. Joanne chose coffee and cake. Holly was still on her mind. She missed her so much.

It didn't seem too long before they were descending towards Sydney. By the time passengers disembarked and collected their baggage, it would be about 6:00 am daylight saving time. Joanne planned on catching a taxi to her flat and seeing how the painting in one room had turned out. Her tenants were on their honeymoon and had no objections to the room being painted in their absence.

Joanne got to her flat and had a quick look around. Everything seemed fine, and there was a hint of fresh paint in the air. The painters had completed the job she organised before leaving for WA. She took out her mobile phone and speed-dialled a number. It rang out. She tried another number, and someone answered after about four rings.

'Colin, this is Joanne,' she announced. 'How are you?'

'Well, well. Look what the cat dragged in,' came the reply.

'You're still a dick, by the sounds of it,' Joanne responded with a laugh.

Both had a chuckle at each other's comments.

'It's good to hear from you,' Colin said more cordially.

'It's been a while, hasn't it?' Joanne replied.

'I heard you left town. Was that true?' Colin inquired.

'Yes, I did, but I've come back to tie up a couple of loose ends.'

'I'm guessing you want my help,' Colin pre-empted.

'Yes,' Joanne replied. 'I need something that is high velocity and accurate.'

'I think we need to talk face to face, not over the phone,' Colin suggested. 'Say in an hour's time. You know where?'

'Okay, I'll be there.'

Joanne ended the call. She had to organise a hire car so she could get around at her leisure and not depend on taxis. There was a car-hire place a couple of blocks away. Joanne picked a compact car, one that would serve her needs. As soon as she got the car, she headed to the other side of town to a disused industrial estate that still had some warehouse facilities available. Colin was at the very end of a long line of buildings, in a warehouse that was rundown and didn't attract attention.

An access door was partway open, just enough for a vehicle to drive in. As Joanne drove in, she noticed some activity at the far end of the warehouse. She approached cautiously and then spotted Colin coming out of an office-type donger. Two other men were milling around, probably keeping a watch on proceedings. Joanne parked the car and got out.

'Well, my dear, you are a sight for sore eyes,' Colin greeted. 'How long has it been?'

'Two or more years, at a rough guess,' Joanne replied.

'It's been too long between drinks, babe—far too long.'

'We didn't part on amicable terms back then,' Joanne said. 'Enough with the 'babe' stuff.'

'Same old Joanne. I loved that about you. No bullshit, straight to the point. And it's water under the bridge. It is what it is,' Colin replied nonchalantly.

'Yes, that's how I see it as well,' Joanne agreed.

'So, about that phone conversation we had. It sounds like you have an operation to perform?'

'Yes, you could say that,' Joanne replied. 'It's called unfinished business, or tying up loose ends. It's highly illegal.'

'Can I ask who the intended target is?'

'Yes, someone who deals in drugs and helped to kill my close friend,' Joanne said.

'I know some people who fit that description,' Colin replied. 'And I have what you need.'

'I knew all along you could help, and you've just confirmed my assumption.'

'Come over here and cast your eyes upon this selection,' Colin encouraged.

Joanne followed Colin to the back of the car's boot. There were three rifles on the floor of the boot, wrapped in cotton sheets. Colin unwrapped all three and laid them side by side.

'There you go. It's your choice,' Colin said. 'There's a Remington 03, a Sako TRG-42 and an Accuracy International AX.'

Joanne looked at the three carefully, and after a few minutes, made her choice.

'I'll take the AX and ten rounds,' Joanne said. 'How much to hire it?'

'You've got some serious firepower there,' Colin observed. 'Who's the target?'

'Roberto Rossetti.'

'Oh shit, really?' Colin queried. 'The Rossettis are serious drug dealers. How did you get involved with them?' 'I didn't. My friend did, and now she's dead.'

'You think this guy had something to do with it?'

'I don't think. I fucking know it.'

'Okay then,' Colin said, realising Joanne had a grudge to sort out. 'Shooting is extreme.'

'Maybe, but very effective,' Joanne replied in a stern voice. 'How much for the AX?'

'Seven hundred dollars, and I'll give two hundred back on its safe return. When are you planning on carrying out the deed?' Colin asked.

'I'm not sure at this stage. I need to follow his movements, then pick a prime position.'

'Let me help if you like. There are contacts who can soon find out the lay of the land,' Colin suggested.

'That's a kind offer. I'll give it some thought,' Joanne replied.

'Joanne, we go back a bit, and we had a reasonably good working relationship when you first started security,' Colin said. 'I'd even say that as a team, we were way above the rest.'

'You really think we made such a good team?'

'I can't forget the incident we had with those car thieves selling off parts. You had my back that night. If it weren't for you, I'd probably have died.'

'I wouldn't put such a dramatic spin on it,' Joanne replied. 'We were both lucky that night.'

'Yeah, but you nailed the guy who had a bead on me first,' Colin reminded her. 'Luck had nothing to do with it, just clear thinking and reacting positively.'

'You make it sound like it was easy that night,' Joanne opined.

'No, it wasn't, but we got through it unscathed,' Colin said. 'And thanks to you.'

'We had some angst occasionally. I have to admit that,' Joanne agreed.

'Let me see what I can find out about this Roberto fellow and work on a plan. I'll even spot you. It's the least I can do for you, Joanne,' Colin offered.

Joanne considered Colin's offer and then relented. She knew he was right. Any help in seeing this through would be a blessing. It could even make things move faster, allowing her to return to WA sooner rather than later.

'Okay, agreed. I'll wait until I hear from you,' Joanne finally said. 'Keep the rifle until we're ready.'

'Okay, you've got it,' Colin said. 'I'll let you know what's going on as soon as I find out.'

It seemed like a done deal. Joanne pulled out a wad of cash and counted seven hundred into an envelope. She handed it over. Colin quickly counted it and put it in his pocket. He closed the boot of the car and shook Joanne's hand.

'Great to be working together again, even if it is on the wrong side of the law.'

Joanne grinned and got into her car. Colin signalled to his 'guards'. Once all was clear, he joined her in his car. Joanne drove off, followed by Colin, who wasn't far behind. She headed back into the city to find somewhere to stay. She couldn't stay at the warehouse, and the flat had been leased to the honeymoon couple starting today, so that wouldn't do.

Joanne found a hotel close to her flat, booking in for four nights. She hoped this would give her enough time to tie up the loose ends she had to deal with. If Colin comes through, it should work out well.

***

Ashcroft was running a little late for work that morning, but he had some news regarding the Rossettis that he had just learned from a reliable source. He was only about ten minutes late and highly motivated, hoping to make an arrest today. As he entered the conference room, he was surprised to see Parker, a couple of junior detectives, and the Superintendent already seated, staring at the display board.

The pictures on the board featured Dominic Rossetti and Roberto Rossetti front and centre, surrounded by Vinnie, Mario, and Teresa.

On one side of the display were pictures of Tammy O'Lachlin, Milton Clark, Holly Jamieson, and Emily Spain. Just this morning, they had added Holly's picture to the board.

'Morning, Ashcroft,' Parker acknowledged sarcastically. 'So glad you could join us.'

'Sorry for being late, Sir, but a reliable source of mine has given me some information about some of these people,' Ashcroft began.

'Oh? And what info is that?' Parker asked.

'Well, first we guessed the Chinese are trying to take over the drug trade here by eliminating small-time pushers, then the bigger players like the Rossettis.'

'Yes, we are aware of the conflict that is occurring at present and the aim of it all,' the Superintendent interjected.

Ashcroft pointed at Vinnie's photo. 'The Chinese have set up a warehouse near the place where this guy was shot. It's also rumoured that a Shanghai-based cartel is behind it, and maybe they're trying to stop the supply from Beijing to the Rossettis here.'

'Well, that would throw a spanner in the works,' Parker observed.

'The bit that concerns me is it looks like we're now facing two gangs with the same intent,' the Superintendent said. 'You say there's a warehouse already set up by the Chinese?'

'Yes, that's right, and apparently we're supposed to know about it already,' Ashcroft said.

'What makes you say that?' Parker asked.

Ashcroft replied that someone had seen Detective Mitch Fleming enter the warehouse with one or two Chinese involved in the operation.

'So they assume we are aware of the operation and the contents of the warehouse,' Ashcroft suggested.

'I think it's time to give all of this a big push. I'll start with the magistrate to issue search warrants,' the Superintendent said. 'We'll tackle the warehouse first, then see if we have reason to serve a search warrant for the Rossettis. Also, we need to find out what the Chinese are really up to. One step at a time, people, and make it count.'

The Superintendent left the room and returned to his office. He immediately got on the phone and rang a magistrate to sign a search warrant for the warehouse. Time was crucial. Once word got out, the police were moving against the drug suppliers. Many would run for cover, making it difficult to bring them out of hiding.

The Superintendent completed the signing of the search warrants, and they were ready to be executed. He then called Parker and Ashcroft.

'Parker and Ashcroft, you can go by the courthouse and pick up the search warrants,' he ordered. 'Get a uniform to provide backup while you execute them. The warrants cover the warehouse, inside buildings, vehicles, sheds, the lot!'

'Very well, Sir,' Parker replied. 'Sounds terrific.'

Both Parker and Ashcroft picked up their coats and headed for the door without a word. At last, something was happening. The detectives had already informed the uniformed police about the raid and were prepared to go to the midday warehouse raid with them.

The police collected the warrants, and three police cars headed to the warehouse. They arrived amid a furore emanating from inside. The police entered, weapons drawn, and shouted in unison:

'Police! Get on the floor now!'

'I want to see your hands stretched out in front of you, now!' Parker yelled.

One man thought he could make a run for it. Unfortunately, he ran straight into a burly police officer, who sat him on his arse. The officer had his weapon drawn and pointed at the runner. 'Don't even breathe if you want to stay alive.'

The man saw that his chance of escape had been forcefully closed and had no choice but to comply. They handcuffed him before he rejoined his colleagues, all facing a wall.

'Let the search begin,' Parker ordered. 'You two officers keep an eye on these four.'

The warehouse had several crates stacked at the far end. A small office and a storage room were off to one side, with a large walk-in freezer at the end. The two officers inside the office were looking over some paperwork on the desk and in the drawers.

The storage room had a wardrobe and a mattress on the floor. Someone had left women's clothing scattered to one side. There was little else apart from a bookshelf with a couple of books haphazardly placed. The freezer, however, was another story.

'Detective Ashcroft, I found something!'

Ashcroft was there in a flash and recoiled at what he saw. The officer had opened the large walk-in freezer and stumbled back once he realised what was inside.

'Oh, my God!' he exclaimed.

Propped up in the corner of the freezer behind some carefully placed crates was the corpse of a woman, frozen solid and scantily clad.

Parker, who had been questioning one of the Chinese men who spoke reasonable English, saw the contents for himself.

'I was just about to call you over,' Ashcroft said. 'Look in here, behind these crates.'

Parker approached slowly and then stopped dead when he too realised a woman was sitting upright behind the crates. She had clearly been there for some time, with ice thick over much of her body. The next challenge was to identify her and determine how long she had been in the freezer.

Parker returned to the man he had been interviewing.

'Do you know anything about this?' Parker asked.

'I don't know what you're talking about,' the man replied.

'You mean you use this warehouse and know nothing about the dead girl in there?'

'We were told to stay away from that part of the warehouse by one of your men. It was of no concern to us,' he said.

'Which one of my men was that?'

'Fleming. He told us all to stay away from there.'

The mention of Fleming surprised Parker, especially regarding the freezer and its contents. This raid had far-reaching consequences.

They opened some crates and discovered that they contained coffee beans. But upon opening the beans, however, were plastic bags containing white powder. So far, six out of ten crates had been opened. Another dozen remained. One crate contained bags of pills and one bag of 'ice' crystal meth.

Ashcroft joined Parker as he interviewed the Chinese man. Both looked at each other in disbelief at the find and at the allegation involving Detective Mitchell Fleming. They weren't making progress with the other Chinese men, who supposedly had a language barrier. That was a deliberate ploy to hamper the police.

'Arrest this lot and get them down to the station,' Parker finally ordered.

They bundled the men into a couple of paddy vans and took them away. They found more powder and pills. It was a major haul, estimated to be worth millions on the street. The Chinese were serious about launching a major drug distribution ring. Parker was concerned there were more than just these four involved.

'Ashcroft, get hold of forensics and have them come down here straight away. Examine the freezer's contents,' Parker requested. 'Also, have the drug squad come down and start sorting this lot out.'

Ashcroft made the calls, and both units confirmed they were on their way. Parker wondered who the woman in the freezer was, why she was there, if someone had killed her elsewhere, and whether Mitch Fleming might be involved.

It didn't take long for the two crews to arrive. Forensics had to wait for the freezer to thaw enough to move the corpse. The drug squad had their work cut out, grappling with the sheer quantity of drugs discovered, surpassing eight million dollars, possibly ten.

'There's something that bothers me,' Ashcroft said. 'Where is the BMW these guys had, and who owns it?'

'That's a good question, and one we hope to solve,' Parker agreed. 'Let's go back to the station and check the progress of the interviews. It took the forensics and drug squads most of the night to sort this lot out. I'll ask the Superintendent if he's in favour of issuing an arrest warrant for Fleming.'

'Do you think he will?'

'Multiple individuals have mentioned Fleming several times, so we must proceed regardless of the outcome.'

Parker and Ashcroft returned to the station just as the Superintendent was leaving for the day. Parker mentioned he had the warrant for Fleming and would look into it first thing in the morning. With the information they had about Fleming, they could issue a warrant based on that alone. The Superintendent bid both Parker and Ashcroft goodnight and said he looked forward to tomorrow being an eventful day.

***

The day started in a panic. When Parker arrived at work the next morning, Ashcroft was talking to the Superintendent.

'Ah, Parker,' the Super said as he spotted him. 'We've had a fatal shooting in the early hours of this morning.' 'Did anyone try to call me?' Parker asked.

'No,' the Super replied. 'There wouldn't be much accomplished by calling you in when someone already on duty could handle it, and you've already worked quite a few hours recently.' 'Who was the victim?' Parker asked.

'Three victims,' Ashcroft clarified. 'Fleming, and one of the Rossetti gang members, Mario Sandrini, and his wife, Antonia.'

'Oh, my God!' exclaimed Parker. 'Do we have any idea who the shooter was?'

'It's thought there were three gunmen, based on the number of spent cases at the scene,' Ashcroft replied. 'We think they used a Chinese AK-47.'

'That is some serious firepower for an execution like this,' Parker suggested. 'Are there any witnesses to the shooting?'

'Yes, there was. What we have been able to establish so far is that the three victims had just left a nightclub. A dark-coloured BMW pulled up, and three men got out and mowed them down,' the Super replied.

'The BMW that went missing from yesterday's warehouse raid,' Ashcroft added.

'We may have to concentrate on the Chinese rather than the Rossettis,' Parker said with a smirk. 'At this rate, there won't be any Rossettis left to arrest.'

'Unfortunately, that isn't what we are trying to achieve,' the Super replied.

'Yes,' Parker agreed, 'you are correct, and the Rossettis take priority.'

'I wonder why Fleming was with them,' Ashcroft speculated. 'Maybe he was playing the Chinese off against the Rossettis, and the Chinese found out.'

'That could well be, but confirming it may not be so easy,' Parker suggested.

'Whatever the outcome, both of you keep investigating the Rossettis,' the Super ordered. 'We'll tackle the Chinese once we gather more information about them.'

'Very good, Sir,' Parker responded, and he and Ashcroft headed to his office. 'I'll find out how the interviews are going, and you can try to find the whereabouts of Roberto Rossetti.'

'Okay, I'll get on it straight away,' Ashcroft replied.

After several phone calls to his contacts, Ashcroft had drawn a blank. It was as if Roberto had gone into hiding after the Mario shooting. It was obvious he would lie low. He had only a couple more informants to contact, but these were a long shot, and he had little faith in finding any useful information from them. As predicted, Roberto Rossetti would have to surface sometime.

# Chapter 21: Goodbye, Arsehole!

Joanne awoke early, lying in bed for a moment, contemplating how the day might unfold. She thought about what she was trying to do in Sydney, besides shooting Roberto, and why. Would his involvement in Holly's death be sufficient reason to kill him? She was only surmising that he had a hand in it. Maybe it was his father who ordered the hit. She had received information that the police had cornered the killer and fatally shot him, the Russian she had seen with Roberto that night, she met Holly in the nightclub.

When Joanne flicked on the TV, the 7:00 am news showed the gunning down of three people outside a nightclub. She sat up in surprise and immediately thought of Roberto. Would this make it harder to find him? The Rossettis would reel from the shooting and probably consider going into hiding themselves.

After the news bulletin finished, she got dressed and thought about having breakfast. Bacon and eggs would start the day off nicely, especially when someone else was doing the cooking and cleaning up afterwards. As she finished her coffee, Joanne wondered if she would hear from Colin today. She didn't want to be sitting in a motel room for the next three days twiddling her thumbs.

No sooner had she finished her breakfast and was leaving the dining room when her phone rang. It was Colin.

'Morning, sweetheart,' Colin began. 'Did you have a good night's sleep?'

'I did, actually. Why do you ask?'

'We have a midnight rendezvous with your proposed target at the Mariner,' Colin replied.

'What are you implying?' Joanne quizzed.

'It appears business as usual for them,' Colin said. 'Apparently, there is a scheduled pickup out at sea that they can't afford to miss.'

'How do you know this info is correct?' Joanne asked.

'Let's meet at my place and I'll give you the details, rather than over the phone,' Colin suggested.

'Brilliant idea. I'll be there in the next half hour.'

Joanne got into her car, heading out to the place where they had met yesterday at the warehouse. Joanne knew Colin would come through, and his quickness in getting a result impressed her. Hopefully, there would be enough time to test-fire the rifle before actually attempting to assassinate someone. They had all day. When she arrived at the warehouse, Colin was already there.

'Well, isn't it a lovely day to plan an adventure?' Colin opined.

'What are you talking about?' Joanne queried, caution creeping into her tone.

'Come inside. I've got more to tell you,' Colin requested.

'Have you heard that someone shot one of the Rossettis' principal man last night, along with his wife and Detective Fleming?'

'Oh! Really?' Joanne replied in surprise. 'Where was this?'

'In front of a nightclub. That's why I said, 'It's business as usual,'' Colin repeated. 'My sources say that Roberto will head out from the Mariner in his cat just after midnight to pick up a consignment. They cannot afford to miss this, as it is the largest yet.'

'If he didn't pick it up, what would happen to it?' Joanne asked.

'Someone may retrieve it, or it will wash up on the beach somewhere,' Colin surmised.

'I want to do this before the pickup, not after,' Joanne said.

'Is there any reason you're thinking like that?'

'I don't want to compromise the opportunity to shoot him,' Joanne replied. 'He may pull into another mariner or rendezvous with someone up the coast.'

'That could well be, especially with the shooting and so on. The police will be all over them,' Colin surmised.

'So, what have you found out about the location?'

Colin gave Joanne the information that the boat was moored securely at the Manly Mariner, in the waters of Port Jackson.

'The car park has a kiosk at one end and will be closed. There are some small shrubs along the fence facing the Mariner, which will give us some cover.'

'Did you say 'us'?' Joanne queried.

'Yes, remember I'm spotting for you,' Colin insisted. 'That way, I get to see Roberto Rossetti finally taken down, and most importantly, if the police are aware of his movements, they're watching as well.'

'I had planned to do this on my own. Get no one else involved,' Joanne defended.

'Considering the danger of getting caught, I think my proposal is valid,' Colin insisted. 'Plus, there could be a bonus. The Chinese may get blamed for the shooting in light of what happened early this morning.'

Joanne thought for a while and could see the logic in what Colin implied. She also knew she was venturing into dangerous territory. Getting caught was something she wanted to avoid at all costs. Maybe Colin was right again. A spotter was an option.

'So, what's the plan now?' Joanne asked tentatively.

'I've booked the Hornsby rifle range for 2:00 pm. A member of the club will oversee our practice shooting from five hundred metres,' Colin informed her.

'Using this rifle?' Joanne queried. 'This isn't a 'standard' rifle for target shooting.'

'Yes, I know, and I've told him it's a 'test' weapon and police sanctioned.'

'You think he'll let me use this rifle on the range?' Joanne asked, somewhat bemused that Colin had organised it.

'Yes, and he's a friend as well,' Colin replied, reassuring her. 'As long as we play by the rules, no one will be any the wiser.'

'Right, that sounds good to me,' Joanne replied, agreeing.

'Good, I'll see you at the range at a quarter to two.'

Joanne felt a little uneasy as she left Colin at the warehouse. His arranging the rifle, offering to be her spotter, and now having an arrangement to use a rifle range made her feel like she wasn't in full control. After all, she wanted to kill Roberto; she had to organise a rifle for the job, and she had to find a suitable location. The Mariner wasn't her first choice, but it made sense to use it and not a location with witnesses abounding.

She sat back in her motel room and read a book, something she hadn't done for quite some time. The rifle range at Hornsby was a good twenty to thirty-minute drive for her. While she continued reading, a loud crash of someone emptying a bin outside suddenly startled her. She looked at her watch. It was five past one. She had dozed off to sleep.

Joanne bounced out of bed, splashed her face with water in the bathroom, brushed her teeth, then grabbed her car keys. She took one last look around to make sure she had everything, room keys included, before leaving. She then got into her hire car and drove off towards the northern part of Sydney.

Joanne arrived at the rifle range just as Colin got out of his car and opened the boot. He grabbed the gun bag that held the AX, along with a packet of bullets.

'Brilliant timing. I just got here myself,' Colin announced. 'Let's sign in.'

Both went inside and signed the register. Someone was waiting for them. He approached Colin, greeting him.

'Hey Josh, how are you?' Colin greeted him, shaking his hand. 'This is

Joanne, who will shoot a couple of shots with this rifle.'

'Hi Joanne, pleased to meet you,' Josh replied, also shaking her hand. 'Okay, let's set you up. We'll use target two on the five-hundred-metre range over there.'

They followed Josh out onto the range. Joanne was feeling butterflies, and she wasn't comfortable with that. Nevertheless, she had made a commitment to herself, for Holly's sake and her own. There was no turning back now.

'You said you wanted to try the three-hundred-metre distance first?' Josh asked Colin.

'Yes,' Colin confirmed. 'We'll probably need to shoot only about half a dozen rounds to confirm its accuracy.'

'Okay, I'll leave you to it,' Josh replied. 'I'll be back at the next mount sorting out some communication wiring.'

Colin unzipped the gun bag and handed the contents to Joanne. She quickly inserted the breechblock, set up a sandbag to rest on, and then laid out six rounds. Colin set up the monocular, advising Joanne he would confirm the drop of the shot.

Both were ready, and Joanne loaded the first round. She wriggled a bit and got comfortable. She then squeezed the trigger. There was a loud *crack* as the rifle discharged the round. The rifle recoiled into Joanne's shoulder, which shook her a bit at first. Compared with her experiences, its responsiveness was unexpected. Mind you, it is a high-powered sniper rifle.

'That shot hit to the right and low by about fifty millimetres,' Colin said.

Joanne adjusted the ratchet screws on the scope, one for up and the other to move the gun to the left. She reloaded the rifle and squeezed off another round. This time she was ready for the recoil, and she felt a sensation rush through her body. She found the power of the AX amazing, and she believed she could easily orgasm at the fourth shot.

'Height's good, but you need to go left a bit more by about fifteen millimetres,' Colin advised.

Joanne readjusted the scope and reloaded the rifle with the third round. She squeezed off the round without effort. The reaction of the rifle and its power exhilarated her, something she had not experienced with other rifles before today. She was looking forward to the fourth shot.

'Same height but still about ten millimetres too far right,' Colin again advised. 'There's a slight crosswind from left to right, so if you get the shot on the edge of the bullseye, that would be perfect.'

Joanne adjusted and loaded the fourth round. This time, it did exactly what Colin had hoped for. It hit the target close to the edge of the centre ring.

'We hope there's no crosswind tonight, so leaving the rifle set like it is now will probably allow it to hit the centre of the gained target tonight,' Colin opined.

Joanne didn't reply. She loaded the last two rounds and squeezed them off. Colin was impressed.

'They hit a little closer to the centre than the last round. Nice shooting.'

'I have to confirm that,' Josh's voice came from behind them. 'Is that an AX sniper rifle?'

'Yes, it is,' Colin confirmed.

'What do you plan on using that for?' Josh asked.

'We'll use it for pig shooting, among other things,' Joanne replied.

They said nothing else. Josh looked a bit bemused by Joanne's accuracy with the rifle, which was now back in its bag and out of sight. All three then headed back to the club rooms, where Colin thanked Josh and they said their goodbyes. Colin and Joanne then left, returning to their vehicles.

'How do you think it went?' Colin asked once the rifle was back in the boot of his car.

'I'll tell you tonight after I've dispatched the target,' Joanne replied. 'The kiosk staff are all gone by ten-thirty, so be there just before eleven,' Colin suggested.

'Okay, I'll see you there around eleven tonight.'

***

Joanne arrived at the Mariner as arranged. Colin was already there, walking around and surveying the area. He came over to her car as she opened the door.

'Well, at least it appears all quiet,' he informed her. 'I'll set up the rifle for you and choose a spot to shoot from.'

Joanne got out and walked past the kiosk to a small hedgerow some twenty metres from the shopfront. She looked out toward the pens where all the boats were moored. Colin came and stood beside her, pointing at the large catamaran moored about a hundred metres from where they were standing.

'That's Roberto's Cat over there,' Colin pointed out. 'He's not here yet.'

Joanne looked for a suitable spot with cover on both sides and with a clear view towards the front, overlooking the bay.

'The Cat will travel along the far side of the groyne and then head into the bay once it is clear,' Colin pointed out. 'I think this is a suitable spot for you.'

Colin unzipped the bag, and Joanne began setting up the rifle. She felt uneasy, with the butterflies quite active in her stomach. But it had to be done. She finished setting up the rifle as a car drove into the Mariner car park, quickly turning off its lights before it even stopped. The driver sat there for a while, as if checking for any activity on the Mariner that might stop him from carrying out his task. Joanne recognised him as Roberto. Her heart started pounding.

Roberto finally got out of the car carrying a small esky, hurried to the boat and got on board. A pale-coloured light came on in the cabin as he got ready to depart. They waited about five more minutes before the engines of the Cat sprang into life. Roberto appeared in the wheelhouse and was organising himself for the trip, with the esky stowed next to him.

'I've got my rangefinder. I'll call the distances as he sails out of the Mariner,' Colin advised Joanne.

'Good,' she replied. 'That will take out the guesswork. Thanks.'

'Not a problem, sweetheart,' Colin replied. 'We've got this.'

The "sweetheart" bit wasn't to her liking, but it set the mood and eased some of her angst.

Roberto released the mooring of the Cat and drifted away. Joanne put a round in the AX's chamber and rammed the breechblock home. She flicked the safety on, wriggled a bit to get comfortable as she usually did, and waited to take the shot as Colin called the distance.

'One hundred and eighty metres,' was Colin's first call.

The catamaran slowly slipped along the groyne in front of them. As it reached the end of the groyne, it turned to starboard, heading into open water and out of the Mariner. Colin gave the next reading.

'Two hundred and fifty metres,' Colin reported.

Joanne flicked off the safety catch and put the crosshairs of the scope on the back of Roberto's head. There was no breeze. If the settings were correct, they were spot on.

'Three hundred metres,' Colin said as he read the rangefinder readout.

A loud crack filled the night air for a split second. It echoed around the Mariner and across the bay. Joanne had taken the shot. She saw the results through her scope. Roberto turned his head slightly to the left. The bullet struck the back of his head and exited above his right eye. The velocity of the bullet made the front section of his forehead leave his skull, along with blood and brain matter, slamming against the windscreen of the Cat. He fell forward against the controls first, then his lifeless body slid back onto the floor of the wheelhouse.

Joanne quickly looked away, remarking on the shot she had just executed.

'That was a great feeling!' she said out loud. 'Goodbye, arsehole!'

Both Joanne and Colin backed away from their positions. It was time to leave. The shot had caused more excitement than they had first thought, as the water police appeared to come out of nowhere. Two boats came from either side of the bay, with a third from across the bay itself, all with lights flashing and sirens wailing. The police boat that reached the Cat first swiftly got a man aboard. He froze upon seeing a body on the floor with the front section of the forehead gone. He reached over to turn off the engine.

As the police realised what had happened, searchlights started playing across the Mariner and the area where Joanne and Colin had been earlier. Both found refuge behind the kiosk.

'We had better get out of here, as the place will crawl with cops soon,' Colin suggested.

'Yes, that will be fine with me too,' Joanne confirmed, her heart pounding like never before.

The searchlights went darting off elsewhere, and that was the opportunity for them both to get to their cars. Colin placed the bag in the car's boot, Joanne going over to hers.

'I'll ring later,' Colin said as they both got into their vehicles.

Colin backed away with no lights until he got to the exit. Joanne did the same. They had only travelled a short distance when police cars with sirens and flashing lights made a beeline for the Mariner in the opposite direction to theirs. With Joanne's heart pounding, this was something she would remember for some time. Being on the other end of the law was an experience she never wanted to revisit again.

Colin rang Joanne's phone.

'Are you okay?' he asked.

'Yes, I'm fine,' Joanne replied. 'The adrenaline is slowly dissipating.'

'I'll meet you tomorrow at the warehouse. I have something for you, as arranged,' Colin requested.

'Okay, I'll see you there in the morning,' Joanne replied. 'I want to leave as soon as I can.'

'Right, see you then.'

# Chapter 22: My Lawyer is a Woman

The water police scoured the Mariner for any movement but found none. Hoping to determine where the shot came from and flush out any suspects, they relied on the police in uniform. They had secured the catamaran and covered Roberto's lifeless body. They hadn't expected that he was going to be shot, but they had been ready to apprehend him on suspicion of drug trafficking. The Cat was now destined to be moored at the water police office for forensics to examine. The coroner would take possession of Roberto's body.

Anglers just outside Sydney Heads contacted the water police base, believing they had discovered something that would interest the police. The third boat that was across the bay acknowledged the call and volunteered to investigate. The patrol boat was fast, and they didn't want the fishermen to wait too long because the anglers clearly wanted to go fishing and get back home as soon as possible.

A police launch motored past the Heads and into the open sea. They recorded the coordinates given to them in the GPS, and the boat headed on a direct course to the location. A couple of minutes later, someone used a light to get the attention of the police. It was the fishermen.

'Over here!' one of them shouted, waving frantically.

The fishermen were soon caught in the police launch spotlight. There were three occupants on the fishing boat, all wearing life jackets as required.

'Pull alongside that boat,' the sergeant of the police boat ordered.

The fishing boat was a thirty-two-foot single-hull vessel with an inboard engine. It had a flybridge and was quite a nice-looking and well-appointed boat.

'You guys got a problem?' the sergeant yelled out.

'Yes and no,' one man replied. 'We found a package afloat that someone had thrown off a container ship about an hour ago.'

The police boat then came alongside Roberto's vessel, and were tied together with ropes.

'How do you know it came from the container ship?' the officer asked.

'We saw a man in a red checker blazer throw it overboard.'

'Are you the skipper of this boat?' 'Yes,

I am,' the fisherman replied.

'Can I have your full name and those of your crew?' the officer asked. 'It's just a formality.'

'I'm Harold Roberts and here's my skipper's ticket,' he replied as he handed the officer the ticket.

'Thank you, sir,' the officer replied. 'Do I have your permission for us to come aboard at this time?'

'Permission granted.'

The police officer got on board the fishing boat and introduced himself and his partner.

'I'm Sergeant William Frost of the Sydney Water Police, and that is Constable Shayne Morris.'

'Pleased to meet you, Sergeant. Constable,' Harold replied, nodding. 'These are my fishing buddies, John Walsh and Robert Collins.'

'Thank you, Mr Roberts,' the sergeant replied. 'May I call you Harold?'

'Harry will be fine too.'

'Okay, Harry. You witnessed this package being thrown from a cargo ship?'

'Yes, it was a Chinese ship,' Harold confirmed. 'It had Chinese lettering on the back, so we presume that's its origin.'

'Where did it go?'

'In through the Heads, and I would believe to dock at one of the container handling facilities,' Harold explained.

'Okay, we'll radio the harbour master and put a quarantine on the ship so no one leaves or gets on board without our permission,' the sergeant replied.

'There is something else that concerns us,' Harold continued. 'We've been fishing these waters up and down the coast for some time, and we know the excellent fishing spots, but something unexpected came up on a hook on one of our lines.'

Harold retrieved a plastic bag from the storage locker on the boat. It contained what looked like a piece of material from a shirt or jacket, and some hair. He handed the bag to the sergeant.

'Where did you get this from?' the sergeant asked.

Harold checked the GPS and said,

'About three hundred and fifty metres north of our current position. We've drifted south a bit since we contacted you guys,' Harold advised.

'Give me the coordinates and we'll investigate the source of this material.'

'The scary part is that it looks human to me,' Harold said, voicing his opinion.

'We'll do some tests and see exactly what it is,' the sergeant replied. 'I think you could be right.'

There was silence for a moment. Everyone had gaunt looks on their faces and wondered what else was down there.

'We'll load the package you picked up onto our boat, and we'll head back to shore,' the sergeant suggested. 'Here's your skipper's ticket.'

'Thanks. We won't be far behind you either,' said Harold. 'It's been a night to remember.'

They made sure everything was secure and released the lines. The police launch took off first, and Harold started his boat's engine and followed in the same direction.

***

They quarantined the container ship and mobilised the drug squad to do a complete sweep. The crew had to remain in their cabins while the authorities circulated a description of the man in the checker windcheater. They needed to question him and possibly arrest him and his accomplices if found. The captain was utterly shocked when the police came on board. He offered them as much help as possible and confirmed he wanted the culprits caught as well.

The Super greeted Parker and Ashcroft with recent developments involving the Rossettis when they arrived at the station together. The Super asked them to step into his office.

'I have some important information that we need to act on,' he began. 'First, there was an incident last night where Roberto Rossetti got shot with a high-powered rifle.'

'Oh, for shit's sake!' Ashcroft exclaimed. 'What else is around the corner? I'm guessing it was fatal?'

'Absolutely,' the Super confirmed. 'It entered the back of the head and exited above the right eye. The water police said it was quite a mess.'

'I'm sure it would be,' Parker agreed. 'Where did the shooting occur?'

'It took place at the Mariner around midnight. It is believed that Rossetti was going for a drug pickup outside the bay around midnight.'

'Was it the Chinese again who perpetrated this one as well?' Ashcroft asked. 'I'm betting it was.'

'We cannot confirm who it was, or the motive,' the Super replied. 'Go down there before it becomes too crowded and see what you can find. The uniformed police have cordoned off the area they believe the shot came from.'

'Alright, we'll get right on it,' Parker said.

'Before you go, there is more I need to tell you,' the Super continued. 'We have identified the woman in the freezer at that warehouse as Emily Spain, missing for about two weeks.'

'I recall we identified her as a pusher for the Rossettis,' Parker said. 'About four months ago, we arrested her, but we could not establish a link with the Rossettis.'

'I found out she's been depositing money into her account every week,' Ashcroft added. 'But I wasn't able to establish where the funds disappeared from her account. The bank could not supply the information on time.'

'I would suggest an account held by the Rossettis,' the Super suggested. 'The autopsy report suggests she either overdosed on heroin or someone administered it to her. I am thinking possibly of the latter.'

'I would suggest that someone stripped her naked and placed her in the freezer in the sitting position we found her in after she was already dead,' Parker surmised.

'Yes, I'm sure that is the case, but we have made no connections yet with the Rossettis,' the Super said, agreeing with his suggestion.

'I think the drug connection will come to light once we investigate the Rossettis further,' Parker suggested.

'Yes indeed,' the Super replied. 'I've also received a preliminary report from the Sydney Water Police. They wanted to intercept Roberto Rossetti last night on his return from wherever he was going. Also, some fishermen saw a package being dropped from a container ship, and the Water Police said it had sixty kilograms of drugs in it. Currently, the authorities are investigating the crew of the docked ship.'

'Wow,' Ashcroft responded. 'The boys had a busy night all round.'

'Well, I guess we need to start at the mariner?' Parker queried.

'Yes, that would be first,' the Super agreed. 'I also have the interview report of the Chinese we detained from the warehouse. You can have a read of that later.'

'Well, it should make interesting reading,' Parker replied.

'Oh, one more thing I was told about,' the Super continued. 'The anglers also snagged what appears to be some sort of clothing and human hair on one of their hooks. The Water Police are organising a dive team to investigate the area.'

'I can see where this is going and what they may find,' Parker replied.

'I'm thinking the same. We'll talk more later when you get back from the mariner,' the Super said.

Parker acknowledged and then motioned to Ashcroft. It was time to visit the mariner. Both went to their respective offices and grabbed their coats. They arrived at the mariner and introduced themselves to the two uniformed police monitoring the area.

'Senior, the cordoned-off area is where it's believed the shot was taken. That section over there,' one officer informed them.

'Thank you,' replied Parker.

He and Ashcroft looked around the area in front of the kiosk. It was a lawn area with some seating that flowed to a fence-type hedge about ten or twenty metres from the kiosk. Sections of the hedge had gaps where you could easily walk through and down to the mooring area. There were five gaps in the hedge line. Ashcroft stood at each one and checked the view towards the bay.

'Not this one,' he said to himself. 'Nor this one, but maybe this one, as it has a clear view.'

'What are you surmising?' Parker asked him as he watched him for a couple of minutes.

'I believe the shooter took the shot from here,' Ashcroft suggested. 'Where was the victim hit?'

'The bullet entered the back of his head.'

'That being the case, he would have been side-on to the shooter until he entered the bay at the opening to the mariner,' Ashcroft explained. 'It is at that point his back is towards the shooter. These positions here have yacht masts to contend with, but here is an open passage.'

'Yes, I think you are correct with your assessment,' Parker said, agreeing with Ashcroft.

'The only thing is there is no evidence of someone having been here with a rifle.'

'I think you'll find it almost impossible to find evidence if this was a professional hit,' Parker suggested. 'They would have cleaned up after themselves.'

'Do you think the Chinese were involved?' Ashcroft asked.

'Could be, but we need to confirm that somehow before we make that assumption.'

'It appears it was a professional hit,' Ashcroft surmised.

'Yes, or a well-planned hit by someone that may have wanted revenge,' Parker added. 'People who are desperate enough can execute a well-thought-out plan like a professional.'

Both stood there for another couple of minutes, looking out into the bay from the Middle Harbour Yacht Club. They may never find the person who took the shot unless someone witnessed something and gives the police that information.

'Let's go back and report in,' Parker suggested. 'There's not much we can do here.'

Before they left, Parker told the two uniformed police there was nothing else to be done here and to take down the cordon tape and clear the area.

When Parker and Ashcroft returned to the station, the Super greeted them.

'More breaking news,' he began with a smile. 'We've identified a second lot of DNA found in Tammy O'Lachlin's flat. It belongs to Dominic Rossetti.'

'That is breaking the case open,' Parker admitted.

'I've sent two officers to arrest him,' the Super informed Parker. 'They should be back soon.'

'Thank you for letting us know, Sir,' Parker acknowledged. 'Today will be a wonderful day, after all.'

When Parker got back to his office, he looked over the record of interviews with the Chinese whom the police apprehended at the warehouse. Three of the five were illegal immigrants, and the Department of Immigration was very interested in dealing with them. The other two individuals faced charges of importing a prohibited drug intending to sell, which is the major offence the Department of Immigration was interested in dealing with.

The interview revealed nothing more than what they were already aware of, and the activities seemed in line with a major thrust to establish a drug trade, beginning in Sydney and then spreading to the other capitals. It came as no surprise that they mentioned Fleming twice as a key figure in setting up lines of distribution. The Chinese realised his connection with the Rossetti group, and that did not sit well with them, hence Fleming being gunned down as well. They perceived him as a potential thorn in their side.

'Dominic Rossetti is in the interview room,' the Super said as he poked his head around Parker's office door. 'Take Ashcroft with you.'

Parker got up immediately and followed the Super down the hallway to Ashcroft's office. The two detectives went to the interview room, where they found Dominic a little impatient with the proceedings. Parker sat down and read some notes the Super had handed to him. Ashcroft sat alongside.

'Mr Rossetti,' Parker began, 'I'm Senior Detective Parker, and this is Detective Ashcroft. Please be aware this interview is being recorded and, for the record, please state your full name.'

'Dominic Joseph Rossetti.'

'Mr Rossetti, do you know the reason for your arrest?' Parker asked.
'Some bullshit about a murder I know nothing about,' Dominic

replied. 'To make things even worse, my son was killed early this morning, and you cops have taken no action to catch his killer.'

'Mr Rossetti, the death of your son is being investigated to the fullest of our resources as we speak,' Parker said.

'Someone brutally murdered him.'

'That brings us to why you are here, Mr Rossetti,' Parker continued. 'Do you know a Sergio Stromnikov?'

'Should I?'

'Someone found his DNA in the flat where the murder of Tammy O'Lachlin took place the other week.'

'How does that concern me?'

'We also found your DNA there. Can you explain that?' Parker pressed home.

'I'm not saying anything until my lawyer gets here,' Dominic finally requested. 'My lawyer is a woman, too.'

'What do you mean by that statement, Mr Rossetti?' Parker asked. 'We didn't mention that Tammy O'Lachlin was a lawyer.'

Dominic's face briefly lost colour as he realised he might have accidentally disclosed sensitive information and implicated himself. He said nothing further.

'We'll be back once your lawyer has arrived, Mr Rossetti,' Parker informed him. He and Ashcroft then left the interview room, leaving Dominic on his own.

# Chapter 23: They Found Three Bodies

Joanne thought she was early heading out to Colin's warehouse, but to her surprise, he was already there. That suited her fine, as she could get to the airport in plenty of time to catch a flight back to Perth. Colin was still in the car and got out as Joanne pulled up alongside him.

'I'm glad you're early as well,' Joanne said as they both got out of their cars. 'I was hoping for an early start.'

'The thought crossed my mind that you might be eager to get organised and return to WA,' Colin agreed.

'My flight leaves in about four hours, so I have enough time to sort things out,' Joanne replied.

'There isn't much to sort out between us,' Colin said.

'I have to pay you for your help with my problem we solved,' Joanne replied.

'All you owe me is the cost of bullets,' Colin showed, 'nothing else.'

'Didn't we agree on the cost of hiring the rifle?' Joanne queried.

'Sweetheart, I know you don't like being called that. However, with the number of times you've had my back in the past, I feel I owe you instead of you owing me,' Colin pointed out. 'And I enjoy calling you Sweetheart.'

'So, what are you proposing?' Joanne asked tentatively.

'One hundred dollars will cover the costs incurred, and we're even,' Colin suggested. 'And I'm returning your earlier payment. My choice.'

'That is very admirable of you, and considerate as well.'

'You're a good person, Joanne. I'm glad I could help you for a change,' Colin said. 'We have history forever.'

'We do indeed.'

Colin handed back the money. They both looked into each other's eyes. Colin shook her hand, then drew her close for an affectionate hug and kissed her on the cheek.

'Take care, my sweetheart. All the best for the future,' Colin said with feeling.

'You too, Colin,' Joanne replied. 'Thank you for being a good, firm friend.'

Joanne returned to her car, a little choked for the first time in longer than she could remember. Colin, leaning against his car, waved as she reversed up and swung around onto the road. The business of the day was done. Now she had a plane to catch. Colin watched as she drove away. He realised she had gotten away again. He would always have a place for her in his heart and hoped she realised that.

*****

Parker returned to his office and continued reading the interview record with the Chinese. He wasn't at all surprised to read that Fleming had overstepped the mark with them. They suspected him of being involved in a shooting that resulted in one of their number being shot by him. He had also sustained a bullet wound on his right side because of the incident. They put him on the hit list not long after that.

Parker got up and went to the Super's office to see if he could view the autopsy report on Fleming again.

'What are you hoping to find?' the Super asked.

'During the interview with the Chinese, they mentioned Fleming had sustained a gunshot wound to the side,' Parker informed him. 'I wanted to check whether the report mentioned it.'

'You can take the report with you if you like,' the Super suggested. 'By the way, here is an interesting report from the Water Police. As we expected, some fishermen handed something in, and they are planning to do some diving.' 'And what is the result?'

'I'm still waiting for a result. The clothing material and human hair that was dragged on the end of a fishing hook,' the Super said.

'Thank you,' Parker acknowledged, then returned to his office.

The autopsy report on Fleming mentioned an injury sustained from a previous incident but did not elaborate on the injury itself, as it had nothing to do with the cause of Fleming's death. Parker finished reading the interview record with the Chinese and was a little surprised they had divulged so much detailed information, most of which centred on Fleming's activities. There was nothing about how the drugs got to the warehouse, the point of origin, or who brought them into the country.

Parker then started reading the Water Police report just as Ashcroft came into his office and made himself comfortable in a chair.

'What are you reading?' Ashcroft asked.

'This is the Water Police report on the shooting of Roberto Rossetti,' Parker replied. 'There is also an amended report from two officers who answered a fisherman's call. It makes for interesting reading.'

Ashcroft read the report, raising his eyebrows twice at its content. The analysis of the cloth and hair samples had yet to be completed. It seemed to be of some importance if they were engaging divers to investigate further. Ashcroft surmised it to be human hair.

'According to this, the Water Police will dive on the site later this week, tomorrow, actually,' Ashcroft read.

'I think they will find more than they bargained for,' Parker suggested.

Just then there was a knock on the door, and the Super opened it and entered Parker's office.

'A couple of developments already,' he began. 'Dominic Rossetti's solicitor has arrived, so we can continue our interview with him. Also, the Federal Police have been involved with drug drops at sea, and they have arrested four men. They go by the names Styles, Thomo, Hanson and Joe. According to them, Thomo was the individual observed throwing the drugs overboard.'

'Well, looks like things are hastening a change,' Parker observed. 'Let's see what Mr Rossetti has to say.'

Both Parker and Ashcroft got up and headed for the interview room. The Super offered to close the office door. Dominic, with his solicitor, finished chatting as Parker and Ashcroft came in.

'Mr Rossetti,' Parker began, 'now that you have your solicitor present, are you prepared for further questioning?'

'I will, as advised by my solicitor,' Dominic replied.

'I'm Miss Joan Atwell, Attorney at Law,' Dominic's solicitor introduced herself.

'Miss Atwell, it's a pleasure,' Parker replied. Ashcroft nodded as well.

'Mr Rossetti, can you clarify why your DNA was found in Tammy O'Lachlin's flat?' Parker asked straight off.

When Tammy's name came up, Miss Atwell appeared somewhat surprised. Ashcroft saw the look on her face and realised that she knew of Tammy, but didn't know there was a connection to the Rossettis. She wriggled in her seat, getting more comfortable.

'I do not know,' Dominic replied. 'Perhaps someone placed it there.'

'We discovered Stromnikov's DNA in her bedroom, where she was shot. You were the one who hired him as a hitman,' Parker said. 'There was a witness to this murder, and you spoke with that person the next day with your son.'

'I speak to many people on some days, but I can't remember talking to a woman about a murder,' Dominic replied.

'I said it was a person you spoke to with your son. There wasn't mention of a woman.'

'If the person was with my son, then it could only have been a woman,' Dominic replied.

'I think you are trying to avoid the fact that you were involved in Tammy O'Lachlin's murder with Stromnikov,' Parker said, making a point. 'Your DNA confirms it.'

'That doesn't mean he was there when the alleged murder took place,' Miss Atwell put forward.

'But according to the witness, she spotted him there simultaneously Stromnikov shot Miss O'Lachlin,' Parker replied.

'Is there a point to this interview?' Miss Atwell asked impatiently. 'It seems we are going around in circles.'

'Yes, there is,' Parker began. 'Mr Dominic Rossetti, I'm placing you under arrest for complicity in the murder of Tammy O'Lachlin.'

'This is bloody outrageous!' Dominic shouted and turned to his solicitor. 'Do something!'

'My hands are now tied,' she replied. 'An officer of the law has formally charged you, and the process of a hearing is now in play.'

'Detective Ashcroft, please escort Mr Rossetti to a holding cell,' Parker requested.

'I thought you were better than this!' Dominic yelled at Miss Atwell.

Ashcroft frogmarched him out of the interview room, accompanied by two uniformed police, and down the corridor to one of the holding cells in the station. Dominic complained about being manhandled, not defending himself properly, not being represented effectively by a female solicitor, and being arrested on prefabricated evidence.

'Tomorrow,' Ashcroft informed him, 'you will face arraignment and appear before a magistrate for a committal hearing. You can then speak and defend yourself.'

Ashcroft locked the cell door with Dominic still protesting. On his way back to the interview, he met the Superintendent along the way.

'Do you know whether Parker is in his office or the interview room?' the Super asked.

'I can check the interview room, Sir,' Ashcroft offered.

'Yes, please do. I'll meet you both in my office.'

Parker was just finishing saying his goodbyes to Miss Atwell when Ashcroft approached.

'The Super wants us in his office,' Ashcroft informed Parker.

'I wonder what now,' Parker said. 'I guess we'll find out.'

The Super's office door was open, so Parker and Ashcroft went in.

'Take a seat,' the Super invited. 'I've just received a report from the Wentworth police that will interest you.'

Parker glanced at Ashcroft and settled back in the chair.

'There is an abandoned property west of Wentworth that still has a house and farm sheds on it,' the Super began. 'A couple of young lads made a gruesome discovery in the old house. Two bodies with bullet wounds to the head and a burnt-out dark blue BMW with the remains of three AK47 rifles. There was enough unburnt panelling at the rear of the car to identify the colour. The rifles in the van were destroyed.'

'Oh my God,' was Parker's reaction. 'That throws a spanner in the works.'

Ashcroft sat there for a moment, trying to come to terms with what this all meant. He finally commented.

'I have to agree, Sir,' he said. 'We have been looking for three men who shot Mario, his wife, and Fleming. But now, it's clear that we should look for one man, the one that shot his accomplices.'

'Are you saying you believe these are the same men?' the Super asked.

'If you consider the car, the three rifles, which alone suggests the MO for the shooting of Fleming and co.,' Ashcroft pointed out. 'It would also be easier for one man to slip the country than three men.'

'I don't think there's any value in you both going up there. Forensics are already on site, going over the place,' the Super informed them.

'Work with the reports that come through and see how that ties in with the Rossettis' situation. That's a priority.'

'Very good, Sir,' Parker replied. 'Thank you for keeping us updated.'

Parker and Ashcroft left the Super's office with very little to say. Ashcroft had the look of someone who was going to explode.

'You have a problem?' Parker asked as they stopped in front of Parker's office.

'It's frustrating; the entire case is,' Ashcroft blurted out, gritting his teeth. 'Every time we are on the verge of making some ground, something gets in the way and puts us back. First, someone shot Fleming, then they killed Roberto. Now it's clear that we should look for one person rather than the three Chinese we were searching for.'

'Unfortunately, that's how things go from time to time,' Parker replied, sympathising with him. 'At least we have Dominic Rossetti in jail for now.'

'That's until tomorrow when his solicitor appeals to the court for bail and he is free again.'

'You are becoming cynical, my lad,' Parker replied.

'Comes from the time we seem to have wasted on this case.'

'We have made progress,' Parker said. 'The operation has virtually shut down. We froze bank accounts, and unfortunately, some people involved have met their demise. But we still have a lot of investigating to do. Just because we haven't got more people in jail doesn't mean we wasted our time.'

'Yeah, I guess you're right,' Ashcroft admitted with an enormous sigh.

***

Joanne had gotten to the airport with plenty of time to spare. She settled down near her departure gate to eat at one of the many food outlets. The flight to Perth would take about five hours, and with daylight saving on the east coast, that put Perth three hours behind.

That being the case, it meant that according to the flight plan, it would only take two hours to fly to Perth, but not in reality.

It wasn't long before Joanne was boarding her flight. Sitting in her allotted seat, she breathed a sigh of relief. Having successfully completed her mission, she believed the police did not know about her involvement or her whereabouts. She could return to Geraldton and spend some more time with Lewis. She did not dislike all men; it was a run of bad luck with them that had made her resort to the company of her gender. Maybe things would change for the better.

Joanne closed her eyes and leant back in her seat. Now that the plane was airborne, she was going to relax and maybe watch a movie. Her thoughts drifted to Holly and the relationship they had embarked on. Holly was a fantastic person and had all the hallmarks of a long-lasting relationship with her. She knew Holly had been a little apprehensive initially, but she warmed to the idea of having Joanne as a partner rather quickly. As a result, she saw less and less of Roberto, which eventually pissed him off big time.

She awoke with a jolt and the seatbelt alarm on. She gathered her thoughts and looked at the flight map on the screen in front of her. They had crossed the coast of WA, leaving behind the Great Australian Bight. She noticed the plane was slowly descending, even this far from Perth. There was at least an hour of flying time. At last, she was back in WA and left behind the anguish and uncertainty she had experienced. Unfortunately, close friends were back there as well, something she would deal with in her own way.

Lewis would hopefully play a major part in that. She was confident about the prospect of being with him, and especially with her returning to him, as she had promised. The future looked bright, and she was looking forward to it.

***

Parker and Ashcroft were in the courtroom when the arraignment of Dominic Rossetti was taking place. The prosecution began by introducing itself.

'Your Honour, my name is Matthew Sykes, and I am here to represent the prosecution in this matter.'

'Thank you, Mr Sykes,' the magistrate replied.

'Your Honour, my name is Stephen Gibbs of Wright & Gibbs, and I'm here to represent the plaintiff, Mr Dominic Rossetti, on behalf of Miss Joan Atwell, who is unwell at the moment.'

'Thank you, Mr Gibbs,' the magistrate again replied. 'Mr Sykes, please proceed.'

Sykes presented his speech to the court and recounted the murder of Tammy O'Lachlin and an account of Stromnikov's part in the murder. Sykes mentioned Stromnikov was Dominic's hitman and how he followed a person to WA to kill her. He also brought up how the WA police took him down. He briefly described Dominic's involvement in the drug trade and how the murdered people could have undermined his operations.

'Based on the evidence we collected recently and the DNA found at the murder scene, I suggest we hold Mr Dominic Rossetti accountable and bring him to court,' concluded Sykes. 'Thank you, Your Honour.' 'Mr Gibbs,' the magistrate said, addressing him. 'You wish to reply?' 'Yes, Your Honour,' he replied as he stood up.

He began by saying that Dominic was a model citizen and that much of the information and evidence that the prosecution had was, at best, hearsay and innuendo.

'Mr Rossetti did not take part in any drug transactions, and to make matters worse, he recently suffered the loss of his son, who was allegedly killed by an unknown gunman.'

'Thank you, Mr Gibbs,' the magistrate said, acknowledging his response to the prosecution.

The magistrate flicked through some paperwork in front of him and then looked up after a moment or two and handed down his findings. 'Based on the evidence presented, I believe that Mr Rossetti has a case to answer for,' he began. 'Therefore, I am setting a date for the court to proceed with the charge of murder against Mr Rossetti three weeks from now. I will not set bail and order Mr Rossetti to be held in remand until the trial date, yet to be determined. The court adjourned for the day.'

Dominic wasn't happy and started having a few words with his counsel. He had asked him to request bail as he wasn't happy staying in jail.

'You heard the magistrate. He refused bail.'

'But you could have argued the point!' Dominic insisted.

At that moment, two officers approached Dominic to escort him to the paddy wagon and take him to prison. He wasn't a happy customer, and it showed on his face as he gave Gibbs a stare of disapproval.

Parker and Ashcroft followed the rest of the crowd out of the courtroom.

'Now that was worth seeing,' Ashcroft said with a smirk. 'Mr Rossetti being put behind bars at last.'

'Yes,' Parker agreed, 'there's some relief in that transpiring the way it did.'

'Well, he'll have a couple of weekends to think about his situation,' Ashcroft suggested.

'When we get back to my office, we'll go through the reports we've got,' Parker said. 'There might be some relevant information we've only just glanced over for now. It might be required as evidence in court.'

'At least that will fill in the afternoon,' Ashcroft replied.

When they returned to Parker's office, it wasn't long before the Super poked his head in and gave them an update on the water police diving venture.

'They found three bodies on the seabed that was highlighted as an area of interest,' the Super informed them, 'two male bodies and that of a young female.'

'Young female?' Parker queried. 'What do they mean by young?'

'She seems to be in her late teens.'

'I remember there are several missing teenagers in the system over there, but I suppose there is no ID on them yet,' Parker replied.

'No, not at this stage,' the Super said. 'The bodies are in deep water as well, and recovery is going to be slow.'

'I guess only time will tell,' Ashcroft opined.

'Thank you, Sir,' Parker replied, and the Super left.

'I'm looking forward to a beer,' Ashcroft said. 'What about you?'

'That is the best suggestion you've had all week,' Parker replied. 'Let's call it a day. This can all wait until Monday.'

# Chapter 24: I Thought You'd Never Ask

Ashcroft had a couple of drinks with Parker and the boys on Friday night after work. It was a time to relax, tell tall stories and maybe even reflect on the events that had transpired over the past week. He admitted he had become frustrated with the shootings, false leads and things that kept derailing their line of inquiry with the Rossettis.

Ashcroft relished the thought of sleeping in late for a change of routine. The previous weeks had been harrowing, to say the least. First, Ashcroft investigated the Rossettis' banking activities, then Vinnie got shot with a ricocheting bullet, there was Chinese involvement somewhere along the line, then Tammy O'Lachlin and Milton Clark got shot — which required another weekend of work, then Ashcroft discovered Emily Spain's corpse in a freezer, allegedly placed there by Fleming, and the list went on.

He planned on making the most of his weekend, as he wasn't sure when he would have the privilege of another. Now that Dominic Rossetti was behind bars, he and scheduled to appear in court the following week. They were asked to be available to give their testimony at the trial if needed. The shooting of Roberto was still a big mystery, and the question remained: who had, or could get, a rifle to execute such a hit? No one had offered information, and there were no leads of any substance that would help track down the assassin. It was just something that happened under suspicious circumstances, with no leads to follow.

***

The weekend seemed to go too quickly for Ashcroft's liking. The alarm went off. He rolled over for a moment and then realised it was Monday morning. Getting out of bed, he had a shower, then breakfast, and organised himself for work.

Arriving for the first time ahead of Parker.

'How was your weekend?'

'Great,' Ashcroft replied. 'I went out on Saturday night and had a few beers at the pub.'

'You did a bit of "tomcatting" also, as we used to say,' Parker said jokingly.

Ashcroft smiled as they entered the station. No sooner had they reached the muster room than the Superintendent asked them to accompany him to his office. He didn't look happy.

'What's going on, Sir?' Parker asked.

'A tragedy, to say the least,' the Super replied. 'Last night, they discovered Dominic Rossetti dead in his cell.' 'He is what?!' Ashcroft burst out.

'According to reports, multiple stab wounds resulted in his death.'

'Oh, for fuck's sake, what else can go wrong?' Ashcroft retorted.

'Detective Ashcroft,' the Super said, trying to get him not to curse.

'Sir, really, this takes the cake,' Ashcroft replied as Parker watched on, not knowing what to say for a change, but then gained his composure.

'How did that happen? Wasn't he supposed to be in top security?' Parker asked.

'No, apparently it was the general population area,' the Super replied.

'Who handled that mix-up?' Parker asked.

'Internal Affairs is trying to determine that now.'

'That's a bit late for Rossetti,' Ashcroft interjected.

'I know there is nothing we can do, and it's disappointing that after the effort that was put into this investigation by you two in particular it ends up being a non-event,' the Super sympathised, 'but we've done everything by the book and there's still a lot of paperwork to complete, frozen accounts to investigate, and property to impound.'

'Yes, I have to agree, Sir,' Parker said in support. 'At least we've helped to close that drug cartel down, even though there is no conviction to be had.'

'It's unfortunate, but that's how the dice rolled,' the Super said in response.

'Sir, sorry for my outburst,' Ashcroft said apologetically. 'It's just not the way things should have panned out.'

'I understand your frustration. I'm like that on most occasions,' the Super replied. 'But you learn soon enough that there are no certainties in this job. You just need to stay focused and take whatever opportunity arises.'

'Yes, Sir, thank you.'

'I've also shared some of our findings with the boys in the west,' the Super informed them. 'I thought, out of courtesy, that they'd appreciate knowing how we got the key that started the unravelling of the Rossettis.' They expressed surprise at how important that information was to us.

Just then, the Super's phone rang, and he answered the call. After dealing with the usual pleasantries, the smile on his face quickly shifted to surprise. It was the Federal Police.

'When did this happen?' he asked and then paused. 'Interpol gave you the information.'

Parker and Ashcroft remained glued to their seats. Something unusual was going on.

'I see,' the Super acknowledged. 'Thank you for letting me know as well.'

The Super hung up the phone and looked at both Parker and Ashcroft, a little bewildered. He finally told them the information the AFP had given him.

'Teresa Rossetti returned home to Sicily yesterday. It appears she was deliberately run down in Syracuse, Sicily, by an unidentified hit-and-run driver,' he informed them. 'She died at the scene.'

Ashcroft sat there with his mouth partly open, staring at the Super. Parker sat there with a stunned look on his face. No one spoke for a moment.

'Who do you think was behind it?' Parker asked. 'When did she go to Sicily?'

'No one seems to know, or gives a damn, apparently,' the Super replied. 'It's not our business what goes on over there, but considering what has happened here with the Rossettis, they are trying to link the two together. It was good of them to volunteer the info as well. And apparently, she went home after Roberto got shot.'

'Imagine that,' Ashcroft finally said. 'They virtually wiped out the whole family.'

'Not quite,' Parker replied. 'I believe a daughter is living somewhere in Queensland. She disassociated herself from the family quite a few years ago.'

'Yes, she severed her connection with the family some six or seven years ago,' the Super confirmed. 'Dominic Rossetti had excluded her from the family and his will. Interpol is trying to find her with the Queensland police.'

'Let's finish this paperwork, Ashcroft,' Parker suggested. 'That might put you in a better frame of mind. Besides, we will finish early for a change.'

They both left the Super's office and headed back to their own offices to catch up on the nagging paperwork. Ashcroft pondered the situation for a while, then gave an enormous sigh. At least someone dealt out justice in some fashion. It's a pity the courts didn't get the opportunity to pass down their judgement.

***

Meanwhile, Detective Matt Wilson was sitting in his Geraldton office, shuffling through some paperwork. Steph was on his mind. He sat back, pondering what he should do. He found her attractive, so maybe he should explore that a little further.

While fumbling through his notes, he located her phone number. Whether to ring her was a decision he was weighing. He sat staring at his mobile for a moment, then picked it up and dialled her number. She answered almost immediately.

'Hello,' came Steph's voice.

'Hi Steph, it's Matt,' he replied. 'Can we get together sometime? I'd like to have a talk with you.'

'Mm, yes, definitely,' she replied. 'I thought you'd never ask.'